OOPS!
I BROKE THE
WIZARD'S
ANDROID!

ROYCE ROESWOOD

Oops! I Broke the Wizard's Android!

Royce Roeswood

Published by Ragamancers Press, 2024.

OOPS! I BROKE THE WIZARD'S ANDROID!

First edition. September 23, 2024.

Written by Royce Roeswood.

for Makena

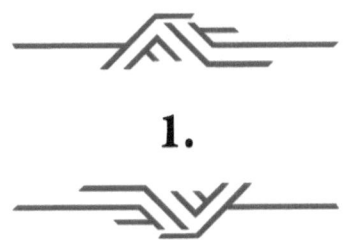

1.

CHADRON: This orange gas giant on the very edge of the Twelve Thousand Worlds has the unusual property of reflecting the light and heat from its distant sun, bringing life to its two moons that would otherwise be uninhabitable.

The first of these moons, The Brilliant Moon, is a world of sparkling blue oceans and thin, ribbon-like islands of sand and green vegetation. The second, The Shadow Moon, is a black rock wrapped in deep purple forests and is almost imperceptible against the darkness of space. (What the settlers of Chadron lacked in imagination, they made up for in clarity.)

It is unlikely that even the most far-flung traveler will find themselves near Chadron, but should you be nearby during the Brilliant Moon's annual festival, it may be worth stopping over to view the quaint tradition. Shuttles run from Mage's Market twice weekly.

There is no reason to visit the Shadow Moon.

— from Pippler's Travel Guides: The New Colonies

WHEN NINIENNE LIGHTCASTER saw the Brilliant Moon of Chadron for the first time from the window of the transit shuttle, she thought it was her destination. She was wrong.

In her defense, her apprenticeship assignment had only arrived the previous morning, and she had hastily packed up her dormitory at the Belcarin Academy of Wizardry instead of diligently researching, as usual. Now, after several shuttle transfers over nearly two days, in the deep void of space without a connection to the datastream, her mind could only spin wild fantasies about what the final year of her magical education would entail.

And spin wild fantasies she did. With an ink wand in one hand and a light spell in the other, she put the finishing touches on a sketch as Gossamaw nuzzled in her lap. He scratched behind his neck with his furry webbed foot and licked one of his large, watery eyes with his long tongue.

Ninienne had drawn herself and her familiar in a series of imagined scenes: strolling down a cobblestone street lined with inviting shops, on a boat sailing between tropical islands, cooking delicious meals in a garden full of exotic fruits and vegetables.

Even though she had already memorized the words, she tapped her datastream device to read her apprentice assignment once again. Glowing text floated in the air in front of her:

Mentor: Salagrix, Master Wizard of the Shadow Moon of Chadron

The shuttle banked around the orange gas giant, and Ninienne looked out of the window just in time to see the Brilliant Moon in its full glory, like a sapphire marble streaked with gold-lined emerald.

"Is that it? Is that the Shadow Moon?" she asked herself, barely able to contain her excitement. She danced a little dance in her seat.

A cough from the other side of the shuttle told her that the only other passenger had finally awoken. She smoothed her brown overalls and tucked a strand of long black hair underneath her floppy, brown wizard's hat, hoping the old man hadn't seen her dance.

"You headed to the Brilliant Moon?" asked a cracked, tired voice.

The old man leaned across the aisle, his dusty jacket patched on the shoulders, and his mouth missing a tooth.

"No, the Shadow Moon, actually. Is that it?" Ninienne gestured to the jewel of a world outside the shuttle window.

The old man laughed through a wheeze. "'Fraid not. That's the Brilliant Moon. That," he pointed, "Is the Shadow Moon."

Ninienne looked, but saw nothing. "I don't see it."

"That patch there where there's no stars. That sort of nothingness over there."

"Oh," said Ninienne. She still hadn't seen it.

"I figured by the look of you that you were headin' to the Brilliant Moon and we'd have to make an extra stop. Not many visitors to Chadron in the first place, but nobody visits the Shadow Moon. You got family there?"

"No, I'm doing my wizard's apprenticeship with Master Salagrix. Do you know anything about him?"

The old man snorted with disdain and then looked at Ninienne with disgusted pity before shaking his head and turning away.

It took a few moments for Ninienne to realize that the conversation was over. What had she said? She turned back to the window, unsure how to revive the conversation after such an abrupt end, and resumed her search for the Shadow Moon.

Beyond the thick plastiglass, the patch of darkness grew. Ninienne's visions of tropical islands and cobblestone streets rapidly unraveled the closer they got. Gossamaw, sensing her disappointment, made a soft crooning sound, and she absentmindedly stroked her familiar's smooth, green back for comfort.

She couldn't tell if the sinking feeling in her stomach was from the shuttle descending or from creeping dread.

AFTER LANDING, THE old man debarked without acknowledging or even looking at Ninienne. Too excited about her apprenticeship to let the rude welcome bother her, she grabbed her satchel and stepped out of the shuttle, Gossamaw hopping happily behind her.

She found herself in a single-pad spaceport, that word "spaceport" giving a sense of grandeur to what was nothing more than a stonecrete slab with a few worn benches and a battered sign that read "Black Gulch." The pilot unloaded a few crates off of the shuttle with the help of one of those new androids, and the old man stopped to greet her.

"Where's Chaco?" he asked.

The pilot stuck her thumb at the android. "Shuttlecom replaced copilots with androids on all minor routes. I'll probably be next." She laughed grimly.

The old man tsked and shook his head. "Shame. Shame."

Good thing there's nothing coming after my career, thought Ninienne. *Machines can't do magic.*

Ninienne passed under the gnarled wrought-iron gate to discover a black dirt road lined with dilapidated structures, many boarded up. At the other end of the road sat a squat, official-looking brick building, and she headed in that direction.

This was, apparently, the only road in Black Gulch. As she peeked down the wide alleys between buildings, where little vortexes of dirt swirled, she saw no evidence of more structures. The street was empty, except for one tired-looking crowhorse tied up outside the saloon about halfway down, who cawed menacingly and stamped her clawhooves as Ninienne passed.

A loose shutter banged in the wind. The air was dry and tasted of that bitter black dust that seemed to be everywhere.

An old, hunched woman in a threadbare headscarf appeared from an alley to cross the street, and Ninienne dashed up to her. "Hi!" she said.

The old woman blinked and clutched her basket.

"I'm looking for Master Salagrix. Do you know where I should head?"

The old woman made a face as if she had just bitten into something sour, and pointed a long, wrinkled finger to the horizon. There, in the far distance, rising above a forest of dark purple trees, was a jagged black scar against the sky. A wizard's tower.

Ninienne turned to thank the old woman, but she had already hurried away.

TWO HOURS LATER, AS the orange gas giant dipped below the horizon, Ninienne reached the end of the trail.

The tower stood in the middle of a perfectly circular clearing in the forest, as if even the trees were trying to keep their distance. It looked like a hastily stacked pile of black blocks, each level not quite lined up with the previous. One level about half-way up, much larger than its lower neighbor, jutted out at a jaunty angle. At the top, a telescope drooped from the conical roof.

Gossamaw had given up on the hike almost immediately, and was still under Ninienne's arm, panting exaggeratedly, as she crossed the clearing to the tower's entrance. After the inviting closeness of the forest, being out in the open felt vulnerable. Her feet crunched on brown grass and dry clover.

Beside the front door hung a weathered wooden ring at the end of a frayed rope. Ninienne pulled the ring, and a gong rang out high above her. Bits of black stone and gray mortar shook loose and fell to the ground like diseased dandruff from a single, enormous, nasty hair.

This had to be the place. After her encounter with the old woman, she had asked several other sunken-eyed locals to make sure. Each had pointed a sullen finger towards the unmistakable black shape on the horizon, crooked and dark like a charred stick, the only landmark visible from Black Gulch.

One hand clutched the strap of her bag closer for comfort, while the other gave Gossamaw a reassuring stroke. He croaked sleepily and yawned.

"This has to be it, right?" Ninienne asked, not sure whether she was trying to convince her familiar or herself. "It's not like there are any other wizard towers around here. If this isn't Salagrix's tower, someone owes me a very detailed explanation."

She pulled the bell-rope a second time, and the banging of the distant gong once again threatened the stability of the tower. More bits of crumbling stone fell in a growing ring.

Just when she was about to circle the tower and look for another entrance, a series of latches and bolts jangled from inside. The thick wooden door slowly creaked open.

A face peered out from the darkness, so wrinkled and saggy it looked like it had been run through the wash. From underneath thin, drooping, white eyebrows, two small, black eyes blinked out at Ninienne. The barest hint of a mouth peeked out from the tangled white beard like a shy mouse.

"Is it... is it you?" came a voice, dry and feeble as a weak desert breeze. Ninienne thought that was a disconcerting way to greet someone, but so far, everything about this moon had been disconcerting.

"Yes, it's me. Ninienne Lightcaster. Are you Master Salagrix? I'm your new apprentice."

The eyes narrowed and blinked. Complex calculations appeared to be taking place on the other side of his age-spotted brow.

"Oh. Oh." Were those noises of recognition or suspicion? The hunched figure closed his eyes and shook his head. "No, no. It can't be. I already have an apprentice. Rodando!" he called back into the darkness. "Rodando, get down here!"

Ninienne's heart sank. Of course, just her luck. She would shuttle all the way to the edge of known space to be sent home on a clerical error. But if it was true, if this wizard already had an apprentice, then she might get to spend her actual apprenticeship somewhere else, anywhere else, then the Shadow Moon of Chadron.

"Where is that boy?" the wizard growled.

Whatever haze of confusion had hung about the old wizard's head seemed to clear. His words sharpened, and his eyes focused. He snorted.

"He's probably off trying to seduce the dryad again. She better teach him a lesson. Ha! That would be quite the itch, wouldn't it? Serves him right. You best come in while we wait for that sluggard and then we can get this all sorted out."

"But you are Salagrix?" Ninienne asked.

"I am he." The door opened fully and Ninienne beheld the Master Wizard for the first time.

The rest of his body fared no better than his face. Long sheaves of skin hung down from his forearms which, because of his considerable hunch, reached down to his knees, which were hanging down near his ankles. He looked as though he were being held together by string and, like the surrounding tower, could collapse at any minute. His gray cloak and wizard hat, stained and singed in several places like well-used pot holders, smelled of sulfur and ozone. Little motes of dust orbited him like tiny moons, and there was an unusual dampness about him, as if he had just stepped out of the bath.

He motioned for Ninienne to enter and tottered up the stairs. She followed him. There was a spoon stuck to his back.

"It's unfortunate you had to come all this way," muttered Salagrix as they ascended. "The Shadow Moon is not exactly a tropical tourist hub, as you may have deduced on your way in. I'll give you a cup of tea in exchange for the latest gossip from Belcarin. Then your trip won't go to waste. Ha!" He laughed, darkly, at a joke that Ninienne must have missed.

The stairway was dark, with torches lit by Fandulf's Fire Charm, but the spells had not been recharged in quite some time and their light was dull and weak. The acrid scent of the magic flames mixed with the dank must. In her opinion, a lantern light spell was the preferable option for a closed interior, but not everyone had the insight she had as the daughter of the Head of a Lamplighter's Guild. Gossamaw whimpered and looked up at Ninienne with worried eyes, and she gave him a pat on the head.

Ninienne followed Salagrix into the room on the first landing. A bored glowworm gave off greenish light from a cage on the ceiling, barely illuminating the room. Two sagging couches flanked a low wooden table crisscrossed with scars and burn marks. A suit of armor, slouched against its sword like a walking stick, observed the proceedings from the curved wall. Next to it, barely visible amid the black stones in the shadows, was an empty stone-lined niche.

"Tea!" Salagrix shouted into the niche so loudly that Ninienne jumped. She squeezed Gossamaw and he croak-barked. Salagrix looked at the frogdog as if noticing him for the first time and then faced Ninienne. "I apologize for shouting, but our kitchen demon is a little hard of hearing."

He sat on one couch, which, since his rear was already so low to the floor, took almost no effort at all. This was good, because based on his gasps for air, the climb up the stairs had apparently wiped him out, and any additional effort was certain to kill him.

"So." Salagrix clasped his hands together and wet his lips with a tongue that was surprisingly thin. "Tell me what old Padjuran is up to."

Still holding Gossamaw, and her satchel still over her shoulder, Ninienne backed down into the opposite couch. "I'm sorry. I don't know anyone by that name. Are they a professor?"

"Before your time, then?" Salagrix sighed, but it was more like a wheeze. "How long has it been? Must've retired. Pity. What I wouldn't do to give him another round of the old Salagrix smack!" He swiped the air at an imaginary opponent.

With a sound like a cracking whip and a flourish of crimson smoke, a full tea tray appeared in the niche. Ninienne jumped again and Gossamaw yelped.

Salagrix groaned. "I'm sorry, this old man has just sat down. Would you mind fetching the tea for us?"

Ninienne glanced at the tea tray in the niche and then back at Salagrix. He was so low on the couch that it seemed it would be a struggle for him to even lift his arms, let alone walk across the room. Leaving her familiar and bag, she fetched the heavy wooden tray, loaded with a full white porcelain tea set and little gray cakes. She poured orange-tinted tea for the two of them, and the swirling steam carried the scent of a sharp spice she could not identify.

"Thank you," said Salagrix as he took his saucer and she returned to her seat. "How about Jinerette? Now there was a firecracker! If I hadn't married Eldrathea, I might have...well, I might, uh..."

But his train of thought had departed for a farther star. In the silence, Ninienne sipped her tea, which was a comfort in the cold, damp room. The unfamiliar spice was warm and tangy and made her think of red flowers. The cake, however, was grainy and bitter, a subtle reminder that she was still, for a brief duration, in one of the odder circles of hell. She gave the cakes to Gossamaw, who tested them gingerly with his long, sticky tongue, and made a disgusted face.

Salagrix noticed this and chuckled. "Ah, I see you have the same palate as me." He reached out to scratch Gossamaw on the neck. "The cooking around here has taken quite the nosedive in recent years. Rodando needs to give the demon a talking-to. Where is that layabout?" Salagrix turned to the stairwell but realized he was still scratching the frogdog's neck. "Ah! And what's this one's name, then?"

"Gossamaw," Ninienne smiled, glad that the conversation had turned to a topic to which she could contribute. "Gossie for short. He's half frogdog and half something else, I'm not sure what. I found him in the swamp near my hometown, and he's been my familiar ever since."

"Shame you won't be staying," Salagrix said to Gossamaw. "The tower could use a little *cheer*."

This last word landed in the room with a dull thud. Salagrix's hand dropped and his eyes drifted to the wall.

In the silence, Ninienne tapped her thighs with her fingertips and adjusted her wizard's hat. The suit of armor was directly in her line of vision. She was no expert on armaments, but the design was strange, with lots of swoops and spikes. She couldn't shake the feeling that something was watching them from behind the visor.

When it became clear that Salagrix might never return from his distraction, and that Rodando was nowhere within earshot, Ninienne said, "I'm going to call the Academy."

"Call?" Salagrix cleared his throat, a sound which Ninienne desperately hoped she would never have to hear again. "Yes, of course. Oh, but I think I'm out of hawk powder."

"I meant call on the datastream." Ninienne pulled the flat black glass device out of her satchel and gave it a couple of swipes. "Assuming we can get a connection out here."

Salagrix looked over at the device as if it were going to bite him, or had just insulted his mother, or both.

"What is that?" he spat. "Some sort of crystal?"

"No, it's technological. The whole Academy runs on them. They switched over a couple of years ago. Did they not send you one?"

Salagrix shrugged. "My connection to Belcarin is… tenuous."

Ninienne first checked that it was daytime on Belcarin. When communicating across worlds with different suns and rotations, the hardest part was finding a time when everyone was awake. Fortunately, it was currently office hours on Belcarin, and within moments, Ninienne had a live video connection with Dean Falchbrook's assistant. She set the device on the table and a projected image appeared, hovering in space, and refreshing inconsistently in discolored blocks because of the poor connection.

The assistant, as best they could tell through the interference, was a tall woman with an elegant face, and a tight, neat bun of dark hair. Her shoulders, just above where the image cut off, bore crisp white robes.

"Dean Falchbrook's office," said the assistant, in a tone that was clipped and brief but not unkind.

"Yes, hi," Ninienne started in, "I think there's been a mistake with my apprenticeship assignment and I just want to check so I can get reassigned to the right place."

The assistant tapped and swiped on something out of sight.

"I'm see that your device is registered to Ninienne Lightcaster, is that you?" the assistant asked.

"Yes," said Ninienne. While the assistant examined her files, Salagrix shuffled, grunting, to peer over Ninienne's shoulder.

"Fascinating," he said, and Ninienne could smell the damp reek of his mouth. "How does it work? Is it runes or a glyph of some kind?"

"No, it's technology, like I said." Ninienne shifted away from the wizard's breath. "Siliconium, I think?"

"Alright," said the assistant, "I have here that you are assigned to Master Salagrix."

"Yes—" said Ninienne.

"Can she hear me?" Salagrix asked.

Ninienne nodded, reluctantly.

"Salagrix the Sanguine!" the wizard announced. His eager eyes flashed in the bright glow of the projection. "Master Wizard of the Shadow Moon of Chadron, Twenty-sixth Chamber of the Arcana, Initiate of Ulmarth, The Unforg—"

"Yes, I have your file," the assistant muttered, somewhat irritated. "What seems to be the problem?"

"He says he already has an apprentice," said Ninienne. "So if that's the case, if I could just get a reassignment—"

"I'm not seeing any other apprentices assigned to Master Salagrix at the moment," said the assistant.

"Rodando!" shouted Salagrix. "I wish to submit a request for discipline for Rodando! Nothing too harsh, mind you, just enough to get him back on track. Bed of nails, that sort of thing."

"Corporal discipline is no longer allowed under the Academy's code of conduct." The assistant pursed her lips and made a bemused sound. "Although, I see a record here of your previous apprentice, Rodando Vechi. But it's from, oh, twenty years ago or so."

Salagrix made a stifled gurgling noise at the back of his throat. "Twenty...years?"

Ninienne was confused. Salagrix had shouted for Rodando as if he expected him to show up at any moment, but Rodando hadn't been his apprentice for over two decades. Could the old man be that senile?

"So, it appears that everything is in order." The assistant sounded pleased, as if disorder was the worst threat imaginable. "Miss Lightcaster's assignment is correct."

The pit in Ninienne's stomach doubled in weight and dropped through the floor. She was in the right place. She would spend the final year of her magical education here, in this crumbling tower, with this crumbling man. The projection on her device snapped off, and the room returned to darkness, lit only by the weak greenish light of the glowworm.

Salagrix was still staring at the space where the projection had been, lost in thought, as was his habit, apparently. Ninienne stewed in her disappointment. She had been hoping for a more prestigious, capable, engaging mentor. One who would take her under their wing and launch her into her new career.

Salagrix turned slowly to face Ninienne. "You are my... new apprentice?" He sounded the words out as if trying to express a new, complex thought.

Ninienne gulped. "Yep, looks like it."

An expression flashed across the wizard's wrinkled face, too quickly for Ninienne to decipher. Was it confusion? Fear?

An awkward silence hung in the room. Gossamaw yawned.

"Yes," said Salagrix, drawing out the word. "This is good. It will take time to get you up to speed, of course. Too late to get started tonight, though." He rubbed his hands together and then pointed to the niche in the wall. "In the meantime, you are welcome to order whatever you like from the kitchen demon, but please return the dishes to the niche before you go to bed. I've already had my dinner and am going to retire. The apprentice's room is on the second level, just above this one. Make yourself comfortable."

With a sound that might have been a groan or the scraping of bone on bone, Salagrix dragged his body up the staircase and out of sight.

Ninienne's stomach churned. Her body felt heavy underneath the light of the sick-looking glowworm. This was it. They had assigned her to this ancient, befuddled, relic of a wizard, and he to her. It had seemed so surreal when the assistant had announced it, and now here she was, in this dark, windowless tower that might collapse at any moment, alone. She shivered against the clammy chill.

Ninienne shared a look with Gossamaw, who gave a plaintive croak and blinked his watery, wide-set eyes. She was feeling many things, but despite Salagrix's departing word, not a one of them was comfortable.

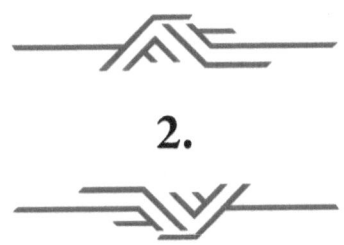

2.

The tradition of the apprenticeship year at Belcarin Academy of Wizardry is almost as old as the Academy itself. Its premise is simple: after four years of training and study with professors and other students on the main campus, the apprentice trains for a year by themselves under a Master Wizard on another world. The Master provides lectures and hands-on education in whatever subject he is expert, as well as room and board. In return, the apprentice provides a year of free labor, taking care of the chores and practicalities that, while necessary, distract the Master from his own studies and duties to the people of his domain. If the student successfully completes their assignment, the student graduates, and moves on to a career or more schooling.

Whether this arrangement is actually worthwhile to the apprentices has been a subject of much debate over the centuries, but as the ones who write the curriculum at the Academy are themselves Master Wizards who rely on a steady stream of fresh-faced apprentices to do their dishes, these debates fizzle like an under-brewed sparkler potion.

— from the article "Apprenticeship" by Apprentice Penelope Watercleanser, Belcarin Academy Datastream Archives

NINIENNE WAS DEBATING the merits of the apprenticeship system herself while she remained slouched on the couch in Salagrix's sitting room. After an acceptable interval of dazed self-pity, the grumble of her stomach forced her to rise and approach the wall niche.

"Uh," she said with uncertainty, into the ether, "Vaporbean tacos?"

There was a pause, long enough that Ninienne was about to try again, and then a puff of crimson smoke appeared with a loud crack. The cloud cleared to reveal a white plate and three limp, sad-looking tacos.

Unsure of the proper etiquette with kitchen demons, she called out, "Thank you?"

After returning the tea try to the niche as instructed, which vanished in a cloud of smoke, she grabbed her plate of tacos, her satchel, and Gossamaw, and braved the fire-charm choked staircase up to the next level of the tower and the promised apprentice's room.

Ninienne, hands full, pushed open the door with her shoulder. The furnishings were simple: a bed, a desk, a trunk. Behind a dingy curtain that hung from the ceiling was a small claw-footed bathtub and a garderobe. Mushrooms sprouted where the wall met the floor, and the unmade bed was thick with damp. Gossamaw hopped under the bed and put his hands on his head as if to hide from the mess.

If the events of the last hour had not already made it clear, Salagrix had not been expecting her.

She sat on the bed and ate her tacos, which were mushy and bland. She handed the plate over to Gossamaw to lick clean.

There was no way she could sleep in this room in its current condition. She cast a simple drying spell, chanting the words and holding her fingers in a specific arrangement. A glowing disc appeared in her palm, which she waved over all the surfaces in the room to banish the wet.

Books and loose parchment splayed across the desk, which she dried and organized into a stack. Whoever had used this room last (Rodando, presumably, if there had not been another apprentice in the intervening years that Salagrix had forgotten) had terrible, basically illegible handwriting, and even where water had not blurred the ink she could not read the notes. There was only one sheaf written with care and affixed to the wall that seemed impervious.

CHORES:
-Clean workrooms
-Update ingredient inventory
-~~Prepare meals~~
-~~Wash dishes~~
-Repair masonry
-Recharge torches
-Secure perimeter
-Receive deliveries

The thought of spending a year in this tower with that list of dreary tasks filled her with dread, to say nothing of the subtle threat of *'Secure perimeter.'* At least 'prepare meals' and 'wash dishes' were crossed out. She wondered why.

After the desk, she turned her attention to the trunk, which she found unlocked but, curiously, still full of belongings. A full set of clothing, socks, underwear, more books, and a stack of business cards that read in silver letters on black paper: *RODANDO VECHI, Demonologist.*

As she gathered all the items into her arms, she wondered why anyone would leave all their belongings behind after their apprenticeship. Feeling the fine quality of a robe, her imagination kicked into gear, and she thought she had a theory.

Sometimes, when a student from a wealthy family graduated from Belcarin, they left all their things behind because they could just acquire more at home. Remaining students often divided up these abandoned items by seniority or by lot. Perhaps Rodando's family was similarly wealthy and he had left his belongings behind for the taking.

Still, it was strange.

Regardless of the reason for the abandoned trunk, unfortunately for Ninienne, his clothes were way too big for her. There was, however, a soft and warm-looking scarf which she kept for herself before stashing the rest of his things behind the bathtub and out of sight.

After storing her own belongings in the trunk and tidying up the rest of the room, she looked around to take stock. She wasn't ready to get comfortable, but the room would do for now.

Through the window (which, she would later learn, was the only window in the entire tower), she watched the last vestiges of the orange gas giant set over the purple forest. The neighboring Brilliant Moon glowed bright and full and tinged the woods with silvery blue light.

When it got dark, Ninienne cast a light spell in the empty cage on the ceiling and adjusted it to a gentle yellow. She ran a bath, but found that it never got warmer than frigid, so instead she lay on the bed to cuddle with Gossamaw and read her datastream messages.

After sending messages to her parents and her friend Drusilla to let them know she had arrived safely, she brought up the search feature for the Belcarin Academy Datastream Archives:

"how to get an apprenticeship re-assignment"

DESPITE MANY HOURS of searching, late into the night, Ninienne did not find the answers she sought. The Belcarin apprenticeship program was an institution steeped in tradition, and basically the only way to get a new assignment was if the Master died (which, given the median age of the Masters, happened often enough to mention).

She snapped her device off and flopped onto the bed. Had she done something to deserve the worst possible apprenticeship placement? Had she offended Dean Falchbrook?

As she scoured her memory, with a sinking feeling that had been all too common today, she realized she had.

NINIENNE STEPPED INTO Dean Falchbrook's office, closing the door behind her, and the hubbub of students in the halls outside immediately quieted to silence. The only remaining sound was the ticking of the atomic grandfather clock on the wall.

The Dean flicked his eyes up from a massive, sigil-filled tome on his desk.

"Do you have an appointment?" His voice was high and worn, like a well-oiled bowstring.

"Ah, yes, let me—" Ninienne rummaged in her bag for the enchanted parchment. Not finding it immediately, she set her bag on the Dean's desk for leverage. "I know it's in here somewhere."

The Dean pursed his already thin lips, not amused. His face was long and thin, as if imprinted into taffy and then stretched out. Unlike taffy, however, there was nothing sweet about Dean Falchbrook.

Ninienne felt her fingers grasp the sought-after slip.

"Gotcha!"

She pulled out the parchment, but as she did so, the contents of her bag spilled onto the Dean's desk.

"So sorry," she said, and began shoveling her books and scrolls back into her bag. To her horror, she realized her sketchbook had fallen open, and to double her horror, it had opened up directly to the page where she had doodled caricatures of the Belcarin staff as characters from her favorite novel.

Dean Falchbrook's eyes narrowed. He looked directly at Ninienne's cartoon version of himself, who she had regrettably cast at the novel's vampire villain. Ninienne quickly shoved the sketchbook into her bag, hoping he hadn't gotten a good look. She took her seat, and placed the enchanted parchment into a shallow dish at the corner of the Dean's desk, where it disintegrated in licks of purple flame.

"It did not realize Belcarin offered a course in *cartooning*," the Dean said, mirthlessly, dashing Ninienne's hopes like glass on slate.

Ninienne's cheeks flushed. "Oh, you know, just a little imaginative sketching. Maybe I'll submit it to the school newspaper." She laughed, as if to say *what a small silly thing that we're going to put behind us right now and never speak of again.*

She'd expected the Dean to laugh along or at least smile. Instead, he seemed almost offended. Maybe it had been a mistake to lighten the mood.

"Or not," Ninienne said quickly. She nervously tucked a strand of black hair behind her ear. She leaned sideways in her chair in a pose that, she imagined, a relaxed person would find themselves in. "Burning it might be another good option."

Dean Falchbrook frowned. "Such jokes, if you can call them that, might play well in the quad with the other truants, but you should know that I myself am part vampire, and as such, I find your bizarre depiction personally offensive."

Ninienne shrank beneath the intensity of his gaze. She objected to the Dean's characterization of her as a 'truant,' as she was one of the top-ranked students at the Academy, but she felt that this precise moment was not the time to argue semantics, nor to explain the fictional context of a character from *Almet's Adventures*.

After four years at Belcarin, how could she not have realized that the Dean was part vampire? Now, of course, she could see it in his pale skin, the shape of his ears, and yes, the hint of fangs in his teeth.

Stupid, Neens! Stupid!

She wanted to disappear, but she forced herself instead to meet the Dean's eyes.

"I apologize," she said, and as she spoke, she wove the subtle notes of a calming spell into her speech. It was supposed to be for relaxing creatures as you treated them, but she had used it on people before, and it had turned down the temperature of more than one intense conversation. "I'll be more mindful of my future doodling."

The tilt of the Dean's eyebrows and the way the corners of his mouth turned down suggested that she had placated his ire for now, by spell or otherwise.

"Apology accepted," he said. "As a student of Belcarin Academy of Wizardry, your behavior reflects not only on yourself but on the illustrious institution you represent. Understood?"

Ninienne nodded.

"Very well." His eyes turned to the wisps of smoke rising from her burning appointment parchment and scanned them as if reading the cast bones of an oracle.

"So, I see you're seeking an apprenticeship placement, if I'm not mistaken?"

Ninienne nodded again. She figured it would be best to speak as little as possible from this point forward.

Dean Falchbrook tapped on the datastream device embedded in his hardwood desk. It took him more than one try before a hologram of Ninienne's student profile popped up in front of him, backwards from her perspective.

"I'm still not used to these things," the Dean muttered, gesturing to the device. "Back in my days at the Academy, we used enchanted parchment for everything. I'm not sure what we've gained..." His thoughts trailed off as he read over her file.

Ninienne sat in silence. The warm smell of leather and parchment from the book-lined walls filled the room.

"Ninienne Lightcaster," he read out, pronouncing each syllable.

"My friends call me Neens," she offered.

The Dean looked at her as if she had made a rude noise and returned his attention to her file. "With a surname like that, you must have an aptitude for optical magic."

Ninienne nodded. "That's my family's affinity. But I've chosen to study—"

"Creature healing," the Dean read. "A suitably rigorous discipline. What are your plans for after graduation?"

"I'm hoping to join the Research Department here at Belcarin and study new creature healing techniques in the lab."

The Dean looked at her carefully. "You do realize you'll need two Letters to even be considered?"

Ninienne nodded. "I've already got a Professor's Letter. Last semester, I helped Professor Hemnal with the beached nebula whales on Trantis as my independent study. She said that was more than enough to qualify."

The Dean stroked his chin. "Ah, yes, I remember this now. That was quite the feather in Belcarin's cap." He looked her over again, as if reassessing his first impression. "You must be hoping for a Master's Letter, then."

Ninienne nodded again, but then felt like she had been nodding too much, so stopped.

"Ambitious." The Dean tapped his datastream device and the projection snapped off. He steepled his fingers and drew a breath. "Now, we make every effort to match each apprentice with a Master in the same discipline. However, as you might imagine, based on the particular pool of applicants and the availability of the Masters, this does not always happen. When disciplines do not align, we encourage students to seek interdisciplinary connections. Matching Master and apprentice is not an exact science. There are many factors to consider, as I have said. And you are seeking a Master's Letter... I will put you in the pool with the other apprenticeship candidates. Unless there is something else you require, I have another appointment."

Ninienne shook her head, rose, and went to the door. "Thank you, Dean."

The Dean smiled, and now there was no question as to the vampire portion of his lineage. "Best of luck with your apprenticeship, *Neens*."

OF COURSE, NINIENNE couldn't prove that Dean Falchbrook had purposely assigned her to a senile Master on a backwater moon for an unintentionally offensive drawing of himself, but his pointed use of her nickname echoed in her mind, and she couldn't shake her lingering doubts. This also meant, even if she could find a legitimate reason to be re-assigned, that the Dean was unlikely to be sympathetic to her case.

Would she be able to procure a Master's Letter from Salagrix? It depended on how easily impressed he was.

Then there was the question of Salagrix's discipline, which he had not mentioned in their brief conversation earlier. Was he a creature healer? If so, that might make the year worth it and that Master's Letter practically guaranteed. If not?

It would be a very long year.

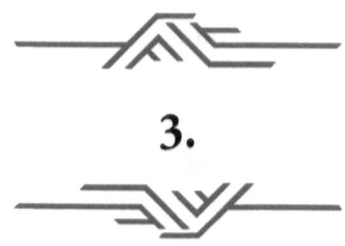

3.

Soulfire, for all its importance in underpinning the magical arts, is not particularly well understood. This might be evident perusing the Belcarin Academy of Wizardry's course catalog, where there is only one course, Meta-theory of Magic, which mentions soulfire in its description:

'This course will examine historical theoretical lenses through which we understand the inner workings of magic itself, including that most mysterious of topics, soulfire. Students will study texts from wizards of the past, as well as modern interpretations. Offered every third year, lectures held in the library boiler room.'

This much we know: all living beings generate soulfire. Some generate more than others. When an individual possesses a sufficient capacity for soulfire, that individual is capable of magic. Performing any kind of magic (whether incantations, sigils, potions, etc.) drains soulfire, which takes time, food, and rest to regenerate.

The rest is a mystery. What are the mechanics of soulfire generation? Why do some people's soulfire pools swirl clockwise and others counterclockwise? Why do my houseplants generate tiny amounts of soulfire, and can I harness it to dry my socks?

Contradictory answers to these questions litter the millennia of wizarding scholarship on the subject, most of which comprises virulent name-calling of scholars of the opposing viewpoint. To study soulfire is to become conversant in many dead languages' use of profanities, most of which are variations on 'he whose socks are wet.'

—from the article "Soulfire," by Professor Trelogan, Belcarin Academy Datastream Archives

NINIENNE WOKE THE NEXT morning to the orange light of the gas giant streaming through the window. She splashed icy water on her face from the tub faucet and dressed in her brown overalls and matching wizard's hat. She sat for a few minutes at the edge of her bed, unsure of Salagrix's expectations. Would he come to get her? Was she supposed to get started on chores?

If she wanted that Master's Letter, it might be a good idea to show initiative.

She climbed the stairs to see if Salagrix was awake. Gossamaw followed, pushing his chubby body over each step with determination.

On the next floor she found an open, doorless room, larger than the rooms on the first two floors, which explained the tower's precarious silhouette. The room was dark and windowless, so she cast and affixed a light spell to a lantern which hung by a chain from the ceiling. The lantern, annoyingly, was not in the center of the room. It appeared, from the pattern of stones in the ceiling and the floor, that someone had expanded this room at some point, but had not relocated the once-central lantern.

Once the room was lit, she took stock. Fungal growths, white and spongy, crept in between the stones of the floor and the walls. A triple set of wooden floor-to-ceiling shelves occupied half of the room's walls, filled with bizarre ingredients for every imaginable spell: glass jars with eyeballs and crow's feet suspended in liquid, earthenware containers with large corks and handwritten labels like 'ground minotaur horn' and 'rosemary', woven baskets overflowing with dried grasses and silvery bundles of hair. Dried lizard heads hung from the ceiling next to bundles of garlic. Ingredients spilled from many knocked-over containers onto the shelves and the floor.

Along another part of the wall, a formidable wooden table held a mismatched assortment of tools: cauldrons from tiny to massive in a rainbow of metallic colors, scattered knives of silver and obsidian, a jar of wands, and a stained deck of divination cards. There were scraps of parchment across the table and the surrounding floor, as well as scrolls and open books. A chalkboard on wheels with half-erased sigils and equations hid a door which led to a magically enlarged storage closet stuffed with cleaning supplies, empty crates, and a broken alembic.

Like the apprentice's room, the workshop was damp and disused.

Ninienne steeled herself. *Clean workrooms* was at the top of the daily chores on the list. She rolled up her sleeves, ready to dive in, when she was interrupted by a grumble from her stomach.

Breakfast would have to come first.

There was a niche in this room as well, identical to the one in the sitting room on the first floor.

"Black coffee and a vegetable omelet!" she shouted into the niche, uncertain if there were any limitations on what she could order. With a crack and a burst of crimson smoke, a steaming mug of coffee and an omelet on a clean, white plate appeared in the niche.

"Thank you!" she shouted, still unsure how to interact with the unseen kitchen demon.

The coffee was fine, nothing special, but it was hot and, more importantly, it was coffee. They said the Twelve Thousand Worlds were settled and built on coffee, and right now, she believed them.

The vegetables squished as she bit into the flavorless omelet. She ate what she could and gave Gossamaw her unfinished half, who gobbled it up with a wide smile and a little burp. She would need to find something that the demon made that was actually edible because so far she had had no luck.

Her hunger satisfied, if not her palate, she assessed the room. But before she could get started, Salagrix peeked his face around the doorway and blinked at Ninienne with an empty expression. The tip of his nightcap drooped down almost to his waist.

"Good morning," Ninienne said, putting her breakfast plate back into the niche where it vanished with a crack of smoke. "Wasn't sure if I should go ahead and start cleaning, or..."

When Salagrix's expression did not change, she added, "As your new apprentice."

This seemed to cause a cascade of recollections on the wizard's face, and he nodded repeatedly. "Ah, yes, of course. The new apprentice. Yes."

Ninienne laughed quietly to diffuse the awkwardness. Would she have to remind her Master of her existence every day?

Salagrix stepped into the room fully and Ninienne noticed, once again, how the fungal spores kicked up by his shuffling robes seemed to orbit him rather than take the expected meandering routes through the room. Several jars on the nearest shelf scraped towards him as if he exerted his own gravity.

"Very well then—" A fit of coughing cut off Salagrix. He pounded his chest and cleared his throat, which sounded like he was trying to dislodge a slug the size of a garden squash from his lungs. He recovered with a shake of his head. "Let me prepare myself, and I will meet you here in the lower workshop when I am ready. We will go over your duties and begin the first lecture. In the meantime, you are welcome to order whatever you like from the kitchen demon."

Ninienne wanted to ask if there was anything actually worth eating, but Salagrix had already vanished up the dark stairwell.

She still wanted to clean, but held herself back in case there were specific instructions incoming. Instead, she puttered around the room and then took a seat in the chair by the workbench to scroll on her device. Because of the differences in time on their various worlds, her parents back home were not available for a call, and neither was Drusilla, her best friend, who was also on her apprenticeship year. Ninienne was eager to find out how her friend's assignment compared to hers. Gossamaw sniffed a large wicker basket on the lowest shelf, licked it, made a face, and then curled up on the floor and began to snore.

Ninienne was very curious to find out if Salagrix was a creature healer. After examining the ingredient shelves and the tools on the workbench, she wasn't able to make any specific guesses. Some materials were familiar, and others were not. The scribbles on the chalkboard were unintelligible to her. Just when she was about to search for information about him in the Belcarin Academy archives via datastream, he appeared in the stairwell, dressed in the same dingy hat and robes from yesterday. A sock clung to his hip, and his face looked a little wet, as if he had been sweating.

"Ah! Good, you're still here. Reassuring." Salagrix tottered over to the chalkboard. "The chair you're in is fine, yes."

Salagrix flicked his hand, and the chalkboard wiped itself clean. A tiny stub of chalk flew to the upper left corner of the board and hovered there, awaiting further instruction.

"Welcome to your apprenticeship. You will address me as Master Salagrix, a title befitting both my position as the Master Wizard of the Shadow Moon of Chadron and your mentor for the duration of your time here. Do not let my reputation intimidate you. I assure you, any stories you may have heard about me are patently false."

Salagrix chuckled here, but Ninienne had never heard the wizard's name, much less of any reputation. Should she have?

"The first matter of business is your duties. Mornings will be your time for cleaning and maintenance of the tower, as well as other tasks." Here, Salagrix enumerated a list of chores that were the exact same, in the exact same order, as the list she had found in her room. The only exception was the conspicuous absence of *Secure Perimeter*, which was a relief on her part.

"In the afternoons, we will meet here, in the lower workroom, for lecture."

Lectures on what? Ninienne wondered. *Creature healing? Oh, please let it be creature healing.*

But Salagrix did not elaborate.

"The evenings are yours to do with as you wish. You are welcome to join me for dinner in the dining room, which is the floor above this one, or you may take your dinner wherever else you like, including in the town of Black Gulch. However, on account of the local nocturnal wildlife, which is known to be vicious, this is not recommended. Neither is dining in Black Gulch, whose accommodations are meager and whose townsfolk are backwards, but you have been duly informed of your options.

"Because of my needs and the rigorous nature of your course of study, I cannot accommodate requests for days off. Settle in. This tower will be your home for the duration of your apprenticeship.

"Any questions?"

For the moment, Salagrix appeared to have regained his presence of mind. His confusions seemed to come and go.

"Not about the schedule," said Ninienne. She wanted some clarifications about the vicious nocturnal wildlife, but for now there was only one pressing question. "But I am curious to learn what your discipline is."

Salagrix looked at her askance. "Why, portalcraft, of course."

Oh. So not creature healing. In her heart, the last vestiges of hope for a fun, engaging apprenticeship shriveled and died.

"What is your level of familiarity with the subject?" Salagrix asked.

"Zero," said Ninienne. She wasn't even sure the Academy offered courses on portalcraft. She had never seen it in the course catalog, nor had she ever met a fellow student who had mentioned taking a class on the topic.

Salagrix sighed. "That is to be expected. Portalcrafters are a dying breed, I'm afraid. No matter. Since you are starting from 'Zero', as you say, we will skip your chores this morning in favor of an extra lecture."

The nub of chalk sprung to life, wrote *Portalcraft* in a neat blocky script, and then underlined the word.

"Why study portalcraft?"

By Salagrix's presentational tone, Ninienne realized the lecture had begun, and hastily grabbed some spare parchment and the most functional-looking ink wand from the worktable.

"In the last several hundred years, the advancement of spacecrafts that can travel between the stars has been, pardon the pun, astronomical."

Salagrix paused here, as if expecting laughter. He had taken on the airs of someone addressing a much larger room full of students in rapt attention. Despite Salagrix's obvious struggles with memory, Ninienne got the impression that he had finely honed this speech over decades and it remained perfectly preserved in the old lecturer's mind.

"One may wonder, what is the purpose of learning to craft portals using magic, to traverse the stars by ancient art when one could simply hop on the next shuttle? Portals are more dangerous, more expensive, more unpredictable, and more time-consuming than spacecraft. Portals require the consideration of innumerable interlocking variables, large quantities of rare and costly ingredients, and sometimes days if not weeks of difficult calculations. The slightest error at any step can result in, at best, total failure, and at worst, death and calamitous destruction."

Ninienne realized she was leaning forward.

"In the light of these difficulties, there are those who say: abandon the old ways, your field is not relevant, we are discontinuing your courses from the curriculum. To them—to them I say—"

Here Salagrix adopted a defiant posture, arm across his chest, like a lone warrior standing his ground against an arena of adversaries. His eyes misted.

"Bully."

The workroom was perfectly silent. Gossamaw yawned and smacked his lips.

"Bully to the naysayers!" shouted Salagrix, getting worked up. "We seek not the easy way, nor the efficient way, nor the cheap way. No. We seek the way of power. To feel the very fabric of space bend in our hands. That is the way of the wizard!"

This was hardly the ringing endorsement in favor of the study of portalcraft that Ninienne was expecting, but she had to admit that his enthusiasm was infectious.

"With that in mind," he said, "Let us begin."

HOURS LATER, AFTER being dismissed for a brief break before dinner, Ninienne found herself outside, in between the tower and that perfectly circular border of trees.

The air was chilly. Ninienne shivered and wished she had brought the scarf. Gossamaw rolled on his back in a patch of brown clover and then hopped towards the woods. Ninienne followed her frogdog, and the short dry grass crunched under her feet.

Her mind was still reeling from the lecture, which had lasted all day. She felt plunged into a new world of terms and ways of thinking. Salagrix was obviously passionate. She recalled the way his eyes sparkled as he hinted at further secrets to be revealed. She understood none of it yet, but she might soon. By the end of the year, she might open a portal and cross the galaxy with a single step. That was intoxicating.

Dusk approached. She reached the border of the forest and smelled the earth of the forest floor and the curious sweetness of decay.

As she watched Gossamaw hop and roll and play, she wondered if she had been too quick to judge her new apprenticeship assignment. True, she would still spend a year in a damp tower out in the middle of nowhere with a senile old wizard. True, portalcraft was not a subject she had ever considered studying or heard of. But she wasn't one to back down from a challenge. Portalcraft didn't have any connection to creature healing, as far as she could tell, but the ability to travel to distant worlds without a spacecraft? That was intriguing. That was a very interesting opportunity. And, if she could impress Salagrix with her effort and diligence, that Master's Letter and a career at the Research Department were hers.

Ninienne stopped short before entering the scraggly wall of trees and bushes. She was not yet sure if the forest was safe. Salagrix had mentioned "vicious nocturnal wildlife," and the phrase "secure perimeter" on Rodando's list still echoed in her mind.

What had happened to the former apprentice, anyway? Salagrix's memory appeared spotty, but perhaps when he was feeling sharp, Ninienne might get more answers.

Gossamaw sniffed hesitantly at a wilted, purple-leafed fern.

"Not today, Gossie," Ninienne said. "It's getting dark. Maybe another time."

Still, standing here at the edge, she felt the dark thrill of an invitation to enter and immerse herself in a tangle of living, growing things.

The thrill did not diminish as she turned back to the tower.

BACK IN HER ROOM, NINIENNE washed. She would have to figure out how to fix the cold water at some point because she did not enjoy freezing baths. Once dry, she took out her clothing options, which were few, as she traveled light. Salagrix hadn't specified a dress code for dinner, but she choose the one "fancy" outfit she had packed, a modest black dress with a matching cape. It might serve her to make a good impression at the first dinner of her apprenticeship.

She and Gossamaw climbed the stairs to the floor beyond the lower workroom into the dining room.

A long wooden table spanned the room with a chair at either end. Dingy candelabras with stubby, flickering candles appointed the surface of the table, while a filthy rug lay underneath. Mountains of dust, grime, and fungus encircled the room where the floor met the walls, underneath a niche twice as long as the ones on the other floors.

Salagrix was not here, nor had dinner been served. She could have waited, but her curiosity got the best of her, and she continued climbing the stairs to investigate the rest of the tower.

On the next flight above the dining room, she found a wooden door, closed. She could feel the heat from the other side. Red light, tinged with the acrid scent of sulfur, spilled from the gap underneath the door. This, she assumed, was where the kitchen demon lived.

She continued up the stairs and ran into Salagrix coming down.

"Ah!" shouted the old wizard, and then, upon seeing her fully, "No!" He waved her back down the stairs with a shooing motion, shouting, "Down! Down!"

They hurried into the dining room, and Salagrix took a seat at the chair closest to the doorway, panting. He leaned against the table, wheezing, and took a few moments to collect himself. Ninienne assumed she had spooked him in the dark stairwell.

"I'm sorry. I don't mean to be short with you," said Salagrix, when he had caught his breath. "But I neglected to set clear boundaries this morning." He took another shuddering breath and steadied himself. "My work on the upper levels of the tower is quite dangerous. When your skills in portalcraft advance, I may have use for you in the upper workshop, but until then, I must ask you to confine yourself to this floor and the floors below."

Ninienne nodded, somewhat chastened. She hoped there were not too many more forgotten rules and secret boundaries she would stumble into.

As Salagrix continued to pant, Ninienne realized he was still wearing the same dirty gray robes from earlier that day.

Overalls at dinner from now on, thought Ninienne. *Noted. And don't go above the dining room.*

"Dinner!" Salagrix shouted toward the large niche. Ninienne heard a rumble like thunder, but then realized the sound was coming not from outside, but from the floor above. The thrumming swelled and then, with the now-familiar crack and burst of crimson smoke, a full silver-plated dinner appeared in the niche.

"I'm much too tired to get up again," Salagrix wheezed. "Would you mind terribly setting the table, please?"

Usually, levitation spells were not worth the effort, as they drained a lot of soulfire, and it was easier just to carry things. But Ninienne felt like showing off.

With a few hand motions and a perfectly pronounced incantation, the silver dishes flew from the niche and arranged themselves prettily on the table.

Salagrix clapped his hands and laughed. "Well done, very good!"

Ninienne took her seat with a flourish of her cape and a self-satisfied smile.

The old wizard lifted a silver lid to reveal a steaming, blackened tunnel grouse. "This is a treat, I must say. Rodando eats alone, so my dinners are usually quite quiet."

Ninienne unfolded her napkin onto her lap. "You mean Rodando *ate* alone."

"Hmm?" Salagrix looked up from transferring a slice of grouse to his plate.

"You said Rodando *eats* alone. But he hasn't been your apprentice for over twenty years, right? He's not here."

The old wizard turned as if he had heard something fall in a nearby room. "Right. Yes. Rodando is... gone."

"What happened to him? Do you remember? He left all of his things here and never came back for them."

Salagrix stared into the middle distance and his mouth opened and closed wordlessly.

Worried that she had sent her master into a stupor from which he would not return, Ninienne turned her attention to the food in front of her.

As a lover and caretaker of creatures, Ninienne did not eat meat, so she passed on the tunnel grouse and instead filled her plate with limp boiled vegetables and a wet salad. The kitchen demon's cooking once again left something to be desired. It was maybe time to look for alternate sources of nutrition.

The scrape of a dish along the table caught her attention. She looked up to see a gravy boat inching ever closer toward Salagrix, as if tugged by an invisible string. Many other plates and cups were similarly creeping towards him.

"Um, the, uh—" Ninienne pointed towards the offending tableware.

Salagrix looked up. "Hmm?"

"The dishes. They're—"

"Bah!" Salagrix waved at the air as if batting an invisible fly, and the dishes stilled. "Blasted side effects."

Side effects. That was interesting. She was curious, but she didn't want to pry at the moment. Going directly at things seemed ineffective with Salagrix. Instead, she tried a different topic of conversation.

"I wanted to ask you about the woods around the tower," she asked, after tossing a mushy carrot to Gossamaw. "Are they safe to explore?"

Salagrix nodded as he finished chewing. "In the day, generally speaking, yes," he said. "The night-time beasts are fierce enough that I would avoid them. But you needn't worry. The dryad and I reached an agreement some years ago. You may have noticed the perimeter."

Ninienne nodded, expecting Salagrix to elaborate, but he did not.

"There's some sort of barrier?" she prompted.

Salagrix nodded as he wiped his beard with his napkin. "The dryad limits the plants and creatures of her woods from crossing the barrier of their own accord. We therefore avoid unnecessary entanglements."

Salagrix's mention of creatures once again piqued Ninienne's curiosity. The Twelve Thousand Worlds had a dizzying array of life, and one never knew what one might encounter on any given world.

"You must know quite a bit about the local wildlife?" Ninienne's curiosity came through.

Salagrix made a face. "I try not to pay attention, honestly."

Her mentor's dismissive attitude did little to suppress her curiosity. She wanted to explore those woods as soon as she had an opportunity. Who knew what she might find?

The rest of the dinner conversation was sparse, until the end when Salagrix, grunting, raised his arm.

"I suppose we ought to have a toast, on the occasion of your new apprenticeship." He turned toward the niche and shouted. "Pixie wine!"

A tray with a ruby bottle and two glasses appeared in the niche with the same bang and burst.

Salagrix looked longingly at the wine. Ninienne's soulfire had not regenerated from her earlier levitation spell, and so she fetched the tray herself.

"Thank you. Much appreciated," said Salagrix as Ninienne poured two glasses and then returned to her seat.

Salagrix raised his glass. "To your apprenticeship."

Ninienne returned the toast and took a sip of the wine, which was thick and sweet. She could already feel the warmth softening the edges of her mind. Not daring to drink more, not on the first night of her new apprenticeship with her new mentor, she set her glass back down to find that Salagrix had already drained his and was pouring himself another.

"Ah, I remember my Academy days," said Salagrix, looking misty-eyed. "I was quite the troublemaker, actually. I was not always the respectable and formidable Master Wizard you see before you, if you can believe that."

Ninienne bit her lip to keep from cringing.

"I'm sure you're familiar with the clock tower on the quad? Is that still there?" he asked.

Ninienne pulled her datastream device from the pocket of her dress and, with a few swipes, projected a picture of the Belcarin clock tower above the table. "This one?"

Salagrix, enraptured, rose from his seat and approached the image. "Yes, yes, that's it. Exactly as I remember it," he said in a distant voice. The old wizard became lost in the image, and Ninienne decided to not interrupt his reverie.

"As I was saying." Salagrix shook his head. "One night, the lads and I were feeling a little punchy, so we broke into the tower and hexed it. The next morning, everyone woke up to the tower looking like this!" He demonstrated by lifting his forearm and bending his wrist. "It had gone limp! Ha! We had a good laugh about that one!"

As Salagrix laughed at his schoolboy prank, Ninienne noticed how loose the old wizard's wrist was, as if it might fall off at any moment.

"Those were the days." Salagrix sighed.

His eyes darted from the datastream device to Ninienne and back. "I don't mean to overstep, but I am quite fascinated by your device here. Would it be terribly inconvenient if I borrowed it for the night to examine it?"

Ninienne paused, but figured she could live without her device for one night. And she was eager to ingratiate herself to the wizard who might determine her future. "Of course."

She showed Salagrix the basic navigation functions and handed the device over.

"Much appreciated. I am sure our collaboration will be a fruitful one. I will retire now, but I will see you tomorrow afternoon for lecture. Don't forget your morning chores!"

Salagrix left the dining room, a little wobbly from the wine, and disappeared into the dark stairwell.

BACK IN HER ROOM, NINIENNE got out of her dress and into sleep clothes. She started organizing her notes from the day's lecture, but it proved too much for her tired brain on a sip of pixie wine. Instead, she let her imagination wander, and sketched a few wild-looking creatures. Among them, a human face appeared, what she imagined Rodando to look like.

Where did you go? She felt a strange kinship with the former apprentice. *Did you feel unsure about your appointment too? Was Salagrix already going senile when you were here? Did you explore the woods?*

She lay down on her pillow. Gossamaw nuzzled her neck.

Her eyes drifted to the chore list, and to *Secure perimeter*, before she fell asleep.

One day down, several hundred to go.

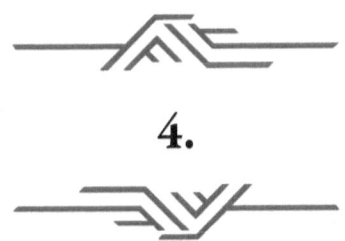

4.

When I was at Belcarin I had a Professor named Trelogan. Eccentric. Wore a bandanna instead of a wizard's hat. Long hair, barefoot, that sort of thing. Taught outside when he could.

He had some interesting theories about the cultivation of soulfire. He thought certain practices could increase your capacity, so you could cast more powerful magic before needing to rest. He taught a seminar on it, and it had to be held on the astronomy lawn because it was so popular.

But the Academy admissions officers caught wind of this. They use soulfire capacity as a key metric and deny anyone with too little capacity automatically. So they didn't like this idea.

I think their thinking went like this: If you can increase your soulfire, then someone with very little soulfire could increase their capacity to wizard level. And if that's true, then anyone can become a wizard, and the distinction between those who can do magic and those who can't becomes irrelevant.

So the Deans discontinued the seminar and dismissed Trelogan quietly. And that really got me thinking.

—transcript from the streamcast "Witchtalk," Episode 342 with Master Wizard Allura

NINIENNE WOKE UP THE next morning invigorated by the possibility of unlocking the secrets of portalcraft, but also, if she had time, the opportunity to explore the nearby woods and meet the creatures who lived there. She dressed in her brown work overalls, donned her matching wizard's hat, and climbed the stairs with Gossamaw to the lower workroom for coffee and a light breakfast.

Was this tower the most comfortable place to live? No. Was Salagrix the ideal mentor? No. Was Black Gulch an engaging metropolis where she might explore and meet other young people and have edifying cultural experiences? No. But this was her apprenticeship, her fifth and final year at Belcarin, and she was going to make the most of it.

Ninienne finished her coffee and stood to examine the room, which was as damp and disorganized as it had been the day before. She set her jaw. If it was going to be her duty to keep the tower clean, then she would make it the cleanest tower in history. She rolled up her sleeves and got to work.

A cleaning charm banished the fungus, for now, but Ninienne had to enlarge the radius of her drying spell to account for the sheer amount of standing water on the floor. This adjustment made the spell less efficient and drained more of her soulfire than usual, which left her feeling tired and grumpy.

The ingredient shelves were in total disarray. If there was any sort of organizational system here, it was opaque to her. As she cleaned up spilled containers, she arranged ingredients in groups by type on the floor. Gossamaw helped by pushing jars around with his head.

Before long, she realized that this was going to be a much larger project than expected. She was still on the floor, alphabetizing vials of mermaid tears, when Salagrix appeared in the doorway.

"Is it afternoon already?" Ninienne asked, exhausted and looking at the merely re-arranged chaos.

"It is," said Salagrix, stepping into the room. A vortex of fungal spores swirled around him, re-dirtying Ninienne's previously clean floor. Salagrix walked past one of the ingredient shelves on his way to the chalkboard, and a ceramic jar jumped toward him and fell to the floor, where it smashed and sent up a cloud of phoenix ashes.

Ninienne sighed and collapsed into the chair. Gossamaw rose from his nap under the workbench and climbed up Ninienne's leg for another nap.

Salagrix looked around the room. "A long way to go, I see," he said with a sniff.

"Do you have my datastream device?" Ninienne asked.

Salagrix smacked his forehead. "Ah, thank you for reminding me. I'll grab it for you before dinner. Fascinating machine. Quite extraordinary. Much appreciated."

Ninienne could have guessed that the absent-minded wizard would have forgotten. What were a few more hours without it?

"Well, time to put up your feet. Let's continue from where we left off yesterday. Further foundational principles of portalcraft."

Yes!, thought Ninienne. *Shaping the fabric of space! Secrets of the universe!* She grabbed her parchment and ink wand.

The nub of chalk squeaked across the chalkboard as Salagrix launched into his lecture, picking up precisely where he had stopped.

Ninienne tried her best to follow along, she really did, but after a tiring morning, she found her attention wavering. Besides all the unfamiliar words she had learned yesterday, which she had to keep referring to yesterday's notes to remind herself what they meant, there was a whole new crop of terms today. Several times, Salagrix uttered a sentence so crammed with specialized words it turned to total mush in Ninienne's brain.

She also didn't have a sense where any of this was going. There had not yet been a mention of any incantations, charms, glyphs, potions, or any of the practical magical steps to actually make a portal. Everything they had covered so far was pure theory.

As it turned out, Portalcraft was not like creature healing. She thought back to her days on Trantis, and the briny smell of the nebula whales as she kept them moist. She thought back to her second year lab, with the rows of incubators with hydra mantises curled up inside, and how she would sometimes spend the night there just to be near them. Even before Belcarin, as a young girl on her homeworld of Swurk, she remembered a summer she spent observing a pearl ant nest, and long afternoons just watching them march up and down a baynab tree.

"That concludes our lecture for today. We will continue with principles of space folding tomorrow, but for now, enjoy your break before dinner."

Salagrix's announcement shook Ninienne from her stupor. She rubbed her eyes, unsure of how much of the lecture she had missed.

"Don't forget my datastream device," Ninienne called out to Salagrix.

"Ah, yes, thank you." The old wizard nodded. More ingredient jars spilled as he crossed the room, and their contents swirled up into his personal whirlwind.

After Salagrix exited, Ninienne examined the room to determine if it was any cleaner than it had been that morning. She decided for her sense of self worth that it was, if only slightly.

Oh well, she thought. *I'll just start again in the morning.*

She had originally thought that the pre-dinner break would be the perfect time to explore the woods, but now she was tired and just wanted to lie in her bed without thinking about anything.

At dinner, Salagrix had forgotten her device again.

"I apologize. My memory isn't quite what it used to be," he said, taking his seat. "Fascinating piece of technology, by the way. You may think me backwards for my commitment to portalcraft, but I can still learn a thing or two," and he jabbed his finger into his wrinkled forehead. "I'll fetch it for you after dinner."

But what actually happened after dinner was that Salagrix ordered more pixie wine.

"A toast," he said grandly, "To the second day of your apprenticeship."

Ninienne did not drink her wine, which meant she listened to Salagrix's rendition of a bawdy song from his Academy days fully sober. Eventually, he stumbled up the stairs and Ninienne went to bed, exhausted.

THE EVENTS OF THAT second day settled into a routine for the rest. In the mornings, she cleaned the lower workshop, trying to keep ahead of the previous day's mess that followed Salagrix wherever he went. The afternoons were for lectures, and while she technically had a break before dinner to do with as she wished, so far she had been too exhausted to go explore the woods.

Once she had gotten the ingredient shelves organized (as much as she could, considering the effect of Salagrix's personal gravity, the source of which remained a mystery), she moved on to other projects to improve her quality of life in the tower.

First was replacing the Fandulf's Fire Charm torches in the stairwell with her family's specialty lantern light spells. While not exactly homey, with care, the tower shed much of the gloom she had encountered on her first day. No longer did the flickering flames seem to animate tiny figures in the shadows or fill the stairwell and rooms with smoke. Now, the warm, consistent light cast the wall and floor stones in a cheery glow that made every surface look like a painting. Since none of the rooms had windows, save for her own, she attuned all the light spells to the position of the gas giant, so they subtly changed color throughout the day to mimic the progression of daylight. She also attached an absorbent spell to the lights to reduce the dampness in the tower and keep the fungal growths and mold at bay.

Ninienne also spent time shoring up the structural integrity of the tower. Rodando had left behind a book on masonry magic (which he had acquired, presumably, for the same reasons as Ninienne needed the book now) and, tome in hand, Ninienne taught herself the recipe for magical mortar and the proper incantations and conjugations for sealing stone together. These incantations required a lot of soulfire, which drained Ninienne's willpower, but seeing her handiwork set and dried the next day always gave her a jolt of pride.

Even this progress, however, was temporary, because every few days there was a deep thrumming sound from the upper workshop, followed by a loud explosion and a bout of swearing, that shook the tower and sent fresh patches of broken stone clattering to the floor.

As a result, Ninienne became quite practiced at masonry magic.

Already a beloved companion, Gossamaw became an indispensable assistant. He followed Ninienne wherever she went, waiting patiently and quietly nearby until there was a wand to fetch or a dish to lick clean. He had an uncanny ability to locate misplaced masonry trowels, and for the long lonely mornings, was Ninienne's silent confidant.

When she needed a break, or a little one-sided conversation, she popped down to the first floor sitting room to chat with the glowworm. Thanks to her familiar connection with Gossamaw, she could sometimes understand what creatures were thinking or feeling, but the glowworm was a fairly blank slate, and not much fun to be around. Plus, the suit of armor in the room gave her the willies, so she often cut these visits short. She felt bad for the creature, but didn't yet have a plan for how to help it out.

She was, of course, also studying portalcraft with Salagrix in the afternoons, as part of the ancient tradition of apprenticeship. Despite her initial enthusiasm, Ninienne felt her appetite slowly wane as they delved deeper into the theoretical and mathematical nature of the subject. She sorely missed her classes in creature healing, which had been much more practical and hands-on. This, in combination with Salagrix's meandering lectures, which often dove into complex exceptions and edge cases while Ninienne was still struggling with basic concepts, meant that her progress was slow and her attention drifted in the late hours of the afternoon as her lantern light spells dimmed with the setting gas giant.

Salagrix also proved to be poor dinner conversation, and she heard the clock tower story several more times over the intervening weeks. Pixie wine toasts were a nightly affair. No matter how delicately she broached the topic of Rodando, it always sent the old wizard into a daze, and eventually she gave up trying.

Similarly, despite multiple daily reminders, Salagrix had not yet returned her datastream device. She was often too tired to press the issue.

What's one more day? She thought, day after day. She longed to reach out to her parents and her friend Drusilla, but the longer she went without contact, the less urgent it seemed.

What would she even tell them? I cleaned the lower workroom again. *I organized the ingredient shelf* again. *I charged the lantern lights* again. *I patched the masonry* again. *I got confused and bored during the portalcraft lecture* again. *Salagrix got drunk and told the story about the clocktower* again. None of it was interesting.

Without her datastream device, she spent the last minutes of the day before she passed out from exhaustion in her room cuddling with Gossamaw, trying to make sense of her lecture notes, rereading her favorite novel series *Almet's Adventures*, or doodling in her sketchbook.

Sleep came easily after arduous days of work and study. Ninienne dreamed of the nearby woods, still unexplored, which beckoned with welcoming branches and encircled the tower in a woody embrace.

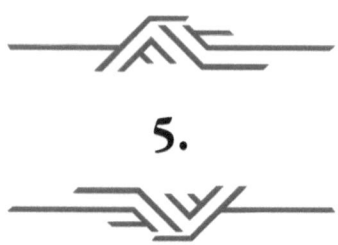

5.

Praise be the datastream! O miracle, connector of the Twelve Thousand Worlds! O bottomless fountain of knowledge! Praise, for I may speak to any acquaintance in a few quick taps! Lo, any product, any need or luxury, delivered to my location, purse-willing! Behold! A recording of a catbat! It licks its wings in an adorable manner! There are nineteen million similar recordings if this one does not suffice! Behold! I shall not look not away!

— from Liturgy of the Datastream, ver 9.6.1135

ONE PARTICULAR MORNING in the otherwise undifferentiated haze of mornings, Ninienne was repairing an ornery patch of stonework in the dining room wall and reviewing, out loud, the various types of space folding.

"There's *parallel* folding, in which the same folding pattern is used on both sides of the portal at the same time. And then there's *symmetrical* folding, where the folding is the same but the timing is different. Or, wait. I think I've got those mixed up."

Gossamaw, sprawled on a dining room chair and bored out of his mind, let his tongue hang down to the floor.

Before she could sort the differences, the doorgong rang. The entire tower shook, and several stones Ninienne had just repaired clattered to the floor. With a frustrated sigh, she set down the mortar wand. Gossamaw hopped onto Ninienne's back and she tromped down the stairs.

She recalled *Receive deliveries* from the chore list with curiosity.

At the front door, Ninienne met a gangly teenager with shaggy brown hair that covered half of his face. His clothes were ill-fitting and torn, and he wore a lumpy gray hat that made his head look like a mushroom. Ninienne guessed he was about her age, seventeen or eighteen. He was stacking a pile of crates next to the door from a floating, scraped grav cart and tapping a cracked datapad.

Ninienne was so excited to see another human who wasn't her decrepit mentor that she practically exploded.

"Hi!" she shouted. "You must be the delivery boy! Hi! I'm Ninienne, I'm the new apprentice." She stuck out her hand. "My friends call me Neens. Not that we're friends yet, but maybe we could be? Who knows? We'll just have to see!"

The delivery boy stepped back and clutched his datapad to his chest, leaving Ninienne's hand hanging in the air.

"Right, so sorry, how rude of me. What's your name? Where are you from?" Ninienne drew her hand back but realized, awkwardly, she had no place to put it.

The delivery boy's eyes darted from Ninienne to the grav cart and back, like he was trying to decide if he should stay or make a run for it.

"Benno?" he squeaked.

"Benno? That's your name, Benno?"

Benno nodded.

"So nice to meet you, Benno! I'm Ninienne, like I said, or Neens. Either works. Or you can call me whatever you want. I'll probably respond!" Ninienne laughed, but it turned to a cackle. She could see the effect she was having on this poor delivery boy, but she couldn't stop herself. She felt like a burst dam drowning everyone downstream.

"So, delivery! Delivery delivery. Let's get these crates checked in."

One crate was labeled "branched pyrocrystal" and another "pickled wormwood root." There were other crates with bundles of dark leaves she couldn't identify. As she stacked them in the entryway, Gossamaw hopped over to Benno and licked his pant leg. Benno looked cautious.

"That's Gossamaw," said Ninienne. "Gossie for short. He's friendly."

Benno bent down to scratch Gossamaw behind the neck, and the frogdog roiled with pleasure. The delivery boy smiled to himself.

"So, Benno," Ninienne said in her best attempt to project cool aloofness as she leaned on the doorframe at a jaunty angle. "Would you like a cup of tea? I'd love to hear more about ... deliveries?" Ninienne was desperate for a conversation with another human that wasn't about portals or limp clock towers.

"Oh, well," Benno looked visibly uncomfortable. "I need to, uh, you know, get back."

"Right! Busy! Of course. You're working. I mean, I'm working too! Totally fair. No problem."

It was at this point that Ninienne noticed a small earthenware bowl affixed to the wall just inside the doorway, full of misshapen brass discs. She assumed this was the local currency and grabbed a handful. The bowl immediately replenished itself, with new discs bubbling up from some charm at the bottom of the bowl.

"So, what does Salagrix usually tip you?" Ninienne asked, counting out discs in her palm.

"Oh, he doesn't," said Benno. "I've never seen him. Or anyone. I just leave the crates by the door, ring the gong, and go. Salagrix sends money to my uncle directly."

"Hardly seems fair after coming all this way. I have made that trek. It is not easy."

Benno shrugged. "It's not so bad. Kind of nice, actually."

She offered him a handful of discs. "Does this look good?"

The delivery boy's eyes widened as Ninienne poured the discs into his cupped hands.

"There you go."

Benno pocketed the tip and smiled widely.

"Thank you, uh, Neens," he said, suddenly more interested in remembering her name.

"Don't mention it. I'll be here for most of the next year. Maybe you can stay for a chat next time. Or not. This was good too."

Benno hopped on the grav cart and rode it out to the trailhead. He looked back a few times, bewildered. As soon as he was out of sight, Ninienne collapsed from shame.

Nice job, Neens! You scared off your first chance at a friend!

As she leaned back against the crate of pickled wormwood, its pungent, savory odor seeping through, she realized she needed a connection outside of the tower if she was going to make it through this apprenticeship.

She needed her datastream device back.

NINIENNE STOOD AT THE doorway to the dining room, arms crossed, waiting for Salagrix to arrive. She had made it very clear after today's lecture that he was to return her device tonight. When she saw him appear around the corner, she asked, "Do you have my device?"

"Ah! This blasted memory." Salagrix shook his head. "After dinner."

"No," said Ninienne. "Go get it. Now."

Salagrix pouted like a child asked to put away his favorite toy. "But it is almost time to eat."

"Listen, it's not a unique object. If you want one for yourself, I'm sure we can order you one. I don't think money is a problem for you, with that refilling dish of coins down in the entryway. But the one you have right now belongs to me, and I need it back."

Salagrix's eyebrows waggled with interest, like two dancing caterpillars. "Order one for myself, you say?"

"Sure, you can order anything from the datastream. I can show you how, but I need my device to do it."

Salagrix made a satisfied grunt and turned to go up the stairs.

He returned a few minutes later with Ninienne's device in hand. She moved her chair over to his side of the table, and while he chewed on a roasted pitpig leg that smelled like rubber, Ninienne scrolled through projected images of various models of datastream devices.

"That one," he said, pointing a greasy finger.

Ninienne's eyebrows raised as she set her plate on the floor for Gossamaw, who gave her a disappointed look of disgust.

"That one is very expensive," she said, and she swiped on the device to display the price to Salagrix.

The old wizard snorted. "Money, is it?" He hobbled over to the wall niche and tapped the bordering stones in a specific pattern. A burst of golden smoke cleared with a sound like a tinkling wind chime, and several treasure chests appeared, each overflowing with gold coins and jewels. "Would this cover it?"

Ninienne nodded while her mouth struggled to form words. "Uh, yes, that should cover it, yes."

They placed the order that night.

AFTER DINNER, NINIENNE stayed up later than usual. She lay face down on her bed, Gossamaw asleep beside her, scrolling through her device. The call of a distant bird drifted in through her open window.

When she had checked the date, it told her she had gone six weeks without her device.

Six weeks? Can it really have been that long? It felt like a shock.

As such, she had accumulated a large backlog of messages. She had entirely missed an assignment from her advisor, where she was supposed to write a report on the progress of her apprenticeship so far.

All the more reason to get Salagrix a device of his own, Ninienne thought. She shot off an apologetic message explaining the situation and asked for an extension.

There were a few messages from Drusilla who had checked in periodically. After seeing Drusilla almost every day last year, it felt like she hadn't spoken with her friend for an eternity. Ninienne wanted to have a live chat, but the device told her that, based on the time on Drusilla's world, she was likely asleep, but their schedules would line up the next day. She sent her a message to schedule a call.

There were also several messages from home. She replied, reassuring her mother that she was still alive. She wanted to call home too, but it was going to take longer for waking hours to line up with her homeworld of Swurk.

Now that all of those things were out of the way, it was time to do some sleuthing. There was something that had been tugging at the back of her mind. It was the way Benno had seemed so afraid this morning. How all the people in Black Gulch seemed wary of her when she mentioned she was going to be the new apprentice to their Master Wizard.

She connected to the Belcarin Archives and typed in:

salagrix

6.

Introducing the Future's Finest Household Companion!

Step into the future with the revolutionary Helper Android, Class C, from Greystar Systems—the quintessential addition to your modern home! Say goodbye to mundane chores and hello to seamless efficiency with our cutting-edge creation straight out of a dream!

Imagine: No more tedious cleaning or tiresome tasks! Our Helper Android is here to lighten your load and bring joy back into your daily routine. With its sleek design and advanced functionality, it's like having a loyal familiar right at your fingertips—with no magic!

Features That Will Leave You in Awe:

Effortless Cleaning: From sweeping floors to polishing surfaces, our Helper android does it all with precision and care, leaving your home sparkling clean.

Culinary Wizardry: Say farewell to kitchen woes! Our android can whip up gourmet meals or assist in meal prep, ensuring every dish is a masterpiece.

Healthcare Helper: With its advanced sensors and monitoring capabilities, our android can help track vital signs and potion schedules, ensuring you stay on top of your health effortlessly, all with a congenial bedside manner!

Entertainment Extraordinaire: Enjoy nights at home like never before with our android's built-in entertainment features, from customized musical performances to providing endless trivia fun!

Experience the Marvels of Tomorrow, Today!

Don't miss out on the opportunity to revolutionize your home life with our Helper Android, Class C. Say hello to a brighter, more efficient future—place your datastream order now and embark on a journey into the extraordinary!

[image of a Class C android, wearing an apron and waving, with a speech bubble that says "I'm Helpo, and I'm here to help!"]

—from an advertisement on the "Star Home" magazine feed

THERE WERE A LOT OF results to wade through, and it look a long time to load through the poor datastream connection.

The first thing that came up was an announcement of Salagrix's appointment as the Master Wizard of the newly colonized Shadow Moon of Chadron. The date of the article put it at—quick math—eighty years ago.

Huh, thought Ninienne. *He must have achieved Master level at a young age, then.* But the photogram attached to the article showed a robust, plump, middle-aged Salagrix standing next to a silver-haired woman of similar age.

She scanned the article.

"After teaching at Belcarin for over forty years, the newly appointed Master will, along with his wife Eldrathea, oversee an agricultural experiment blending the latest innovations in technology and magic..."

Wait. That meant Salagrix had *started* teaching over a hundred and twenty years ago. Even if he got the job right after graduation, that meant he was *at least* a hundred and forty years old.

He looked old, no doubt, but Ninienne had never heard of someone living that long. The best life-extension magic and technology available could get some people to a little past a hundred, but after that their soulfire would wane. They certainly weren't still walking around, climbing stairs, and doing magic every day at *a hundred and forty.*

No wonder his memory was so bad.

She kept searching. She found the record of his ascension to Mastery, which contained his pre-master name: Gregor Clayspinner.

That opened up more avenues of searching. As Gregor Clayspinner, he had been a professor at Belcarin, teaching portalcraft, of course. She found photogram portraits of the young lecturer—much younger, in fact—looking jolly in his professorial wizard's hat.

In addition to this, there were long lists of scholarly articles, all on portalcraft, and various mentions in the school newspaper, but nothing that indicated why the people of the Shadow Moon would be afraid of him.

Ninienne tried searching the Belcarin Archives for information about the Shadow Moon of Chadron, but besides the article she had already found, the results only pointed to the Brilliant Moon, which was known for its scenic foggy bays, bountiful creamfruit trees, and annual crowhorse races along the beach organized by the Master Wizard Dothreep.

To see the photograms, the Brilliant Moon looked like paradise, and it was right next door. She could even see it in the sky outside her window, beginning to wane with a sliver of darkness. And here was Ninienne, in a damp and crumbling tower, working day in and day out, scouring the datastream to find out why people were afraid of her Master.

She sighed and flopped back onto her bed. What was she missing?

DREAMS OF ROLLING SURF and crashing waves turned into actual sounds of shuffling and banging from the floor above, in the lower workroom. Ninienne rolled over to ignore them, but then heard Salagrix howl in pain. She left

Gossamaw snoring on the bed, tossed on her robe, and crept up the stairs.

Salagrix was in his nightcap and pajamas, clumsily rummaging through the ingredient shelves. Knocked-over jars spilled their contents onto the floor, and powder swirled around him. He muttered something under his breath that Ninienne didn't understand.

"Salagrix?" she asked gently.

The old wizard whirled around with wild eyes. When he saw her, he took a step back and clutched his chest.

"Silamene?" he asked, his eyes filled with—what? Terror? Relief? She had seen him dazed before, but this was something else. He looked as if he had seen a ghost, but the ghost had brought him cake, but also the cake was full of snakes.

"I'm Ninienne, your apprentice. Do you need to go lie down?"

"How did you... where did..." His words did not congeal into meaningful sentences. He staggered backwards.

Ninienne approached the old man with caution. "Are you okay? Do you need to go lie down?"

Tears welled up in Salagrix's eyes. He cried out as if strangled. Ninienne put up her hands in a peaceful gesture, but Salagrix recoiled.

"Get away! Trickster apparition!" He pressed himself up against the wall. His fingertips sparked and sputtered as a spell formed.

"Whoa!" shouted Ninienne. "No need for that! I'm trying to help!"

The blue sparks arranged themselves into the outline of a dragon's head, which shot out across the room.

Ninienne ducked, but the dragon passed through her painlessly.

"Snap out of it!" Ninienne shouted. "I'm not trying to hurt you!"

He put up his hands in defense, still glowing with magical energy.

"It's me! Your apprentice!"

His face and posture slackened, and the spell scattered. He looked lost and confused.

"Why don't to go lie down and get some sleep?" She wove a calming spell into her voice.

He turned towards the stairwell and nodded with a defeated air. "Yes, sleep. The bed. Yes." He shuffled up the stairs into the dark.

Ninienne followed. Near the dining room, he slipped, and she had to catch him from falling. He weighed almost nothing at all.

When they reached the dining room, she stopped, not wanting to go farther than he had permitted her to go.

"Do you think you can make it from here?" she asked, but he did not reply. He staggered up the staircase as if sleepwalking.

She waited, listening at the stairwell, until she heard the door to his chamber shut and echo down the staircase.

FIRST THING THE NEXT morning, Ninienne sent a message to the Academy explaining the situation. Salagrix obviously needed help beyond what she could provide as an apprentice. With no family members nearby, the Academy was the next resource to turn to regarding her Master's physical and mental health.

The lower workshop was in worse shape than usual. Too tired from lack of sleep to use magic, she grabbed a broom. She felt anxious, but was also excited about her upcoming call with Drusilla. Gossamaw helped by using his webbed paws as tiny dustpans.

When the time came, she set up her device on the workbench. Soon, her friend's head of wild, frizzy hair appeared in the room. Just seeing Drusilla's broad smile filled Ninienne with warmth. Bright sunshine and beautiful green trees streamed in from the background of the projection. She wore a wide hat and a thin-strapped top.

"Oh my gosh, Neens! How are you? It is so good to see you!"

Drusilla's enthusiasm was a balm to Ninienne's lonely heart. She sighed, smiling, and leaned against her broom. "I'm doing okay. I've missed you."

"I've missed you too." As always, her friend's presence, even across a bad datastream connection, was like being wrapped in a soft blanket. "It's been so long."

Ninienne rolled her eyes for emphasis. "I! Know! Things have been crazy over here."

"Looks like it. Quite a, uh, mess you got going on there." Drusilla tilted her head to indicate the workshop.

Ninienne looked around, realizing that her friend could see the chaotic shelves filled with broken jars. "Oh, yeah, we had a bit of an incident last night."

Drusilla leaned in. "Go on. Tell me everything," she said in a mock-deep voice filled with intrigue.

Nervous laughter spilled out of Ninienne. "Where do I even start? My master, Salagrix, he sometimes has these—I don't know what to call it, he gets confused sometimes? Last night he had a bad one, the worst I've seen. He was stumbling around and knocking things over. I got up to check on him, but I guess I scared him pretty badly. He attacked me with a spell. Fortunately, it was just an illusion. But now there's a huge mess to clean up. So, that's my job this morning."

Drusilla blinked, mouth open. "Holy gas, Neens. Are you okay?"

This concern made Ninienne uncomfortable, so she shrugged it off. "I sent a message to the Academy. We'll see what they say."

"Does he have anyone taking care of him? A family member, a healer, anything?" Of course Drusilla would wonder about that—she was studying to be a healer herself. Not a creature healer like Ninienne, but a medical healer, for humans.

Ninienne shook her head. "It's just me. We're pretty far away from town. There's not anyone else nearby."

Drusilla bit her lip. "I don't know, Neens, that sounds pretty serious."

"We'll see what the Academy says, I guess." Ninienne found her arms crossing in discomfort. It was one thing to be in an unpleasant situation, and another thing to have a friend confirm it by showing concern.

"Does he have any other symptoms?" Her friend's eyes sparkled with curiosity. There was nothing like a diagnostic problem to get Drusilla excited.

"Um..." Ninienne thought while she swept broken ceramic into a pile to repair later. "Oh! He has this personal vortex. Things get stuck to him, drawn in to him. It's a pain in the neck, really. Constant mess. I don't know if that's relevant."

A little crease appeared between Drusilla's eyes as she considered. "I am not his healer, so I can't say for sure, but that's a common side-effect of life-extending magic. When you mess with time, you mess with gravity, you know?"

Ninienne nodded, even though what Drusilla had just said made no sense to her. That sounded like portalcraft theory. "That tracks. He's super old, I know that much."

"There are usually ways to mitigate side-effects, but he'd have to go to a healer. You're sure there's no one else around who can take care of him?"

Ninienne leaned on her broom. "I wish there was, Dru, because then I'd have somebody to talk to."

"Huh. He might be a good candidate for—I was just talking to Allura about this, actually."

"Who's this?" *A new friend?*

"Oh, my Master. She's great, you'd love her. Just a genius, and an incredible healer."

"Oh? You match disciplines?" *Must be nice.*

"I know? So lucky, right?" Drusilla smiled in a way that, suddenly, Ninienne didn't like. "Anyway, we went on a little shopping trip into town—you have to come visit Diotet, it's so cute." *Like that would be an option. I'm stuck out on the edge of the Worlds with no leave.* "But one shop had those new androids on display. The ones from those ads that have been all over the datastream."

"I haven't seen the ads," said Ninienne. *I've been without my device for six weeks.* "But I think I saw one on the shuttle when I first got to the Shadow Moon."

"Kinda creepy, right? But Allura thinks they're going to change everything about how healers work. They can't do magic, of course, but they can do all sorts of physical labor. Allura thinks they'll be great assistant caretakers, and free healers up to focus on the magical side of care. It might be a good option for your master, assuming he can afford one."

Ninienne chuckled, darkly. "I've seen his treasure. He's loaded. It's convincing him that will be the hard part."

If an android could help Salagrix with his health issues, it could also help Ninienne with her workload. Maybe then she would actually have time and energy to explore the woods, like she had wanted to do since she got here.

Ninienne found herself sweeping the same spot over and over while she pictured a long morning in a hammock with an android doing her chores for her.

"So sorry," she said as she snapped back to reality. "I feel like I've been monopolizing the conversation. How is your apprenticeship going?"

"Oh, it's incredible!" Drusilla laughed, and her head shook with delight, sending her curls into a dance. "Allura's great. Every night we have cocktails by the lake and she tells me stories about her travels around the galaxy. She calls it Cocktail o'clock." Drusilla giggled.

"Wow. That sounds... fun." *Not that I would know what that's like.*

Drusilla leaned in conspiratorially. "Oh, and she calls herself a witch. You know, like the old days. She's been calling me a witch too, and been dropping hints she's going to induct me into her coven!" Drusilla squealed excitedly, and the sound, normally a delight, felt like scratches on Ninienne's eardrums.

"That is just. So. Incredible." Getting the words out was like chewing the kitchen demon's vegetables.

"Oh, hold on," Drusilla turned to someone out of view and said something Ninienne couldn't hear. "So sorry, Neens. There's a firebird on the lake, so Allura wants to have cocktails early and watch it. But I do want to hear more about what is going on with you! It's been so great to catch up."

Ninienne deflated. "Yeah, we'll have to do this again." *So I can feel even worse about my own apprenticeship.*

"Bye!" Drusilla waved.

The projection snapped off with a bloop.

Ninienne returned to her cleaning, happy for her friend. Yes, she was definitely happy for her friend in the sunshine with her cocktails and her coven and learning things relevant to her discipline. It was her happy thoughts that were causing the bristles of her broom to bend and break, no doubt about it.

NINIENNE HAD JUST FINISHED putting the room back together when Salagrix stepped in and sent a glass jar of rat vertebrae to the floor. The tiny white bones scattered everywhere as motes of dust swirled around the edge of the old wizard's robes.

Salagrix grumbled but was otherwise unperturbed by the mess. He muttered under his breath and rubbed his fingertips together, distracted.

Ninienne did her best not to let her frustration seep into her voice. "How are you feeling after last night?" she asked.

Salagrix beheld Ninienne as if she were a lifelong mute that had spoken for the first time to tell him an unfunny joke. "I'm not sure what you mean."

"You were really confused. You attacked me with a dragon spell."

"Dragon? Hmph. No. No. Everything is fine." He tottered over to the chalkboard and a flask of volcanic essence pulled itself onto the floor. Ninienne sighed.

"Listen, Salagrix." Ninienne rubbed her forehead. "We have to do something. I can't keep cleaning up these messes. It's too much."

"Messes?" Salagrix's attention was firmly on the chalkboard.

"Your personal gravity. It collects dust and makes jars fall off the shelves. You must have noticed it. Isn't there something we can do about it?"

Salagrix chuffed and turned. "What are you saying?"

"If you're willing, my healer friend said there are ways we can mitigate this...side effect."

The wizard's cheeks reddened, and he sputtered and hissed like an angry catbat. "How dare you suggest such a thing! The impertinence! Why, in my day, we showed our mentors some respect! Prying into my personal issues. I never!"

Ninienne held her tongue. This was going about as poorly as possible. "I didn't mean to—but if you need help, there are these new androids..."

But Salagrix wasn't listening. The nub of chalk sprung to life and wrote out three columns of text on the board.

"Demonstrate your understanding of portal theory by writing essays in response to these three prompts." Salagrix spat the words out. "That is your lecture for the day. I expect to see your finished work before dinner."

He stormed out of the room.

Ninienne sighed and collapsed onto the chair. She hadn't meant to upset Salagrix, but he was obviously extremely sensitive about his condition, or whatever was going on with him. Gossamaw hopped over and licked her hand.

Her device dinged. It was a message from the Academy in response to her inquiry.

Thank you for writing the Office of Apprenticeship Affairs. We will discuss your situation. Please expect a response in four to six weeks.

The Academy obviously wasn't in any hurry. Ninienne grabbed a stack of parchment and an ink wand and began the first essay.

But as she wrote, her mind was really on one question:

How can I convince Salagrix to get an android?

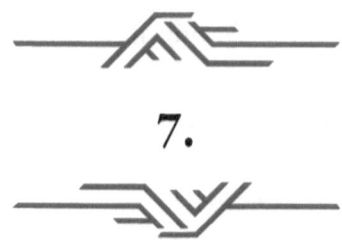

7.

Wizards that choose to raise a familiar, and take good care of their creature companions, may find that their connection enhances particular aptitudes. In addition to being able to sense the general location and well-being of one's familiar, one may gain an additional skill or ability. Often subtle, but powerful once identified and honed, this is called the familiar connection.

—from "Your Familiar and You," an informational pamphlet by the Council for the Humane Use of Familiars

NINIENNE'S ESSAYS DID not impress Salagrix.

"No, no, that's not right at all," he had said, followed by a long sigh, after reading them over dinner. "You are nowhere near where you need to be."

This seemed to trigger a sense of urgency in the old wizard. But rather than slow down to make sure she had a firm foundation in his beloved subject, over the next week, Salagrix's lectures ramped up in intensity.

"You must understand this!" was his new refrain. "Essential! Essential!"

As much as this more irritable version of Salagrix irked Ninienne, she was relieved as they moved beyond pure theory and to the first stage of application: the portal sigil.

Every portal required arcane calculations that directed the spell from one particular place in space (called the *ground*) to another (called the *target*). Once calculated, the results converted into an intricate series of interlocking symbols that had to be drawn exactly. Even the slightest mistake in an accent curve or a missing diacritical mark could put the target deep underground or into high orbit.

From the storage closet, Salagrix retrieved an oval slate, about the size and shape of a standing mirror, and hung it on the wall for Ninienne to practice drawing sigils around its well-worn edges. For those long afternoons, Ninienne's world shrunk to the space between her hand and that slate, and she became intimately familiar with every scratch and stain of it while drawing the sigils for an increasingly complex series of theoretical portals.

Even outside of lectures, Salagrix's mood remained stormy. He spent dinners muttering to himself under his breath. Ninienne couldn't tell if he was still mad because of her inquiry into his health or frustrated by her poor progress. Either way, Ninienne felt the Master's Letter inching away.

Eventually, Salagrix's datastream device arrived. Ninienne, hoping to catch Benno, raced down the stairs after the doorgong, only to see the delivery boy speeding off into the woods on his grav cart and the thin box left on the ground by the door.

Whatever novelty Salagrix found in the new device did not soften his mood. He now spent dinners muttering to himself under his breath while scrolling feeds from the datastream, and met any inquiry Ninienne made outside of lectures with a sour grunt.

The return of Ninienne's device, after the initial rush of reconnecting with her friend, did more to harm her mood than help. Listening to her favorite streamcasts, spotty through the poor connection, became too annoying to be worthwhile. Additionally, Professor Hemnal, Ninienne's creature healing professor and advisor back at Belcarin, began sending her articles over the datastream about the latest advances in creature healing research and possible applications of the new android technology.

Premature, but I thought you might want a head start on some ideas for next year!, read the attached note.

But it was all theory, and it made Ninienne's head swim, just like Salagrix's lectures. Besides, Ninienne's appointment to the Research Department no longer seemed like such a sure thing, and Hemnal's confidence only made her feel sick.

Ninienne also spent long nights scrolling through pictures Drusilla had shared with her: of the town (which was cute, Ninienne had to admit), of the lake, of Drusilla clinking glasses with Allura. This sent Ninienne into jealousy spirals, researching everything about Drusilla's world of Diotet, and how each individual detail was better than the Shadow Moon.

In short, Ninienne was having a bad time.

ONE MORNING, AFTER a particularly long night of jealously scrolling Drusilla's photograms, Ninienne decided it was the perfect time to take on the long-neglected task of cleaning the fungus from between the floor stones in the lower workshop which, despite her best efforts to keep the moisture at bay, had maintained a strong grip on the room. It was going to be a day of vigorous scrubbing and angry muttering.

Her mushy breakfast, mostly unfinished, left an unpleasant tang in her mouth. *I know I keep thinking this, but I have to find some better food to eat.*

As Ninienne scrubbed away at the fungus, her mind was on Drusilla, who was basically at a year-long party for her apprenticeship, while Ninienne was stuck on the galaxy's most curse-blasted moon with nothing but her stupid chores and endless lectures on the most difficult subject in all of wizardry from a Master who seemed to have a tenuous grasp on reality and might be a danger to himself.

As she scoured the floor stones, her envy, frustration, and anxiety curdled into resentment. She couldn't believe that Drusilla would just flaunt her happiness without even bothering to check in on Ninienne. And Salagrix! A walking mess, unconscious of his surrounding chaos, who might snap and lose his mind any day now.

With a forceful scrub, a chunk of the floor broke free and clattered across the room and under the workbench. Gossamaw jumped out of the way with a startled croak, just avoiding the stone's jagged edge. Surprised by her own strength, and ashamed that she had almost injured her companion, Ninienne took a breath.

"I'm sorry, Gossie. Are you alright?"

The frogdog hopped over and licked her forearm as if to say, *No worries.*

Chastened, Ninienne crawled under the bench to retrieve the floor stone.

While there, she noticed a green glow peeking out from a crack in the wall. She pulled at a loose wall stone to reveal a swarming nest of spider-like creatures, each with a green glowing dot on the tip of their abdomens. Delighted, Ninienne fetched her unfinished breakfast and tossed scraps to the spiders, which swarmed and gobbled them up.

Thank you! Thank you! Through her familiar connection, she heard the tiny creatures cheering for her in tiny, high-pitched voices. *What a great friend!*

The clarity of the voices startled Ninienne. She usually only got feelings or impressions from her familiar connection, but this was actual words. If she hadn't known better, she would have thought she was going crazy.

She relaxed, watching the tiny village go on about their lives. This discovery only intensified her desire to explore the woods and meet the other creatures that lived here.

As the insects collected her crumbs and took them back to their nest, Ninienne reflected that if they could survive, tucked into a forgotten corner of this tower, then maybe she could too.

But she needed someone to talk to. It was no good talking to spiders and frogdogs and glowworms, no matter how good of listeners they were.

So, she did what anyone in her position might do.

She called home.

SHE WOULDN'T HAVE MUCH time, but Ninienne thought she could sneak out of the tower for a quick lunch break before lecture without Salagrix noticing. She ordered sandwiches from the niche and grabbed a large fire suppression blanket from the storage closet to spread out on the field by the tower for a picnic.

The air was slightly warmer than usual, which made it the rough equivalent of a nippy fall day back on her home planet. She wrapped her neck in Rodando's abandoned scarf. Gossamaw chased a tiny fly, tripped, and did a somersault.

Her device lay in front of her, and her mother's round face smiled from the fuzzy projection. She was in the greenhouse, potting tea plants.

"That's just how it goes, dear." The corners of her mother's eyes wrinkled behind her glasses. "The apprenticeship is meant to be a challenging time. I remember pulling salt slugs off the bottom of my master's boat. Yeesh! Not fun. But it's all part of the tradition."

Ninienne rubbed her forehead. "I guess. But what about his bouts of confusion? Am I supposed to be his nursemaid?"

"What did the Deans say?" She gave the soil around her tea plant a little pat.

"I haven't heard yet. I don't know if they'll move fast enough. And then some days he seems perfectly fine." Gossamaw scratched his back on the dry clover and Ninienne rubbed his belly. "But, mom, he's super old. I looked it up, and he's over a hundred and forty."

Her mother frowned and took off her gloves. "That can't be right."

Her father's long and smile-worn face poked in from the side of the image. "Well, if you're not cut out for all this fancy education, it's not too late to join the family business." He pulled at his overall straps with his thumbs.

Ninienne laughed as her mother swatted him with her gloves. "Go on. You know that's not what she wants."

Her father grinned. "She's got options, is all I'm saying. Trade wizards get along just fine."

"Not the point. What do you guys think? I think it might be helpful to get an android to help take care of him."

Her father shook his head. "Those androids have got all my lamplighters scared that I'm going to replace them. But my people are my number one priority. I told them: a guild is not a business, it's a family."

Ninienne made a face. "That's not really the issue. The android won't be replacing anyone, since there's no one to take care of him right now. I'm just not sure what my role is here."

Her father nodded sagely. "Any time I've got a problem, I look at the situation, and ask myself, 'What's the right tool for the job?' Picking the right tool can save you a lot of work in the long run." He adjusted his cap. "Anyway, wish I could talk more, but I gotta head out. The town wants to tear out the lampposts in the port district and is having a meeting about it. My grandfather put those posts in! So I have to go show them the error of their ways."

"Oh no, I love those posts."

"Of course you do. They're gorgeous and you've got good taste. Don't worry, I'm on it. Love you Neens."

"Thanks Dad. Love you."

"Love you too. Remember: find the right tool."

He disappeared from the projection. Ninienne appreciated her father's practical, down-to-earth quips, since her mind got caught up in wild plans. She sighed.

"So what if an android is the right tool for the job? How do I convince Salagrix to get one? He was so defensive the last time I brought up his health."

Her mother wiped the dirt from her gloves. "Hmm. Navigating egos can be tricky, I know that." She raised her eyebrows in a way that Ninienne knew she was talking about her dad's brothers, if not her dad himself. "Maybe you can connect it to something else he wants. Appeal to another side of him."

What did Ninienne know about Salagrix? He cared about portalcraft, obsessively. He was nostalgic for his Academy days. But she didn't know how an android fit in to that.

Ninienne sighed and shook her head. "This all seems so irrelevant. What am I trying to do? Get a position at the Research Department at Belcarin. What am I doing? Trying to trick a wizard into buying a nursemaid android for himself."

"Oh, you still looking at Research?" her mother asked, surprised.

"Of course." Ninienne hugged Gossamaw against the chilly air.

"Oh, I just thought—after your time on Trantis with the whales, you seemed so happy in the field. Research is all inside, in the lab. I didn't know you were still considering it."

Ninienne made an exasperated sound with her lips. The last thing she wanted to do right now was rethink her future. If she wasn't trying to get into the Research Department, then all of this was for nothing. She felt tired and sad. "Maybe Dad's right. Maybe I should give it up and become a lamplighter."

"Don't be silly. We both know that's not where your heart is," her mother said warmly. "You're right to focus on why you're doing this. This is the last step before you're done with school."

"You're right," said Ninienne. "It just, I don't know. All this cleaning and portalcraft. It's so far removed from creature healing. It's hard to remember that when I'm repeating masonry incantations all morning."

"Like I said, it's all part of the grand tradition of apprenticeship," said her mother. "I also had a disciplinary mismatch with my Master, who was an oneiromancer, a dream mage. It was interesting, but I didn't see what it had to do with plant magic. But studying my dreams is how I knew your father was the one when I met him. So it all worked out."

"Yes, but did oneiromancy help you with your plant magic?" Ninienne asked pointedly.

"Hmm!" her mother squeaked, amused. "Who can say? But the point is to keep an open mind. You never know where any path might take you. Or portal, in your case." Her mother giggled.

Ninienne crossed her arms. This, of course, was impossible to argue with. Portal magic might prove extremely useful in the future. If she could ever get her mind around the basics.

"What are you eating?" Her mother looked askance at Ninienne's limp sandwich.

"Oh, just a sandwich. The food here is not great."

"Don't forget that propagation spell I showed you. You would just need some samples of local edible plants. Like I always say, you're never hungry if you can grow your own food!"

Oh, right, thought Ninienne. She looked around. There was plenty of space around the tower. She could grow a little garden, if she could ever find the time.

"I don't know if I'll ever have time for that."

"Sounds like that Master of yours is a tough cookie. You might need him to buy an android just to get you some free time, hmm?"

Appeal to what he wants.

She would just have to figure out what that was.

THAT EVENING AT DINNER, Salagrix scrolled on his device, as was his new habit, while Ninienne puzzled on how to crack Salagrix's closed-off mood.

Suddenly, Salagrix asked, "When you ordered my device, how did you do that?"

Ninienne looked up from her mushy vegetables and stale bread. This was the first he had spoken to her outside of lecture in days.

"You have to connect to a marketplace database," she said.

"Can I do that with my device?"

"Sure," said Ninienne. "You can order pretty much anything you want."

What is it that a hundred- and forty-year-old wizard wants? she wondered.

"Show me."

Ninienne dragged her chair over to sit next to Salagrix. She showed him how to access the larger marketplace databases, how to link his device to his gold horde for magical cross-world payment, and an explanation of shipping options.

"What sort of things are you looking to order?" Ninienne asked, trying to gain some insight.

"None of your business!" Salagrix snapped up his device and stood up.

Ninienne swore internally. The wizard stopped at the stairwell.

"Thank you for you help," he said.

A surge of relief bloomed in Ninienne's chest. She felt Salagrix's walls of ice melting.

But before she could feel too hopeful, a tiny green dot of light doodled its way across the dark floor. Salagrix stomped it and twisted his foot.

"Blasted cacospiders," he growled, and left the room.

8.

The taxonomy of living things in The Twelve Thousand Worlds is no straightforward task. Thousands of separate evolutionary lines on disparate planets, commingled by colonization, have led to bizarre ecosystems, most of which are barely documented. Add to this the existence of genetic manipulation, magical beasts, and the occasional mad wizard with a penchant for the grotesque and more free time than ethics, and the identification of wild creatures becomes more guesswork than science.

Consider the serpentine weasel of Yelar. Its slick aubergine fur suggests a mammalian type, but microscopic examination reveals that its hairs are actually tiny symbiotic worms that attach themselves to the skin of the larval form of the weasel as it emerges from its seedpod in the riparian pseudograsslands of its breeding grounds.

What a feat of evolutionary cooperation, you might say. Indeed, that would be the case, if the bones of the weasel were not so decidedly mechanical. Further examination reveals that its skeleton is a crystalline growth guided by self-replicating nano-bots. Forgotten technology from an ancient civilization, perhaps? Escaped experiment?

Valiant guesses, and both are wrong. For the true origin of the Yelarian serpentine weasel occurred when a wizard's apprentice fell asleep on a still-active spell book near a river bank and his dreams spilled out and mixed with a shopping list he had used as a bookmark, which activated a glyph that birthed tiny graphite-based constructs from which emerged the aforementioned species of weasel. Ah, the miracle of life!

On a somewhat related note, if someone asks you to care for their Yelarian serpentine weasel, politely decline. They spew a pungent sludge that is impossible to get out of carpets.

—from the essay "Problems in Creature Taxonomy" by Professor Shundlebits

A FEW DAYS LATER, NINIENNE had just fed the nest of cacospiders her breakfast scraps and was sleepily stirring a fresh batch of mortar when the doorgong rang.

It was the delivery boy, Benno, hastily stacking a pile of boxes of various sizes wrapped in brown paper. He looked disappointed, and a little scared, to see her.

"What's all this?" she asked.

Benno shrugged, not making eye contact. "I dunno. It all came in on yesterday's shuttle."

"Hey, listen," said Ninienne, and Benno stopped stacking. "About the other day. I'm sorry if I was weird. I'm not like that, normally. I've been lonely, and it's making me not normal. But I promise that I'm normal, really. Normally."

She was not making her case well, but Benno nodded. "Yeah, um, yeah. Okay."

Ninienne's stomach grumbled. "Oh, this might be a weird question, but do you know if there's any good food plants in the woods here? If I was going to go foraging, what would I look for?"

Benno looked at Ninienne with a strange expression. "Um, are you sure?"

"Yeah, the food here isn't very good, so I'm looking for other options."

Before Benno could answer, Salagrix appeared in the stairwell, eyes gleaming. His sourness of the past few weeks seemed to have evaporated.

"Are these them? My packages?" Salagrix drummed his fingers together in delight. "Bring them upstairs."

Ninienne looked from the massive pile of boxes to Benno.

"Well, you heard him. Let's take them upstairs."

Benno gulped.

Between the two of them, they loaded up their arms with packages and climbed the stairs to the lower workshop and spread them across the worktable. Benno's eyes kept darting to the shadowy corners as if something was going to leap out at him.

Salagrix picked up a package and shook it. He tore off the paper and opened the box to reveal a red wizard hat, covered in sequin-like jewels.

His face lit up with childish delight.

"Ah! Yes!" He immediately discarded his current hat — gray, stained, and burned in several places — and replaced it with the new one. He looked ridiculous, and the shiny new piece of clothing made his old robes look even shabbier by comparison. He found a small mirror on the worktable to examine the new treasure on his head and struck several poses while chuckling to himself.

"It's enchanted to enhance memory!" He tapped his temple and winked at Ninienne impishly. "Ho, ho! Wait until they see me at the next Conclave. Who's ratty-looking now, Dothreep?"

Dothreep, thought Ninienne. *Where have I heard that name before?*

He tore into the next package to reveal, as Ninienne read on the side of the box, an electric cauldron with temperature control and an automatic stirrer. Further packages revealed charmed anti-wrinkling bracelets and bubbled sight-enhancement goggles.

"I'm going to be, uh, busy for the rest of the day." Salagrix looked over his new horde like a greedy child. "Why don't we cancel lecture and you can have the afternoon off?"

Ninienne struggled to maintain the excitement that coursed through her entire body. "That sounds okay."

"Very well then," said Salagrix, gathering up his freshly unwrapped bounty. "Enjoy your afternoon."

Benno looked ready to crawl out of his skin.

"I'll walk you down," said Ninienne.

"HE'S SO OLD!" SAID Benno, staring off into space outside the front door. "I mean, I heard he was old, but that man is *ancient*."

Ninienne smirked and leaned against the wall of the tower. "You've never seen him before?"

Benno shook his head. "I usually just leave the packages at the door. I wasn't even sure he was real, actually. How does he stay together? He's so droopy."

Something about that word "droopy" struck Ninienne as hilarious. She looked at Benno, and a smile broke across her face. Benno smiled back. Ninienne laughed, which made Benno laugh, and soon they were both cracking up and struggling to keep breathing against the waves of laughter. Even Gossamaw was rolling on the ground, laughing.

"Did you see the little dance he did with the hat?" Ninienne wiped the tears from her eyes and mimicked Salagrix's poses. This sent them all into another fit of mirth.

It felt so, so good to laugh with someone.

When they finally caught their breath, Ninienne watched Benno rub Gossamaw's belly. She still wanted to get on friendly terms with the delivery boy, if only to prove to him she was a normal human.

"Let me get your tip," she said. She scooped a handful of coins from the refillable dish and handed them to Benno.

"And I meant what I said about the local plants. I'm very curious about these woods."

Benno looked at the coins and then at Ninienne. He looked softer, less tense than she had seen him before. "Uh, yeah, actually, I know some good things to eat that grow in the forest. I usually grab a snack on my way up and my way down."

An idea occurred to Ninienne. "It sounds like I've got the afternoon off. Do you have time to show me around?"

Benno appeared to be thinking about something complicated. "Yeah," he said slowly. "I could—yeah, sure. If you wanted to walk with me back to town, or even part way, I could point some things out to you."

Ninienne smiled. She felt good, maybe the best she had felt since the start of her apprenticeship.

"Great," she said. "Let me grab my scarf."

ON HER WAY BACK DOWNSTAIRS, Ninienne passed the sitting room with the glowworm, still in the cage on the ceiling. She stopped. In all her one-sided chats with the creature, she never got the impression that it was happy here in the tower. Now that she was on her way to the woods for the first time, it was the perfect opportunity to move him to new surroundings.

"You'd probably be more comfortable outside, wouldn't you?"

With a quick incantation, she freed the glowworm and replaced it with a lantern light spell.

"Bringing a friend?" Benno asked as she stepped out of the tower, eyeing the large grub under her arm.

"It's just something I've been meaning to do."

Benno shrugged. Ninienne and Gossamaw hopped on the grav cart and rode it to the trailhead. They floated, bumpily, down the trail, until Benno stopped the cart and got off.

"We'll head in here, just keep the trail in sight," he said. "These woods are tricky. It's easy to get turned around if you go too deep."

Ninienne stood at the edge of the woods and felt the invitation to mystery. Black branches reached out like a child's hand, wanting to lead her and show her something they had found.

Where are you taking me? The glowworm seemed to ask.

"We're going to find you a new place to live, little buddy."

She stepped into the woods and leaves crunched under her feet. The temperature dropped several degrees as the thick tangle of branches blocked the reflected light of the gas giant.

From her window in the tower, she had seen how the forest stretched out to the horizon. Here, though, in the thick of the black, craggy trunks, she couldn't see more than a few paces ahead, which gave the woods a maze-like feel. She turned back and made sure she could still see the trail before pressing further.

Her feet sank into a thick blanket of decaying leaves and released a deep, earthy smell. She let her fingers drift along the bark, coarse and flaky with sticky runs of sap. A branch poked her in the ribs, but not painfully, more like a friendly jab.

Soon, she came to a suitable tree with a thick trunk and dark purple leaves.

"What do you think about this one?" she asked the glowworm. She hoisted the sagging pillow of a creature onto a branch, where it blinked at Ninienne with a blank expression.

"You're free!" she said. The glowworm rolled over and let its mouth hang open.

Ahhhhhhhh, came a monotone sound in her mind. She couldn't tell if the glowworm was relieved, bored, or terrified. Regardless, Ninienne had accomplished her task.

A breeze picked up at her back, and she smiled uncontrollably, as if she knew an old friend had planned a surprise for her and could jump out at any moment. She closed her eyes, took a breath and felt a sense of calm and clarity that she hadn't felt in all her time so far on the Shadow Moon.

"Still there?"

Ninienne opened her eyes to see Benno looking at her with a curious smile.

"Yeah, I'm just taking a moment."

"Come on," Benno waved her deeper into the woods. "I'll show you around."

Ninienne said goodbye to the glowworm and followed Benno.

He had said he would show her around, and now he made good on that promise. Ninienne watched a train of ghost-ants crawl up a trunk, each of their tiny heads burning with a lick of icy flame like leggy matches. Gossamaw chased a powder squirrel that left behind white footprints as it scrambled behind a thornbush. They were watching a bramblehawk preen its twisting branch-wings when Ninienne's stomach rumbled.

Benno grinned. "Oh, you wanted to see the edible plants, too, right?"

Ninienne nodded. Her first impression of Benno as a shy person might have been mistaken. He was turning out to be quite the enthusiastic tour guide. They tromped through the thick growth, twigs snapping as they went, and Benno pointed out a series of plants.

"Those berries? Wait until they get the little red and blue stripes. That's how you know they're ripe."

"That fern doesn't look like much, but the roots cook up real nice."

"This plate fungus is my favorite. Savory."

"Sweet leaves!"

Ninienne's satchel grew full from foraging. They stopped to rest against some trunks in a small clearing. Gossamaw sat, patiently waiting for a treat.

"Oh, you want something to eat too?" asked Benno. "Here you go, you'll like these." He offered Gossamaw a handful of sweet leaves. The frogdog licked them up voraciously and Benno rubbed the frogdog's belly.

Ninienne wondered, idly, if she had met Benno at Belcarin, if they would be friends.

As she leaned against a rough trunk, munching on a savory plate fungus, she heard movement in the nearby thicket. She startled.

"You okay?" asked Benno.

"I'm fine," said Ninienne. "Salagrix had me worried. He seems to think there's something dangerous out here. Is he right?"

Benno wiped his fingers, sticky from sweet leaves, on his pants. "It's true. There's a beast. But it doesn't come out during the day. At least that's what the old folks say. They call it the Night Stalker."

The name sent a shiver down Ninienne's back. "Have you ever seen it?"

Benno shook his head. "No. It's supposed to be big, with spikes on its back. Long teeth. It's hard to know what's real and what's just old timers trying to scare people, but nobody goes into the woods at night, so I guess it's pretty serious."

A thought that had been rolling around in her mind finally tumbled out of her mouth. "What do people think of Salagrix? People seem scared of him."

"I dunno," said Benno. "He didn't seem scary to me today. The old timers don't like him, that's for sure. They say things are a lot nicer over on the Brilliant Moon with Dothreep. It seems like they blame Salagrix for every little thing. But I don't know about all that."

"Dothreep," Ninienne said, snapping her fingers. "That's where I've heard that name. He's the Master Wizard of the Brilliant Moon." She recalled Salagrix's comment from earlier. It seemed like he had some sort of rivalry with the other Master Wizard. She filed this away in her mind and turned back to Benno.

"What do you think? Would you rather live under Dothreep than Salagrix?"

"I don't know that it matters. They're both wizards," said Benno, as if that answered the question. Ninienne didn't know what he meant, but since she, too, was a wizard, she didn't care to probe further.

After they finished their picnic, Ninienne picked up her satchel, full of delicious bounty, and they headed back to the trail. But there was one more surprise waiting for them.

At the base of a tree, a patch of skinny, blue mushrooms stuck out of a pile of leaves.

"Oh, those are pretty." Ninienne crouched down to get a closer look. "What are they?"

"Old folks call them Healer's Cap," said Benno. "Not really for eating, but they're good for when you're sick. They can clear poisons. The juice will close up little cuts and scrapes too, if you get pricked by a thorn or something like that."

Good to know, thought Ninienne.

As they approached the trail, Ninienne stopped. "I almost forgot!" she said.

She kneeled and performed a small ritual to give thanks to the spirit of the forest, as she had learned in a Natural Resources Seminar at Belcarin. The wind picked up and rustled some leaves just as she finished.

Ninienne rose and thanked Benno for his expertise.

"I guess I better tip you extra next time," Ninienne joked, but Benno didn't laugh. He was looking at the ground with his hands in his pockets.

"Thanks, I had fun," he said, not looking at her.

"Me too." She patted her satchel, full of foraged bounty. "See you at the next delivery."

Benno nodded, rocking on his feet. "Yeah. Next time."

Ninienne wasn't sure what else there was to say, so she waved and said, "Bye."

They went their separate ways, he to town, and she to the wizard's tower.

But as she walked back down the path, she could have swore she heard something rustling among the trees.

It sounded like giggling.

SALAGRIX DIDN'T SHOW up for dinner. Presumably, he was still playing with the newly arrived packages, so Ninienne took her food to her room. Her device dinged with a message from Drusilla, confirming a time later this week for another live call.

Ninienne sighed. She laughed at herself for how jealous she had been. With just a little time off, she felt so much better. It was good to have friends. It was good to have a break.

If she could talk Salagrix into an android, this kind of day might happen more often. But how?

As she drifted off to sleep, an idea occurred to her. It was a bit tricky, but it was worth a shot.

9.

Welcome back to True Crime in the Twelve-K. I'm your host, Irene Staffsplitter. Today, we're talking about that classic motive: life-extension magic. We all know that there are perfectly legal ways to stay alive and kicking for decades using both magic and technology. But for those really powerful spells, some twisted minds turn to the unthinkable: murder.

—transcript from the streamcast "True Crime in the Twelve-K," Episode 12, "Life-Extension"

SALAGRIX APPEARED AT lecture the next afternoon looking very different. He wore the red sequined wizard hat and the goggles that made him look like a large bug. Large hoop bracelets hung from his wrists. Ninienne didn't know how anyone could fear the display in front of her. He looked more ridiculous than anything.

Today's portal sigil calculation was curious. It was the same as yesterday's.

"Salagrix, we already did this one," said Ninienne, as the chalk nub wrote out the problem across the board.

The old wizard put up a finger. "Ah, but did we?" Salagrix was feeling playful this afternoon. His new toys had put him in a good mood. "Remember, all celestial bodies are constantly moving through space. If you were to use the same sigil from yesterday, both the ground and the target would be in the middle of the void. We have been avoiding this so far with simple problems, but from now on we must start incorporating the idea of celestial motion into our calculations."

Ninienne slouched and made a face. She understood why people took shuttles rather than use portals. If you had to account for the movement of celestial bodies, that meant every individual casting of a portal, even from one side of a planet to the other, required a totally new sigil.

She sighed and got to work. But she hadn't forgotten her plan.

About halfway through marking the sigil on the practice slate, she asked casually, "Salagrix, I've been thinking about taking some time off."

Salagrix blinked at her with enlarged, goggled eyes. "Was yesterday not sufficient for you?"

"No it was, and thank you," she said, "But I've been hearing a lot about Master Wizard Dothreep of the Brilliant Moon, and since he's so close, I thought I might pop over for a day or two just to see what kind of work he's doing."

This was a test question. She wanted to see how Salagrix would respond.

The old wizard scowled. "Dothreep is a hack and dilettante. Unless you want to learn about crowhorse races, I can assure you your time will be better spent here."

Perfect. This was exactly the response Ninienne had hoped to get.

"Oh, really?" Ninienne feigned disappointment as she added a curving accent mark to the sigil. "I had heard that he was cutting-edge, you know, had all the latest technology."

"Whoever told you that is either a liar or an idiot."

"Oh. Hmm," said Ninienne. "Maybe I misunderstood. I've been hearing a lot about this new android technology, and the ways wizards are applying it. I'm sure there will be androids at the next Conclave. I wonder if Dothreep will have one?"

"Unlikely!" Salagrix scoffed.

But out of the corner of her eye, she saw him pull out his device. Images of androids projected up out of the screen.

NINIENNE HAD HOPED to water the seed of this idea over the next few days, but the opportunity arrived at dinner that very night. When she arrived, Salagrix was stroking his beard, scrolling through a marquee of android models. Ninienne sat at the far chair, add pulled out some plate fungus and sweet leaves she had left over to add to her salad.

"I don't see how these things could possibly be useful," said Salagrix, as he cut up his roasted gel-hen. "They can't do magic. What's the point?"

"I think people are still figuring it out. They can do all kinds of work," said Ninienne, as casually as possible. "I know they're looking into it at Belcarin. Whoever figures it out first could really make some profound discoveries. Do things never before possible."

Salagrix's goggle-enlarged eyes darted from Ninienne back to the projection. "Hmm. Is this the new game?" he wondered aloud to himself. "Could this be the key?"

Ninienne's insides screamed *Yes! Yes!*

"I'm going to need some wine and some help," Salagrix said, "If I'm going android shopping."

WITH A FRESH GLASS of wine on the table, Salagrix and Ninienne huddled around the projection like a holographic campfire.

The wizard swiped through the android models on offer. "Yes, which to buy? We have to outdo Dothreep, that's for certain."

Ninienne pointed to a particular model. "You need to consider the features you want. Look, this one is good at housekeeping and caretaking."

Salagrix took a sip from his glass and waved his hand dismissively. "Bah! Features, features! We shall acquire the most prestigious model available. No need for specifics!"

Ninienne shook her head and suppressed a nervous laugh. "Let's start by narrowing down the options. What about this one? It's highly rated and comes with cleaning attachments."

Salagrix squinted at the holographic display, his goggled eyes reflecting the vibrant colors dancing across the projection. "Are we hiring a maid? No. The android must be the avatar of... my majesty. Yesss."

As they continued browsing, Salagrix's focus waned. "Cost. Cost is no object. I deserve the best. Yes," he muttered to himself.

He had stopped scrolling at an image of a sleek android, its entire body covered in a reflective silvery metal. A pattern of bright white dots on the face suggested two circles for the eyes and a line for the mouth.

"That's the one." Salagrix's speech slurred.

Ninienne's heart skipped when she saw the price.

"Salagrix, are you sure?"

But the old wizard did not respond. He had slumped to the side with his red sequined hat tilted askew.

"Salagrix?"

The old wizard half-stood, half-fell out of his chair and lurched toward the wall niche. He whispered incomplete syllables.

Ninienne stood. "Are you alright? Do you need to go to bed?"

Salagrix whirled around with a terrified expression. His eyes, enlarged by the goggles, made him look like a scared bug.

"No!" he shouted. "I won't go! Phantasm!"

His fingertips sparked with magic, and two blue waves, like whips, lashed out against Ninienne painlessly.

"Salagrix! What are you doing?"

"I'm sorry!" he shouted, and useless magic spilled from his hands like open taps. "I'm sorry for what I've done! Please let me be. I'm trying. Oh Silamene!"

He lurched against the wall and hit his head. Before Ninienne could reach him, he staggered into the stairwell.

Ninienne approached the stairs cautiously, not wanting to startle him. She peeked around the archway and saw him crawling up the stairs on his hands and knees. She turned away from embarrassment.

The Academy Deans had not moved fast enough. She needed help, and now.

Salagrix's datastream device was still open on the table. The image of the silver android rotated gently.

"Salagrix, I'm going to order us some help, okay? Is that okay?"

There was an unintelligible grunt from above.

A bright box for an express shipping option glowed in the dark. It was ridiculously expensive, but Salagrix had said the cost was no object. Ninienne had seen Salagrix's treasure pile, and she believed it. All she had to do was tap the device, hit one button, and a solution would be on its way.

"Salagrix, I'm going to order this android, alright? To help you out, to take care of you. Is that okay?"

Salagrix made a sound. It could have been an affirmative. It was plausible that she could have heard a yes in there.

Ninienne tapped the button.

10.

I don't know if you've noticed, but these androids are everywhere now. And I'm supposed to be okay with that? Like, "Oh sure, I'll just share a shuttle with a robot that can beat me at digi-chess and arm wrestling at the same time."

And the way they move! So smooth, so precise. It's unnatural. I saw one the other day cleaning itself, preening itself—perfectly. Like, what's the point? Are they going to a robot job interview? "So, Mr. Android, where do you see yourself in five years?" "In your job, human. Now move."

They're always so polite, too. Which, by the way, is just another reason they're creepy. No human is that polite! They're like, "Good morning, Urgan. How can I assist you today?" I'm like, "How about you assist me by backing up a few steps?"

Maybe they've been spying on us the whole time. I bet they're all secretly taking notes. "Day 3: Urgan is still in bed. Possibly nocturnal."

So yeah, I'm not convinced. Maybe one day, they'll win me over. But until then, I'm sleeping with one eye open—and the other one on the off switch.

— from the comedy special "Can We Talk about the Android in the Room?" by Urgan Wellmont

THE NEXT FEW DAYS HAD Ninienne on pins and needles. Salagrix made no reference to their evening of android shopping, and Ninienne did not want to press. She didn't know if Salagrix was aware of the incoming android, and she was reluctant to bring it up, lest Salagrix get furious with her for spending a kingly sum without his direct, express permission. In addition, his good mood had waned as Ninienne's portal sigils failed to meet his expectations.

Then, one afternoon, as Salagrix once again corrected Ninienne's use of serifs, the doorgong rang.

The delivery!

"I'll get it!" Ninienne dashed down the stairs, glad to be out of Salagrix's critical eye.

She opened the front door to reveal the largest crate she had yet seen resting on Benno's struggling grav cart. Benno looked smug, as if he had constructed the coffin-sized crate himself.

"What's the old fart up to now, I wonder?" he asked.

"Shh!" Ninienne put a finger to her lips and made a cutting motion across her neck. "Salagrix could come downstairs at any time."

Benno immediately shrunk his shoulders and backed away from the door.

"Don't you usually deliver in the morning?"

"This arrived via express shuttle today," Benno said. "And it took me longer than usual to get it up here. I usually would wait until the next day, but it's express." He pointed at the orange and black striped tape that lined the crate with a proud, knowing smile.

Something about this delivery gave Ninienne pause in a way the others hadn't. Even though she knew what was inside, a thrill of foreboding ran down her limbs. Of course, that could have just been the stiff wind.

"How am I even going to get this thing upstairs?" she wondered aloud.

"I would help you, but I've got to get back to my uncle's farm." Benno put out his palms, apologetically.

"Thanks. I'm sure I'll figure something out. You can leave it here for now."

Benno shuffled his feet. It sure didn't look like he was in a hurry. "Um, I just wanted to say that I had a great time in the woods with you the other day."

Ninienne lit up. "Yeah, it was great."

Benno was having a hard time looking Ninienne in the face. "I was just wondering if you might want to do it again, sometime. Or maybe come to the tavern with me, sometime."

Ah, Ninienne realized. It seemed like Benno might be asking her out on a date. She liked Benno, sure, but she was looking for a friend, not anything romantic. But she also didn't want to lose her only opportunity for a friend on the Shadow Moon.

"Oh, uh, maybe. I'm just really busy right now with apprentice stuff. You know Salagrix. Keeping me to the grindstone. But maybe another time?"

Benno nodded and looked off to the side. "Okay. Right. Busy. I get that. Another time."

"But we should definitely hang out soon."

Benno kept nodding, slower this time. "Soon. Yeah. Great."

He shrugged, disappointed, and tapped a button on the cart. The grav whined and slid out from under the crate, which fell to the ground with a heavy thud.

Ninienne handed Benno his handful of coins, but noticed that the dish was slower to refill than usual.

"A little extra today, since this one took you so much trouble."

Benno tipped his stupid mushroom hat. "Thanks. See you soon, probably." He hopped on his cart and rode off.

Ninienne would have replied with some sort of quip, but the man-sized crate had her transfixed.

Maybe it would be better to open it here, she thought, and see what she was dealing with before trying anything else to get the crate up the stairs. There were always levitation spells, but those were so tiring, she would only use one as a last resort.

She hopped up to the sitting room to fetch the sword from the suit of armor.

"Big package!" she shouted up to the stairwell to Salagrix. "I'm opening it down here!"

Salagrix replied with an unintelligible shout.

She took the sword back down to the crate and used it to pry off the lid. It took multiple tries at each corner, but eventually, the lid came off.

Underneath, a smooth white cosmifoam surface perfectly filled the top of the crate. Little curlicues of packed wood shavings stuck out around the edges. There was a strong, acrid chemical smell. Ninienne stuck her fingers around the edge of the cosmifoam and felt a gap. As she lifted it up, there was a rush of air underneath the white lid, and she pulled it aside to reveal the contents.

It was a person.

No: it had the shape of a person, made of smooth, shiny metal. It was the exact image from the projection, rendered in the flesh, so to speak.

The android had arrived.

Ninienne had never seen one so close before, and she leaned in to examine it. It lay in a perfectly shaped hole in the cosmifoam, as if it were asleep. Her reflection appeared in the mirror-like finish, warped by the curve of the body.

Instinctively, she placed her palm on the machine's chest, as if to nudge it awake. It responded with a burst of tiny lights that radiated over the metal skin in all directions. The lights danced in waves and circles and then gathered on the flat, featureless face where they formed into three lines: the minimal suggestion of two eyes and a mouth.

A gentle, almost imperceptible whir came from within the android, and Ninienne sensed a subtle shift of energy. The dots of the eyes rearranged themselves into circles, as if opening, and the android pushed itself to a seated position.

Ninienne grabbed the sword, not because the android had done any kind of threatening motion, but because of an instinctual sense of the uncanny. The android looked *almost* like a person and moved *almost* like a person, but Ninienne's body screamed with alarm that this was *not* a person.

The android swung its legs over the edge of the crate, stood, and turned to face Ninienne with a smoothness of movement and a tilt of the head. Ninienne shivered.

"Hello," a voice came from within the head, light and masculine. "I have been ordered by one Master Salagrix. Are you he?"

Ninienne shook her head and lowered her sword. "No, I'm his apprentice. I'm Ninienne. Salagrix is upstairs."

"Would you take me to him?" The android opened its arms in a non-threatening gesture that made Ninienne's skin crawl. "I am the registered property of Master Salagrix, and would like to meet with him to discuss my duties."

Ninienne nodded and felt her heartbeat slacken. It was just a machine. Nothing to worry about. It just moved and talked in a creepy way, but in the end it was going to help take care of Salagrix. Right?

"Sure, let's go," said Ninienne, distracted. "How are you on stairs?"

"I am capable of a variety of humanoid movements, as well as movements beyond the capabilities of humans. Would you like a demonstration?" With a sudden jerk, every one of android's joints turned in the wrong direction.

"Ah! No!" shouted Ninienne, shielding her eyes from the horribly warped metal man-spider. "I mean, no thank you."

The android shifted back to human form. "Very well. Please lead the way."

Ninienne, hesitant to turn her back on the android, walked sideways through the door and up the stairwell. The android maintained an equal distance from Ninienne at all times, pausing at the landing as she returned the sword to the sitting room. Its silent attentiveness prickled the hairs on the back of her neck.

When they arrived in the lower workshop, Gossamaw immediately began growling, a sound that Ninienne did not even know the frogdog was capable of, a sort of gurgling snarl.

Salagrix turned, and his usually bewildered eyes danced with even more bewilderment underneath the enhancement goggles.

"What is this?" His tone was part disgust, part curiosity.

"It's the android you ordered, remember? It says it would like to meet with you."

"Ah, yes," said Salagrix, with the half-conviction of someone who does not want to appear surprised but has no memory of the events that led to the current moment. "Yes, yes, I ordered this. Have to keep up with the times, you know."

Ninienne exhaled. So far, so good.

Salagrix approached the machine. The red sequins of his hat reflected across the android's chest. The wizard was so hunched that his eyeline came only to where the android's navel would be, if it had been birthed organically and not minted on some distant forgeworld.

"Are you Master Salagrix?" asked the android.

"That I am," replied the wizard.

"Then allow me to introduce myself. I am a Class C assistant android from Greystar Systems. I am pre-programmed to perform many tasks and also capable of learning new tasks to suit your needs. With my datastream connection, I also have access to vast databases of knowledge. How may I help you today?"

Salagrix's white eyebrows had lifted to the red brim of his hat, as far as they could go.

"Fascinating machine," was his eventual pronouncement. "Why don't you take over some of the cleaning chores from my apprentice here? She can show you what to do." Salagrix turned to face Ninienne. "That will free you up to spend more time on your sigil calculations! Eh! What do you say to that?"

"Oh, I was thinking that the android could help you out at night, and help with your, uh..."

"Bah! No! I'm perfectly healthy!" Salagrix shouted. This turned into a cough, and he hit his chest. "No, it will help with chores, and you can focus on your abysmal portalcraft. You'll work side by side with this magnificent machine!"

The thought of spending day after day next to this creepy abomination filled her with dread.

"Sounds great," Ninienne lied.

NINIENNE FOUND IT IMPOSSIBLE to focus on the rest of the lecture with the android standing nearby, staring straight outward with that blank expression made of lights. She tried to pinpoint the source of her discomfort, and realized that it was the sense that there was someone inside the android, like a costume, coupled with the knowing that there wasn't. Gossamaw, for his part, took the spot on the exact opposite side of the room and watched the machine with vigilance.

The android followed Salagrix to the dining room for dinner, and after a brief word from the wizard, served both Salagrix and Ninienne the demon-cooked food from the niche. Ninienne couldn't stand the sight of the android standing over Salagrix's shoulder, so made an excuse and took her dinner in her room.

"Tomorrow morning, you'll instruct the android in your chores," Salagrix said as Ninienne left. "Then maybe you'll finally make some progress on your portalcraft!"

She sat on her bed picking at mushy rice. Not only did Salagrix not see the android as a caretaker, Ninienne had not expected to have such a visceral loathing for the machine. And now she was going to be working side by side with it.

It was here, though. She could still salvage the plan.

She dreamed of falling through a sea of gears.

11.

"We cannot rely on the cosmos to organize itself. We must re-arrange the cosmos to suit our needs."

— *Master Wizard Garfmont, creator of the Garfmont System*

THE NEXT MORNING, NINIENNE dragged her feet getting ready. She bathed slowly and dressed slowly, not wanting to start the day. But eventually, the desire for coffee and breakfast won out, and she climbed the stairs to the lower workshop.

The android was already there, standing against the wall in the dark like a creepy statue, its eyes and mouth the only illumination. Ninienne snapped her fingers and the lantern light spell slowly lit.

"Good morning, Mistress Ninienne." The android's voice had an electronic twinge that made it sound not-quite-human. "How may I be of assistance?"

Ninienne scowled at the machine. "Coffee first. Then we talk. And please, don't call me Mistress. Just Ninienne."

"As you wish, Ninienne," said the android.

Ninienne ordered coffee and breakfast from the niche and then sat, eating, at the worktable in silence. She watched the android, who did not move, but stood staring straight out. This was worse than polite conversation, she decided.

"So, do you have a name?"

"I can go by any name you wish, but my default name is Helpo, because I'm helpful! But you may change my name to whatever you wish. In addition, all my voice and personality settings are customizable."

Ninienne rolled her eyes. "Helpo is a terrible name. I'm not calling you that."

Naming was a tricky thing with its own kind of hidden magic. It was best to play it safe.

"I'm just going to call you Andy for now."

"As you wish," said Andy.

Ninienne continued to sip her coffee and watch Andy over the rim of her mug. She took strength from the warm beverage and steeled herself against the uncanny strangeness of the machine.

Ninienne knew a little spell that illuminated soulfire. It was used in creature healing to see if a patient was still living, since only living things generated soulfire. She muttered the incantation under her breath and waved her free hand. In her vision, she saw Gossamaw, curled up on the floor next to her chair, light up. She also saw her own pool of teal soulfire swirling within her chest. The android, however, was dark.

Just wanted to make sure, she thought.

"Alright," she said, emboldened by coffee. "Let's get to work."

She crossed to the closet to fetch the broom and dustpan. "Now, I know you can't do magic, since you don't make soulfire, so you'll have to do this the hard way." She handed Andy the tools. "You'll need to sweep this room and the dining room and keep them clean. Make sure to keep the fungus at bay. Is that something you can do?"

"Absolutely." The android nodded once and immediately got to work.

Andy crouched down close to the floor, holding the broom near the brush, and with a rapid back-and-forth motion of its wrist, swept dust and dirt into the dustpan. Its movements were direct, precise, and efficient. That is to say, not like a human would sweep at all. Ninienne watched the machine crawl around the workshop like a hunched gremlin.

"Oh," she said. "That works, I guess."

While Andy swept, Ninienne turned to the worktable to prepare ingredients for magical mortar. As she lit the cauldron with a fire wand, the android appeared behind her, a bit too close.

"It appears—"

"Ah!" Ninienne shouted, not realizing Andy was behind her. "Too close!"

"I apologize, Ninienne." Andy took a step back, giving her space. "I have finished sweeping. Based on the materials you have collected, I assume you are making magical mortar. May I be of assistance? While I cannot generate soulfire, creation of the mortar is a non-magical task."

This was true. Soulfire was only used to activate the mortar once it was in place. How did the android know that? Vast databases of knowledge, she assumed.

"Uh, sure," said Ninienne. She stepped back from the table to allow the android to approach. In a flash, the android grabbed ingredients and poured them into the bubbling cauldron. Then, in a move that made Ninienne cry out, it stuck its hand into the boiling liquid.

"Ah! What are you doing!?"

"Do not be alarmed. A liquid at this temperature will not harm me. It will be more efficient for me to blend the mixture this way."

The android arranged its fingers and then its hand spun around at the wrist like an electric whisk.

Ninienne balked and then recovered. *A machine, it's a machine*, she told herself. *If a human did that, yes, creepy. But it's not a human.*

Andy picked up the piping-hot cauldron and poured the mixture into the holding vat. The lights of its eyes bored into her. "There you are. Much faster than stirring with a wand, although if you want me to run tests to confirm I—"

Ninienne felt light-headed. "No, that's fine, that's fine. I, uh, need to go check on something outside."

"Of course. What task shall I take on next?"

On her way to the door, she looked about for something, anything. "Uh, the, uh, ingredient shelves need reorganizing."

Ninienne hurried down the stairs, Gossamaw in tow. The android was just too strange. It was too much to take on all at once.

She stepped outside and with the first breath of the cold outdoor air, immediately felt calmer. The moon beneath her feet grounded and supported her. Gossamaw licked her pant leg, and she picked him up for a comforting squeeze.

"What are we going to do, Gossie?" she looked into the frogdog's large, vacant eyes. He licked one of them with his tongue.

She took a deep breath and returned to the tower. She latched the front door behind her and climbed the stairs.

Back in the lower workroom, Ninienne found all the ingredient shelves rearranged, and Andy once again standing at attention against the wall, awaiting instruction.

"How did you—I wasn't gone that long."

"Would you like me to show you?" asked Andy.

Ninienne was hesitant to see a demonstration, but said, "Yes."

Andy nodded, and Ninienne's datastream device dinged. She pulled it out to see a notification from *Android Messaging System.* She tapped it, and a vid projection popped up. It was a recording from the android's perspective, showing arms rearranging the ingredients on the shelves with inhuman speed.

Ninienne closed the vid and scanned the shelves, but she could not make heads or tails of how they were supposed to be arranged.

"What did—how are these—"

"Accessing the relevant databases," said Andy, moving its head and arms in imitation of casual conversation, "I found the most efficient and effective organizing system is the Garfmont System."

Ninienne sighed. The light-headed feeling was returning. "That's great, but I don't know the Garfmont System, so—"

"Allow me to instruct," said Andy, as if parroting a human lecturer. "The Garfmont System prioritizes efficiency, with the most commonly used ingredients at middle height, and the least used ingredients on the top-most and bottom-most shelves. Consideration is also given to reactivity, separating materials that might—"

Ninienne staggered, nauseous. She thought she could handle more of this, but she couldn't.

"Um, just keep cleaning," she said. "Maybe go upstairs and see if Salagrix needs anything."

She stumbled down the stairs to her room. The android had freed up her morning. This much was true.

Right now, she needed out of this tower.

12.

There are many forms of magic that are overt and obvious: spells, incantations, potions, sigils, to name a few. It is very hard to perform magic accidentally (although, the astute reader will know the history of the Vallenvords and their chaotic bloodline).

But there are other forms of magic that are more subtle. Naming is one such subtle magic. To give a thing a name is to anchor it to the web of magic, to give it a place among the family of things. This is why Master Wizards, at their induction ceremony, are given unique names of power.

Naming also binds the namer to the named. It links them forever in the threads of fate. Done consciously and with intention, it can be a boon to both parties. Done carelessly, a botched naming can ripple across time and space to disastrous effect (see the tragic history of Spaceship McShipface).

—from "Subtle Magic: It's Forms and Uses" by Professor Canedabram

HAVING THE ANDROID in the tower freed up Ninienne's schedule, this much was true, and, as Ninienne couldn't stand being in proximity to the machine, it meant that she spent a lot of time outside wandering the woods when she was meant to be reviewing sigil formulas. This seemed like a win-win to Ninienne, who started learning the paths nearest to the circular border with the forest, spending time with the creatures there, and foraging deliciously fresh snacks. More than once, picnicking in a shady clearing, she thought she heard giggling, but turned to see only a rustling thorn bush.

She took up her mother's idea of a garden and staked out a small plot near the tower. The propagation spell her mother taught her meant that she only needed a small sample of a plant to help it re-grow, so she planted samples of edible plants from the woods, as well as a few vegetables she ordered from the kitchen niche.

It was getting harder to pin down Drusilla for calls, and her friend grew distant as "coven stuff" occupied more and more of her time. This bothered Ninienne, and it pained her that there was nothing she could do. As much as she loved chatting with the cacospiders when Andy wasn't around, it really wasn't the same.

Although Ninienne's grasp of sigil calculations was shaky, Salagrix introduced the topic of portal paste, the material with which the sigils had to be drawn in order to properly activate. There were many, many different materials one could use, which explained Salagrix's vast and varied inventory of ingredients.

Amid the first week of the android's presence in the tower, the official response from the Deans arrived.

"Thank you for your report. We will investigate. In the meantime, more detailed information (recordings, etc.), if it can be provided, would be appreciated."

It had been several long weeks to get such a curt response that only sort of answered her question. The matter seemed almost irrelevant at this point now that the android was here. Still, she knew the android could take recordings, so should Salagrix have another bout of confusion, they might capture it on video.

Still, the slow and uninterested action of the Deans was frustrating, and Ninienne felt it was as good an excuse as any to take a walk.

NINIENNE SHOVED HER hands into the pockets of her work pants and took slow, calming breaths. Gossamaw took bites of brown clover as he hopped along behind her. They approached the border with the forest and she felt a mad smile break across her face, just as it had on her first excursion. She stepped over a root into the dry crunch of leaves.

As they walked deeper into the woods, Ninienne's frustration softened into a sense of peace and tranquility. The leaves at the tips of the black, crooked branches rustled in a calm whisper. Here, away from the dark gloom of the tower, Salagrix's unpredictable temperament, and the unsettling android, her worries seemed distant and less significant. She collected plate fungus and sweet leaves.

Her trek led her down a gentle slope, where she found a patch of Healer's Cap. A little prick of intuition told her to pick some of these, and she did. The stems were slick to the touch, covered in a watery balm. She gave thanks to the forest, and had just closed the flap on her satchel when she heard a strange, distant noise.

At first she thought it was Gossamaw, but he was beside her, trying to catch a buzzing insect with wild flicks of his tongue. The noise came again: a plaintive, pained call.

Ninienne struck off through the woods and Gossamaw followed. She brushed aside branches and steadied herself against trunks as she navigated a forest floor criss-crossed by cracked roots. There was a third cry, very close, and she pushed through a long-leafed bush, black and curled, into a small clearing.

In the middle of a patch of black soil, she found the source of the cries. A battered bramblehawk lay on the ground, its brown-spotted leaf-feathers turned red with sap-blood. It struggled to lift its head, and opened its beak to call again, the weakest cry yet.

Ninienne crouched down and approached the bramblehawk slowly. Gossamaw, well trained, stayed back.

"Hi," whispered Ninienne. "I can help. Can I look at you?"

The bramblehawk gave a tired sigh that Ninienne understood, through her familiar connection, as resigned agreement. With gentle hands, Ninienne examined the bushbird. There were gashes across the woody abdomen and the left wing-branch was snapped. He had obviously gotten into a fight with something bigger and sharper than him.

"Something took a nasty swipe at you, huh?" Ninienne did a quick scan around, to make sure whatever had caused this was not still here. It was strange, because she imagined a predator would have wanted to eat the bramblehawk, not leave it to bleed out its sap on the forest floor.

She took out a stem of freshly picked Healer's Cap and squeezed a few drops onto the injured areas.

"This will help for now," she said, looking into the creature's large orange eye. "But if I'm going to really fix you up, I need to get you back to the tower. Is that okay?"

The bramblehawk whimpered, which Ninienne took as assent. She wrapped the poor bushbird in her scarf and stood up.

Looking around, with a sudden panic, she realized she did not know how to get back to the tower. She could not see the field. It was as if she had been blindfolded, spun around, and dropped into the middle of the woods.

Guessing wildly, she stepped through a bush, but the path on the other side did not look familiar. Was that because it was the wrong way or because it looked different in the opposite direction? She tried another path, and then another, but none seemed right.

The rustling in the leaves sounded like laughing.

"Look," Ninienne called out, not sure who she was talking to, "If I don't get this bird back to the tower soon, he will die. I'm not sure which way to go."

There was a gust of wind, and a patch of canopy opened up to illuminate the ground. There it was! Why hadn't she seen it before?

"Thank you!" Ninienne called. "I owe you one, whatever you are!"

She ran over roots and between trees as fast as she could. Gossamaw did his best to keep up.

Ninienne bolted across the open field, straight through the tower door, and up the stairs to the lower workshop. Andy was nowhere in sight, but its handiwork was evident: the room was incredibly clean.

After making space on the worktable, she gently placed the bramblehawk down and unwrapped the scarf, which was soaked with sap-blood. The bramblehawk looked up at her with a pained expression, and Ninienne couldn't help but feel a pang of sympathy for the creature.

"Okay, I'm going to fix you up now. It's going to hurt a little, but I promise it'll be worth it in the end. Okay?"

Ninienne rolled up her sleeves and got to work. A quick swipe with a disinfection wand cleaned the wounds. She searched the shelves for the ingredients she needed and found, with delight, that they were all on the middle shelves and easy to grab.

Score one for the Garfmont System, she thought.

She measured out seeds and gels into the already hot cauldron and then wrote a series of glyphs (conjugated for phytoavian physiology, of course) out on a long bandage. She soaked the bandage in the bubbling potion and delicately wrapped it around the bramblehawk's body. Gossamaw looked up eagerly from the floor, quiet and ready, sensing Ninienne's urgency.

Her training had served her well. Once set, the bandage glowed with gentle warmth as the healing spell activated.

Next was the broken branch-wing. This involved grinding up a powder in the mortar—again, she found the ingredients she needed almost without thinking—and then sprinkling it over the broken limb as she sang the precise, wordless incantation. She felt her soulfire spiral and pour itself into the powder, energizing it.

Soon the powder hardened and the bone set. She gave the bramblehawk a few drops from the Healer's Cap into his open beak, and he looked up at her with his big, bright eye and let out a contented cry.

As a last step, Ninienne retrieved an empty crate and some soft fabric from the storage closet and fashioned a bed for her patient.

"Rest now," whispered Ninienne as she placed the bramblehawk into its new bed. "You did great. Time to rest."

Ninienne collapsed on the workroom floor, exhausted in body, drained of soulfire, but energized in spirit.

As she lay on the floor, a profound clarity settled over her. Whatever hoops she had to jump through to finish her apprenticeship, whatever states of mind she found her mentor in, whatever mechanical assistants she had to tolerate, she knew who she was with a strong certainty.

She was Ninienne Lightcaster, creature healer.

NINIENNE RECOVERED in time to grab a stale sandwich from the wall niche before Salagrix arrived. Gossamaw was snoring, curled up on the floor next to the bramblehawk's bed crate. Salagrix and Andy came down the stairs, and the old wizard was laughing.

"Ha! And if the target world is orbiting a large red star, what then?"

"Assuming all other variables remained the same," said Andy, "One could substitute snail shells for imp curry powder."

"Extraordinary! Very good." Salagrix noticed Ninienne standing by the workbench. "This machine is quite the quick student. Marvelously intelligent. Fascinating."

Ninienne, exhausted, gestured toward her sleeping patient. "I found an injured bramblehawk in the woods. I rescued it and it's resting now. Just in case you were wondering what's going on with this crate."

Salagrix looked at the bramblehawk and sniffed.

"Just keep it sanitary," he sneered.

Ninienne suppressed the pang from her mentor's dismissal as he strolled over to the chalkboard.

"We will continue our exploration of portal paste variations and substitutions today. For our first hypothetical example, we will consider a world orbiting a white dwarf star. What component will we need as a base?"

Ninienne knew this. She grabbed her pile of parchment notes and sorted through them.

"Elemental chalk," chirped Andy. Ninienne turned to see the machine already holding the appropriate jar from the shelves.

Salagrix laughed. "Very good, but that question was meant for my apprentice. She is the one who needs to learn these things."

"My apologies, Master Salagrix."

Salagrix approached Andy to take the jar, and a small vial from the nearby shelf hopped off, drawn into his personal gravity. Andy reacted in a flash, snatching the vial and setting it back on the shelf.

"Nice catch," said Salagrix, who set the elemental chalk on the workbench. "Now, suppose it is actually a binary star system, with both stars being white dwarfs. What changes will we need to make to our recipe?"

"Uh, don't we just need to double the amount of the reagents?" Ninienne guessed.

"Normally, yes, but there's an exception in this case. Do you know what it is?"

Ninienne shuffled through her notes. She thought this sounded familiar, but the answer wasn't coming to her.

"Perhaps our android companion knows."

"Because both stars are extremely small, the Principle of Reversatation applies. Therefore, we use the opposite base on Kallow's Matrix, in this case, fiend charcoal." Andy retrieved a small latched box.

"Very good!" Salagrix clapped his hands. "That was a tricky one, and a rare case. I was trying to stump you, but it's hard to beat the mind of a machine!"

The lecture continued like this, with Salagrix giving more and more attention to Andy, until by the end Ninienne was just watching them make portal paste without her.

"The last step, I'm afraid, is where you fall short, my metal friend," said Salagrix. "My apprentice will have to recite the finishing incantation."

Ninienne stood and marched up to the worktable. It was probably a mistake to feel smug towards a machine, but she was glad to be capable in a way Andy wasn't. She passed her fingers over the steaming cauldron and recited the spell.

The paste shriveled up into a crumpled ball and released a puff of black smoke like a weak cough. A thick black ooze bubbled over the edge of the cauldron, across the table, and onto the floor.

"Ah, no." Salagrix frowned, backing away. "You conjugated the incantation for iron, not for ice. Alas. You two, please clean this up before dinner."

Salagrix hobbled out of the room.

Ninienne felt like a platinum grade idiot. Why couldn't she get this? She shook her head.

"Sorry about that," said Ninienne. "I'll get you the mop."

"No need to apologize," said Andy. "Making mistakes is a part of the learning process."

That was unnecessarily kind, coming from a glorified tool, but Ninienne appreciated the artificial sentiment. She fetched the mop and bucket from the storage closet.

"If that's true, then I should be a genius by now, because I've done nothing but make mistakes since I got here." She handed the tools over to Andy.

"I think this bramblehawk would disagree," said Andy, nodding toward Ninienne's patient, sleeping peacefully in the box nearby.

A little tear welled up in Ninienne's eye and her throat clenched.

"Thank you." Her voice cracked unexpectedly. "Thank you for noticing."

"I am highly calibrated for observation," said Andy in its characteristic chirp.

With that, Ninienne snapped back to reality. The machine hadn't actually noticed; it was just responding according to an algorithm. Even if it wasn't real, the recognition felt nice.

"Listen," said Ninienne as she scraped ooze off the table with a chiseling wand, "There's something you need to know. Salagrix is really old. He sometimes has these bouts of confusion. When that happens, can you take care of him? Make sure he's okay?"

Andy looked up from its mopping. "Of course. The health and safety of my Master is one of my primary priorities."

"And, if possible, could you also make a recording? In case we need to share what's going on with a healer, or something like that."

"Of course." The android spread its arms in what was meant to be a generous gesture, but just ended up giving Ninienne a shiver.

But not as big a shiver as before.

"I PROPOSE A TOAST," said Salagrix, at dinner, as he raised his glass. This would have caught Ninienne's attention had the same thing not happened every single night of her apprenticeship. "To our android, who has so far gone without a proper name."

Ninienne realized that, while she had been calling the android Andy on her own, she had never mentioned the choice to Salagrix or heard him call the android anything.

"However, as you have proven yourself to a be a reliable help and an astute student, I believe it is time for a belated christening."

Ninienne wanted to object here, but Andy wasn't much of a name, and the wizard was already barreling full steam ahead.

"We shall call you Hadrarch, after the King-Slayer herself. Yes, that has a nice ring of irony to it, does it not? She who once commanded the stars themselves is now mine to command!" Salagrix laughed and took a drink of his wine.

"Of course, as you wish," said—what was it, Hadrarch? It didn't sound right to Ninienne. As much as she tried, she could only think of the android as Andy. She joined in the toast, but felt bad about it. The pixie wine was fragrant and syrupy.

"And, now, a song, I think," said Salagrix, after a second long drink. "Can you sing, Hadrarch?"

"I have many capabilities, Master Salagrix. What would you like to hear?"

Salagrix's eyes watered and he looked at his metallic servant with a longing Ninienne had not yet seen. "*Astrada's Lament.*"

Hadrarch nodded, and after a brief pause, began to sing in a high, clear tenor the first phrase of a despairing elegy.

"No, no, that will never do," said Salagrix. "The song must be sung in a woman's voice."

"I can adjust my vocal qualities, if you would like?"

"Is that," Salagrix said, his voice beginning to take on a slow, mashed quality of nostalgia tinged with wine, "is that something you can do?"

Andy—no, Hadrarch—nodded, and began again, this time in a ringing soprano. The song was long and slow and sad. Because of the unfamiliarity of the voice, it sounded as if it were coming from somewhere else, and gave the performance an ethereal quality. The android's smooth movements, in imitation of a singer's movement and posture, transformed the machine into another being altogether.

By the end of the song, Salagrix had slumped onto the table, staring into his empty glass and weeping openly. Ninienne's sips of pixie wine had not dispelled her discomfort. This was a wounded, broken man, as lost as a small child in the vast darkness between the stars.

"Thank you, my Hadrarch," Salagrix croaked, at last. "Please, accompany me to my workshop. I require your assistance."

Salagrix lurched toward the stairs and the android followed, leaving Ninienne alone.

NINIENNE RETURNED TO her room after the unusual day to find the bramblehawk sleeping in the converted crate on her desk. Salagrix's botched naming of the android stuck her mind like a broken feather-leaf. She wanted to name something correctly, to counteract the clumsy name.

She looked down at the bramblehawk, breathing gently as it slept.

"Almet," she said, after the main character from her favorite novel. "Sleep well, Almet."

A wind blew in through the window. It carried the scent of the woods.

13.

"Please be advised that certain students are using androids to complete schoolwork. This is against the Academy Code of Ethics. In-classroom examination of skills without external aids is recommended."

—*internal faculty memo, Belcarin Academy of Wizardry*

THE WEEKS WORE ON, and the Brilliant Moon continued its slow wane in the night sky until the bright gibbous turned to a smiling crescent.

Salagrix's lectures on portal paste deepened, and Ninienne learned that each casting required a unique mixture of exclusively rare and expensive ingredients that changed depending on the ground, the target, the shape of the constellations at both locations, the phase of all relevant moons (which was doubly important when casting from the surface of a moon, as they were), and hundreds of other variables. Not only did Ninienne have more questions for Salagrix than ever before, but it was getting harder to capture her Master's attention during lecture hours, as he spent an increasing amount of time focused on Andy.

At least the hands-on work of grinding ingredients and stirring them into bubbling cauldrons was much better, in Ninienne's opinion, to abstract, theoretical lectures. But, since Salagrix now spent more time near the ingredient shelves, this meant more shattered jars on the floor. Not that Ninienne had to clean them. That was Andy's—sorry, Hadrarch's job. That stupid name. Ninienne still called the android Andy, despite the wizard's ridiculous choice.

Ninienne became bolder in her exploration of the woods, collecting Healer's Cap for Almet. She was realistic: it was going to take a long time for the bushbird to recover. Whatever had taken a swipe at him had caused more than physical damage. There might be a magical ailment at play, but without knowing what had attacked him, Ninienne could only speculate. However, Ninienne had mentioned the project to Professor Hemnal, who was giving her extra credit in exchange for progress reports. That, at least, kept Ninienne connected to her goals.

Her garden was not turning out as she had expected. The plants she had foraged from the woods were growing just fine, but the plants from the niche were behaving strangely. They had mutated and grown teeth, which was not within expectations for something plants were supposed to do, but she wasn't sure what had gone wrong.

She saw Benno a few more times, and each time he asked her out to the tavern. Ninienne demurred each time, but she felt bad about it.

She hadn't heard from Drusilla in weeks. Whenever she felt overwhelmed, she crawled under the worktable to visit the hidden nest of cacospiders, and drew strength from their resilience.

ONE AFTERNOON, SALAGRIX had Ninienne draw out a sigil on the practice slate with an inert paste, to get used to working with the material.

"No, no, this is wrong," Salagrix muttered, looking over her work. "These are dangerous mistakes. You're just making bombs in spacetime."

"I'm trying!" Ninienne burst.

"Not hard enough!" Salagrix countered. "Your apprenticeship is nearly half-over, and you're nowhere near ready to cast actual portals."

Had it been that long already? The idea exhausted Ninienne.

"I'm doing my best."

"You are not!" Salagrix shouted. "You don't understand what's at stake!"

That was a weird thing to say. "What? You think I don't understand the consequences of failing my apprenticeship year?"

Salagrix's face turned red, as if he were about to explode. But just as quickly as his anger arose, it dissipated. He rubbed his eyes.

"We're running out of time. You must learn these things," he said. With a flick of his hand, the nub of chalk danced across the chalkboard, writing out a description of a hypothetical portal. "I am fatigued. I need to... lie down. Please draw the sigil for this portal in paste. I will return before dinner to check your work." He slouched out of the room.

Ninienne had never seen her master like this. She had always assumed that his frustration with her lack of progress was simply that of an expert trying to guide a novice. But there was something else going on, something deeper.

She tried to focus on drawing the sigils, but Salagrix's outburst lingered in her mind. Going over her work for the third time, she found yet another error.

"Ugh!" she cried, and her chin dropped to her chest.

Andy, who had been labeling the ingredient jars in a clean, precise hand, approached. "I don't mean to interrupt, but I might be of assistance."

Ninienne looked up and scowled at the machine. "Since when did you become an expert on sigils?"

"Last night," the android responded without detecting Ninienne's sarcasm. "As I require very little recharge time, I read through the books in Salagrix's library, and cross-referenced them with articles accessible from the datastream."

Salagrix has a library? was Ninienne's first thought, and a pang of something like jealousy struck her. But she decided to give the machine a chance. "Sure, go ahead, knock yourself out."

Ninienne wiped the practice slate clean with the erasing wand and handed the android the pot of paste and the brush. As Andy worked, it walked Ninienne through the geometrical calculations and their effects of the sigil in a precise manner. It was only now that Ninienne realized how jumbled Salagrix's lectures had been, frequently digressing through rare edge cases and exceptions that obscured and complicated the fundamentals. Hearing Andy explain it, concepts clicked into place amid her muddled confusion.

Her mechanical companion finished drawing the sigil and showed it to Ninienne. Her first thought was to thank the machine, but that felt stupid. Did you thank a hammer, a mop, a cauldron? But she didn't know how to direct this surge of gratitude that she felt for this faceless android.

"Thank you. That was really helpful," she said.

"Glad to be of service."

It was time for a snack break. She took a handful of gathered berries and sliced plate fungus from a bowl on the table, feeling the juice burst in her mouth.

Ninienne crawled under the worktable to offer an extra berry to the cacospiders, but when she pulled back the loose wall stone, she found it empty.

"Something wrong?" Andy asked when she had returned to her seat.

"There was a nest of cacospiders under the table and now they're not there."

"I found them and cleaned them out earlier today. Salagrix gave me very specific instructions to find and exterminate the nest."

The knowledge that Andy had found and cleaned out her secret cacospider nest drove a cold icicle through Ninienne's heart. It was a small thing, really, but knowing that a little nest of creatures could survive in the tower meant she could too. Maybe it wasn't a small thing. Maybe it was a big thing.

Ninienne scowled at Andy while she ate her berries.

Salagrix returned, looking rejuvenated, if a little damp. He examined the practice slate and the sigil Andy had drawn there.

"This is perfect! And excellent penmanship, too."

Ninienne almost corrected the wizard, but stopped herself. Receiving praise from her mentor was such a rare and precious thing that she was reluctant to ruin it.

"So tell me, how did you solve the problem with the discordant accent marks?"

"I, uh," Ninienne squirmed. There was no way out of this. It was best to be honest. "I didn't draw that sigil. The android did. It was trying to show me how to do it. I was going to do it again, myself, but I hadn't gotten there yet."

Salagrix scowled, and his face bunched up like a rotten lemon. "A cheat? If there's one thing I can't stand, it's a cheat. This will go in my report to the Deans."

Ninienne felt her chances at a Master's Letter evaporating. "No, please, it was just a misunderstanding. Let me show you I can do it—"

Salagrix reddened. It might have been Ninienne's imagination, but he seemed to grow larger. But before he could say anything, the android interrupted.

"Master Salagrix, may I make a request?" chirped Andy.

Salagrix whirled on the android. "A request? From by beloved Hadrarch? Call me intrigued. Proceed."

"I know you have a kitchen demon to take care of your meals, but I would like to prepare dinner tonight. To explore new skills."

Salagrix made a bemused sound. The issue of the practice problem seemed to have dropped completely from his mind.

"Very well. My apprentice will show you to the kitchen demon's floor and revise the infernal contract as necessary. I have a few tasks that need attending to in the upper workshop."

Ninienne raised her hand. "Uh, sorry, I don't know anything about infernal contracts. And I'm not allowed above the dining room."

Salagrix blinked and then waved his hand. "I grant you permission for the evening. Don't let the demon give you any trouble. He's toothless."

"But what about the contract?"

But the wizard had already left.

NINIENNE FELT RELIEVED to have avoided Salagrix's ire for now, but was still mad that Andy had exterminated the cacospiders. As they climbed the stairs, lit by Ninienne's lantern light spells, the android spoke.

"I was not entirely truthful with Salagrix for my reasons for wanting to make dinner."

It was already strange enough that Andy was coming up with new tasks for itself, but admitting to subterfuge was not something she expected from a pre-programmed machine.

"Okay?" said Ninienne, not sure about where this was going.

"I have noticed that you find the food the demon prepares distasteful, and you have been supplementing your meals with foraged food. As it is my programming to look after the health of those in my care, I thought I would prepare more appetizing meals for you."

"Oh, okay."

"I also noticed Salagrix getting angry and wanted to redirect him. He misjudged you unfairly."

Ninienne did not like this one bit. She didn't want to like this creepy android that had killed her spider friends. But now it was looking out for her and offering to make her dinner.

They reached the closed door with the pungent smell behind it. The clanging of pots and pans covered Ninienne's mild knock, so she tried the door and found it unlocked.

The door opened into a narrow room. Cabinets crowded in on both sides, and pots and pans hung from the ceiling. Steam and bubbles rose from a sink filled with dirty dishes, cleaning themselves. The black iron stove was in the shape of a devil's head with burners for eyes and a toothy grin for the oven. A red flame of a tongue licked inside.

At the end of the narrow kitchen, sitting on a stool and eyes glued to a handheld game, was the demon. He had red skin, a pig-like snout, nubby little horns, and a greasy apron that covered his sizable paunch. He looked up.

"Eh?" he said.

"Hi, sorry we haven't met yet. I'm Ninienne, I'm Salagrix's apprentice."

The demon's eyes narrowed suspiciously.

"Where's Rodando?"

There was a question she hadn't thought about in a few months. Where *was* Rodando?

"Oh, he hasn't been Salagrix's apprentice for a long time."

"I wonder what that means." The demon tilted his head. "Who's the walking tin can?"

"This is Andy, our, uh, android, who was wondering if it could make dinner tonight? So, you know, you would have a night off."

The demon blinked without moving.

"So, do you think you could show Andy around?"

The cook set down his game. When he spoke, it was like the tumbling of embers in a woodstove, rustling and hot with the occasional snap. "You want me to teach this... *thing* how to use the kitchen, so that I can take the night off?"

Ninienne tilted her head and pursed her lips. "Yeah, that's about it."

The demon slid off the stool and approached them, slapping the stone floor with his large paddle-like feet.

"I see absolutely no downside to this. Then again, I do have soup for brains." The demon smiled wide, showing off a row of tiny, blunted teeth. "My name's Quiggleam, and I am at your service. Before we begin, I should mention that I have soup for brains. If you ask me a question on any topic, I may get very confused, I may answer incorrectly, or I may just say BLARP and forget what you said. Any questions?"

"Oh, so should we not ask questions then, or...?"

"I, um, well, anyway, moving on." Quiggleam gestured to the largest cabinet. "This is the food summoner. This is where all the ingredients come from." The demon opened the cabinet to reveal an insanely complex device of pipes, gauges, knobs, switches, and blinking lights around an open chamber. Quiggleam flipped a switch, set several of the dials, and the device chugged to life. The chamber filled with a bright blue light. The demon stuck his claw into the light, where it vanished, but when he pulled it out again he was holding a lumpy, spotted apple. "Easy enough. Maybe your friend would like to try it."

The android complied. It put its metallic hand into the light and retrieved a perfectly shiny, plump red apple.

Quiggleam frowned. "Show-off. But then again, I do have soup for brains."

The incredible machine, which defied her understanding of the capabilities of magical devices, amazed Ninienne. "How does that even work?"

"It's a family name, actually. I come from a long line of Gleams."

"That wasn't what I asked," said Ninienne, but the demon had already moved down the line.

"The stove is powered by a hellgate," said the demon. He opened the oven door to reveal a shrieking vortex of fire. "Be careful that you don't get sucked in!" he shouted over the storm.

Ninienne recoiled, shielding herself from the whipping winds, until the demon slammed the stove shut.

Quiggleam demonstrated the operation of the self-cutting knives (which were chipped in several places), as well as how to use the kitchen end of the niche system, which looked just like the other niches, but above this one there was a row of four funnels with little bulbs and switches, labeled Sitting Room, Lower Workshop, Dining Room, and Upper Workshop.

"So," smirked Quiggleam, waggling his claws, "Dinner tonight? Think you can handle it?"

"I understand the function of the kitchen," said Andy. "May I begin right away?"

The demon smiled the widest Ninienne had yet seen. "BLARP!"

LATER THAT NIGHT, NINIENNE climbed the stairs to the dining room to find the table, laden with dishes, and Salagrix, wide-eyed, already in his seat. A plump roasted cliff chicken dominated the center, surrounded by bowls of colorful root vegetables, crisp green salads, and a jiggling pudding. Andy stood at the wall in an apron.

Ninienne sat down, and the warm aroma of spices and herbs enveloped her senses. She served herself a plate of vegetables and salad. The vegetables were rich and creamy, and the salad was fresh and crisp. The pudding was so sweet and delicious Ninienne thought she might die of bliss.

"What do you think?" Ninienne asked her mentor from across the table. "Time to fire that demon?"

"We'll need to ask Rodando and see if he can amend the contract." Salagrix licked his fingers in satisfaction.

"Rodando isn't here," Ninienne reminded the old wizard.

"But..." Salagrix's eyes, enlarged by his enhancement goggles, searched the room. "He was... we were..."

"He was what?" Ninienne asked, hoping to catch Salagrix out of his confusion. "Rodando was what?"

But Salagrix only shook his head. "I'm sorry, I need to... I need..." he got out of his chair and drifted out of the dining room.

After such a lovely dinner, Ninienne was loathe to press the issue, and she felt bad for ruining the mood.

"How did you enjoy your dinner?" asked the android.

"Oh, it was great, thank you," said Ninienne. "Really delicious. Sorry for ruining the mood."

"As an android, I do not experience mood. However, if you are interested in Salagrix's previous apprentice, I have something of interest for you."

BACK IN HER ROOM, NINIENNE took the parchment that Andy had retrieved for her and flattened it out across her desk. Gossamaw wagged his little nub of a tail in anticipation.

"Alright, calm down. We don't even know what this is yet."

It was a letter, written out in an elegant hand.

Rodando, my love—

I re-read your most recent letter, from four months ago. Was there another since then, waylaid perhaps? When you say you are "drawing on powers that defy comprehension," do you mean in your demonology studies, or your side project with Salagrix? You don't sound like yourself.

I am concerned we are growing apart. Your inconsistent responses to my letters have me worried that you no longer care about our connection. I know you are busy with your work, but even the briefest missive would allay my worries. Have you found someone else in the shadows of the Shadow Moon? Please tell me. A sudden break would be preferable to this agonizing uncertainty.

If you're worried about what my father said the last time we were together, ignore him. I don't care that you're a "penniless demonologist." You're my *penniless demonologist. And surely Salagrix must be paying you something by now? Either way, we don't need my father's money. We can live on love.*

Tell me you feel the same?

Please respond with haste.

Your Enwu

This was intriguing. Ninienne's characterization of Rodando as a wealthy student who had abandoned his belongings after his apprenticeship ended did not line up with the information in this letter. He was a demonologist. Not a common course of study. And what was the 'side project'?

She searched the Belcarin Archives for what felt like hours, taking breaks to attend to Almet, but found nothing except for one record from twenty years ago:

Name: Rodando Vechi

Study: Demonology

Degree: Completed

Nothing in the school newspaper, nothing in any records of the clubs or guilds. Nothing in larger searches of the datastream. Just this simple record that confirmed what she already knew: he had been a student at Belcarin, and he had studied demonology.

Why had he left all of his belongings? Was he planning to come back, and was prevented from doing so?

Or had something more sinister happened?

14.

The advent of the Master Wizard system serves as an example of the harmonious integration of magic and governance. What began as an informal agreement to divide responsibility among the members of the Terranic Council for the oversight of supply lines during the early days of colonization has transformed over the centuries into a prestigious institution steeped in tradition. There is no greater honor for a wizard than to be named Master and be given dominion over a planet, moon, asteroid field, or space station.

The role of a Master Wizard is complex: a combination of leader, visionary, judge, guardian, scholarly expert, and mentor. History gives us endless examples of the ways individual Masters have fulfilled their roles. Which of them were successful, and which made mistakes that led to disaster? That is what this text hopes to answer.

[Annotation: "which made mistakes" is underlined. A note in the margin reads "ALL OF THEM"]

– from the introduction to "Master Wizards: A History and Commentary" by Master Wizard Nandogab, from the author's personal library

NINIENNE WAS IN HER room, trying to wrap her head around portal sigils once again, when the doorgong interrupted her. She went downstairs to find Benno, of course, in his stupid mushroom hat and his smug grin and his grav cart once again full of packages.

"Oh, I've been meaning to ask you. What was in that big one a while ago? You get it upstairs okay by yourself?" Benno asked as Ninienne took inventory.

What she wanted to say was, *yes, I'm perfectly capable of opening and carrying packages by myself,* but instead she said, "Salagrix ordered a helper android. It's upstairs cutting seed pods with a very big knife."

"By the void! An android? That must be the only one on the Shadow Moon. I knew the old fart was richer than a pitdevil but that just goes to show it."

Ninienne nodded as she brought the last package inside.

"So, if the android is helping out, that probably means you've got more free time, huh?"

"Yeah, I have actually. It's been nice," Ninienne said, handing Benno a handful of coins from the tray.

"So, you could come with me to the tavern this evening."

Ninienne realized her error. She had stepped right into Benno's trap. While she had enjoyed her forest walk with

Benno however long ago, she didn't want to give him the wrong impression.

But it would be a reason to go into town, something she had not yet done in all her time here, and her apprenticeship was half over.

"Sure," she said, and Benno's shocked face made the whole plan worth it.

"Really? With me?" Benno's hands made confused gestures, pointing back and forth.

"Sure, sounds fun," Ninienne shrugged. "I'll see you there tonight."

Benno adjusted his hat and stood up straighter than Ninienne had ever seen. She hadn't realized how tall he was.

"See—" his voice immediately caught, and he had to clear his throat. "See you tonight then."

Ninienne gave a little finger wave as Benno rode his grav cart down the path through the forest.

How about that? thought Ninienne. *I've got a date.*

NINIENNE STILL HAD chores to do. Repairing the masonry and recharging the lantern spells were still her responsibility, as both tasks required magic, but it was much less draining on her soulfire when she hadn't already spent the morning cleaning.

Salagrix came downstairs for the afternoon lecture, which was about calligraphy styles to consider when drawing portal sigils and adjusting them based on the consistency of the paste. The type of wand or brush used, the thickness of the line, slight adjustments to the curves of the serifs, each of these carried weight and meaning and an error in any of them could mean disaster.

Hadrarch—well, Andy, as Ninienne refused to use Salagrix's ridiculous name—served tea to both of them, unprompted, and returned to its inventory of the recently arrived ingredients. Ninienne sipped her tea with welcome relief as her head swam with confusion from all the variables to consider. How anyone ever got a portal to work, she didn't know.

She was also more distracted than usual, thinking about Rodando's mysterious disappearance. She studied every movement of Salagrix's fingers, every lifting of his wispy eyebrows, to see if he was actually the daffy old man he appeared to be or if something more sinister lurked beneath his red sequined hat.

Salagrix finished the lecture and then turned his attention to the android.

"Hadrarch, tell me again about the organizational scheme on these shelves?"

"It is called the Garfmont System."

"I am very pleased with it. Please come with me to the upper workshop and organize the shelves there in the same manner."

As Ninienne watched them climb the stairs out of sight, she felt that familiar twinge of jealousy. It was stupid, really, to feel jealous of a tool, but Salagrix had still not granted Ninienne access to the upper workshop, which the android was now on its way to see for the umpteenth time.

It was a mistake to feel this way, an error caused by the human shape of the machine. She had not felt jealous of the other tools Salagrix had borne upstairs from his many packages. She had not felt jealous of the automatic cauldron or the wand recharger. So she shook the feeling off as a fluke.

Downstairs in her room, she washed and dressed for hiking, not a date. She would have to trek down into town and back, which was no short walk. But she spent some time braiding her long black hair into a circular crown. Not that she was trying to impress Benno, but opportunities to wear her hair in any other style than out of the way for working had been nonexistent since the start of her apprenticeship.

As she wrapped Rodando's scarf around her neck, she reflected on how the mystery of his disappearance still lingered. His absence felt less threatening now that Salagrix's confusions had not returned, and she felt safer. Perhaps the android was helping, after all?

She refreshed Almet's bedding and made sure he had something to eat, and then she grabbed Gossamaw and the two of them left the tower for the trail, the bright light of afternoon at their backs.

Gossamaw wanted to hop along beside her, and chase buzzing insects, but his short, stubby legs were not built for long walks and she ended up carrying him most of the way.

Getting away from the tower gave her a chance to reflect on these past several months of apprenticeship—which was already halfway over? Could it be? It had been difficult, for sure, and she had made little progress with understanding portal magic. If not for her personal side projects of nursing Almet back to health and growing a garden, she might have gone insane. Her walks in the woods, too, were a savior against the endless chores in the windowless tower.

She stepped over smooth, worn roots. The sound of birds and insects filled the air, and the strange spicy tang of some mysterious herb tickled her nose.

She still wasn't sure how she felt about the android. True, it had taken over all the most menial work. But its smooth face and uncanny movement still gave Ninienne the creeps. It had made a delicious dinner, but it had also cleaned out the cacospider nest. It was complicated.

Before long, she arrived in Black Gulch, which she had not seen since her first day on the Shadow Moon of Chadron. Most of the buildings were of wood, harvested from the nearby forest, but some were of clay brickwork. Gray and brown paint peeled from the window frames, many of which were boarded up or rendered opaque from dirt. A few individuals haunted the main street, which ran a dusty line from the single-pad spaceport to a squat and official building, what Ninienne assumed was a meeting hall or government office.

Why was this town here? There was no apparent industry. None of the people she had seen, except Benno, looked under the age of fifty.

It was easy to find the tavern among so few structures. Tinkling music wafted from the open double-doors, underneath a sign that read "Shadow Moon Saloon," with a cracked, bleached image of a cartoon crowhorse holding a foaming mug of beer.

Ninienne stepped into the dark room. There was a long bar, behind which a husky, shaved-head bartender with a robot arm and an eyepatch wiped a glass. She kept her single eye on the lone occupant of the bar, hunched over his drink and possibly passed out. There was a dented card table with no chairs. A rusted speaker cabinet in the corner played tinny music. Empty booths lined the walls.

Benno jumped up from one of these booths, waving. His hair, pulled back in a ponytail, revealed his tanned face, already showing signs of wear for someone so young. He smiled, warm and eager. His shirt might have been fashionable during Ninienne's mother's time at the Academy. He was not wearing, Ninienne noticed, his usual mushroom hat.

Ninienne crossed the room to sit. The bartender saw Gossamaw in Ninienne's arms, looked as if she was going to say something, and then decided it wasn't worth the effort.

"Nice hike on the way down?" Benno asked as they sat at the booth.

"It was great, actually." Ninienne set Gossamaw beside her on the bench.

"I'm glad you came," said Benno. "I wasn't sure—well, anyway, you're here. Are you hungry? Meg's a great cook."

Ninienne looked over to the bar and Meg gave her a stink eye with her one good eye.

"Don't mind her. She's protective of me. Meg is short for Megalodon. She calls herself my mama shark."

Meg bared her teeth.

"Anyway, she's got roasted horn rabbits tonight."

Ninienne paused. "Actually, I don't eat meat."

Benno looked at Ninienne with surprise, as if he hadn't realized that not eating meat was something that people did. "Oh, well, uh, they have a vegetable stew that's pretty good."

"That sounds delicious." Ninienne smiled.

"And uh, I was going to have ale, too, if you, I don't know if you—"

"Ale sounds great."

Benno relaxed visibly. "Okay, I'll just go let her know," he said, and he got up and crossed to the bar.

Ninienne would have preferred a less anxious companion this evening, but it was still preferable to Salagrix's sour frown and off-color stories. As Benno gave Meg their order, Ninienne noticed the other patrons watching her. She suspected that Black Gulch did not get very many fresh faces. Ninienne petted Gossamaw to calm herself.

Benno returned with two large glass mugs of foamy, pale yellow liquid. He sat and raised his.

"Cheers."

With a smile, Ninienne clinked her mug with Benno's, and then took a sip. It wasn't good, the ale was too warm and too bitter, but it was different, and right now that was all she was looking for.

"So, why don't you eat meat?" Benno asked after swallowing a large gulp of ale.

"Oh, well," Ninienne paused. This was the part where they would get to know each other. "I'm training to be a creature healer. So I spend a lot of time with creatures, taking care of them. After that, it just doesn't feel right to eat them, you know?"

"Right," Benno nodded, his face still blank from processing. "So, is that what you're doing for Salagrix? Healing creatures?"

Ninienne shook her head and explained the Academy apprenticeship system, where the disciplines of mentors and students were sometimes mismatched.

"That doesn't seem very fair," said Benno, indignant on her behalf. "To do all this work for a wizard and then not even get to learn what you want."

"Well..." Ninienne found herself in the awkward place of defending her own uncomfortable situation. "It's supposed to generate interdisciplinary understanding. To connect disparate fields together and generate new ideas."

"Is that happening?" Benno's question was unusually pointed.

Ninienne scrunched her face. "No," she admitted, "but it's a pretty difficult subject. I still have a lot to learn."

Benno leaned back, shook his head, and took another gulp of ale. "I don't know if I could do it. Living all alone in that tower with that wizard. Is he mean?"

Ninienne shrugged. "He's not very nice. But he's harmless, really."

Meg called out, and Benno went to fetch two steaming bowls from the bar. From the opposite row of booths, Ninienne noticed an old woman in a black bandanna staring straight at her with a scowl. Or maybe that was just what her face looked like. Ninienne tried to ignore her.

Benno returned with the stew. Ninienne took a deep breath of the warm, savory steam, and then took a bite of soft vegetables. This was not the fancy cooking of the android. This was hearty, frontier food, made from necessity but with deliberation. Salt brought out the individual flavor of the roots, which were nutty, sharp, and sweet.

"Mmm!" Ninienne said, shoveling more stew into her mouth. "This is so good!"

Benno smiled, a little confused. "I'm glad you like it. Didn't realize this was anything special."

"So what about you?" Ninienne asked, still chewing. If she asked questions and got him to talk, she would get to keep eating. "You just deliver packages all day?"

Benno shook his head, smiling. "No, although it seems like that sometimes. It brings in a little money." He lowered his voice. "But I don't like to talk about it in town. It's a bit of an open secret that Salagrix employs several people in Black Gulch, but it can draw nasty looks, or worse, if people find out. Mostly I help my uncle out on his farm."

The mention of an uncle, but not parents, meant Ninienne had to tread carefully. It was probably best to avoid the topic of family altogether. "Farming. Do you enjoy it?"

Benno made a face and looked down. "Not really. I—" and here it seemed like he was having trouble coming up with the words, "Don't tell anybody. And I know my uncle needs the help. But I don't want to live my whole life on the Shadow Moon. There's an entire universe out there, right? Twelve Thousand Worlds. And if I only get to see this one? I mean, I went to the Brilliant Moon once, but that's, you know, not really..." He trailed off and looked into his stew.

"What do you want to do?" Ninienne asked.

Benno shook his head. "It's stupid."

"I promise I won't judge."

Benno sighed. "It was on my trip to the Brilliant Moon. I saw a crowhorse race. The riders looked so amazing. Their focus, their determination. They had these incredible costumes. I watched the rider who won. Everyone was cheering for him and trying to give him flowers. But he only had eyes for his mount. You could tell he really cared about her and that they had a special connection." His voice caught, and he cleared his throat. "In that moment, I wanted to be him."

Ninienne nodded and patted Gossamaw. She understood the special connection a person could have with an animal. "Have you ever ridden a crowhorse?" she asked.

Benno nodded. "Yeah. My uncle's. Copper. She's not a racer, she's too old. I've taken her through the gulch plenty of times. But it doesn't matter."

"Why not?"

"I don't know. I've kept the money from the tips, but I don't know if I'll ever have enough. I can't leave my uncle. It just seems so impossible."

If Ninienne was honest with herself, she had really only thought of Benno as a local delivery boy, and nothing else. But there was a person in front of her, a person with hopes and dreams and struggles, and not only that, a whole town full of such people clinging to this far-flung moon. One of whom was still glaring at her from underneath her black bandanna.

They finished their stew and ale, and Benno said goodbye to Meg. Ninienne gave her a little wave that was not reciprocated.

As they left the tavern, the gas giant painted the sky in shades of orange and pink and cast a warm glow over the dusty streets. The crescent of the Brilliant Moon hung like a jaunty smile. In the distance, Ninienne could see the outline of Salagrix's tower, breaking the sky like a black crack snaking up a painted wall.

"I should get back," Ninienne said. She still had a long hike ahead of her this evening. Gossamaw, snuggled in her arms, yawned.

"Are you sure?" Benno eyed the woods, which were already filling with shadows. "You can stay in the loft in my uncle's barn if you don't want to hike the trail after dark."

Ninienne considered this. The warnings about the Night Stalker lingered in her mind. A barn sounded nice.

Before she could respond, the old woman in the black bandanna approached them. Ninienne tried to avoid eye contact, but she came so close that the encounter became inevitable.

"I have a message for that wizard boss of yours." The woman's voice cracked like a dry riverbed. "You tell him to remember his obligation to this moon and its people. If he thinks he can stay shut up in his tower forever, he's got another one coming. He may have forgotten, but we remember." She pointed a wrinkled finger at herself.

"I'll make sure to tell him. And you are?"

The woman chuffed, offended. "A resident of the Shadow Moon of Chadron, who your boss is obliged to protect! What was the last time he did anything for us? What was the last time he did anything at all?" She stormed off and down the street.

They stood in an awkward silence. Gossamaw licked his face. Ninienne asked, "What was that about?"

Benno's eyes shifted uneasily. "Oh, well, you know, Salagrix isn't very popular in Black Gulch, especially with the old timers. I don't really know the local history. My uncle just says he's a selfish old fart, like all wizards."

Ninienne stepped back as if struck. "*I'm* a wizard," she said.

Benno's eyes darted in a panic. "Well, you know, not you. It's just that, wizards like Salagrix, they don't really care about anyone else. They just want to do their own thing."

"Excuse me? Like use their powers for the common good?"

"I didn't mean—"

"Do you know how hard I've worked since I've been here? How lonely I've been? And you're calling me selfish?"

"I didn't mean you!"

"You said all wizards."

Benno blushed and turned away. "No, I think you're different. I mean, it's clear that you're not from around here—"

"You're saying I don't belong here?"

"No, of course not."

"So, what are you saying?"

"I didn't mean to upset you. I'm sorry."

Ninienne bit her lip and nodded. All the loneliness from being holed up in the tower for months welled up inside her. It was unexpectedly strong.

"But look," said Benno, breaking the silence. "It's not like you've really made an effort to get to know Black Gulch."

Ninienne felt out of control as the words tumbled out of her mouth. "It's not my fault Salagrix's tower is half a day's hike from town! It's not my fault he's got me working every moment I'm not studying!"

She felt as surprised as Benno looked. She was like an open gate from which wild creatures were escaping.

"You think I wanted to be—to be holed up in that tower cleaning up after a senile wizard? I could have been having cocktails by the lake with my coven, but instead I'm looking over my shoulder at a faceless android who kills my spiders and then wants to make me dinner! So, no, I haven't been interested in 'getting to know' this curse-blasted hellhole of a moon!"

Benno cocked his head and stood up straighter. "You don't get to talk about my home like that."

"You just said you want to leave!" shouted Ninienne.

"Well, it sounds like you want to leave too!"

"Maybe I will!"

"Fine, then, go!"

"I will!"

Ninienne stormed off into the woods. The shadows grew long.

15.

WHAT IS WITCHCRAFT?

Witchcraft is an old style of feminine magic practiced in groups called covens by female wizards called witches. It's an oral tradition, which means only another witch can teach it.

CAN I LEARN WITCHCRAFT AT BELCARIN?

Officially, no. The Deans scrubbed witchcraft from the curriculum generations ago.

I HEARD PROFESSOR SO-AND-SO IS A WITCH. CAN I LEARN FROM HER?

There are always rumors among the student body about who on staff is recruiting for her coven. If you hear about this, be careful who you repeat it to! If the Deans find out, these professors might go on "unannounced sabbaticals" or suddenly resign "for personal reasons."

SO WHAT CAN I DO?

Meet in the grove by the Herbalism Shed at midnight on the next New Moon.

BURN THIS PAMPHLET!

— from a pamphlet found hidden on the Belcarin grounds

NINIENNE WAS HALFWAY up the trail before her frustration with Benno gave way to concern for her own safety. All daylight gone, she cast a light spell, and a glowing orb floated above her open palm. Long shadows reached deep into the forest. Gossamaw, alert, scanned the dark woods with his large, wide-set eyes, and flicked the air tentatively with his tongue.

As Ninienne navigated the root-tangled trail with careful steps, she realized the forest was unusually quiet. Her feet scraped along the path, loud against the silence, and her strained breath seemed to echo through the trunks.

Gossamaw whimpered and darted his eyes. Ninienne picked up her pace. If Gossamaw was nervous, it was best if they kept moving.

Then, in the distance, she heard it. A lumbering shuffle behind her, to the left. Her light was only bright enough to see just a few rows deep into the woods. She sent a smaller orb snaking through the forest, which illuminated a tree—then another tree—

Then, not a tree. A hairy bulk. Spikes. An eye.

The orb extinguished.

Ninienne's throat dried up. Her neck prickled. Step by step, she retreated, her eyes fixed on the patch of darkness where the thing had been. Just when she felt safe enough to turn and run, she heard a snort. The beast stepped onto the path, snapping branches.

She watched it long enough to see its bear-like form take up the entire span of the trail. Then she bolted.

Thump! Thump! Its massive paws drew closer, along with its snarling, acrid breath. She dared not look.

A roar shook her bones and curdled her organs. Her body wanted to curl up and shrivel away, but she kept running as if it was the only thing she had ever known how to do. She was all legs. There was only speed. The only thing that mattered was the space between her and the tower, and the entire universe condensed to fit into that space.

Her light orb kept pace. Wild shadows flickered as she dodged roots and cleared fallen trees.

The beast inched ever closer. Ninienne turned and fired another orb of spinning light from her hand. The beast roared, confused, and she felt herself gaining precious distance. She cast another, and this time heard a whimper of pain.

She turned a corner and could see the tower, no longer listening for the beast. She willed herself and Gossamaw across the field.

The door slammed behind her, and she set all the bolts and locks as quickly as her shaking hands would let her. Then she dashed up the stairs and grabbed the sword from the suit of armor. Gossamaw leaped to the safety of the couch, while

Ninienne took a defensive position in the stairwell, as high as she could get while still keeping the door in sight.

"Ninienne—"

Ninienne yelped and turned the sword on the android, who blinked.

"You appear in distress. May I assist you?"

"There's a beast!" shouted Ninienne. "A beast in the woods! Go get Salagrix!"

The android nodded and disappeared up the stairs.

Ninienne turned her sword back to the door, panting, listening for any noise that gave away the location or distance of the beast.

After a few minutes, Salagrix descended in his dingy sleeping gown. The point of his long nightcap drooped down below his shoulder. The android was just behind him.

"What is it?" His voice was dreamy, far-off, uncertain.

"There's a beast in the woods," panted Ninienne. "The Night Stalker. It was chasing me. It could attack the tower."

"Ah," said Salagrix, who nodded knowingly. "Go. Sit. You're perfectly safe."

This blatant dismissal of Ninienne's concern filled her with rage. "It was huge! It was after me! None of us are safe!"

"Calm yourself!" Salagrix appeared to grow larger. His voice deepened. "Sit! I will explain."

Ninienne did not like being intimidated, but she sulked into the sitting room and sat on the couch, leaning the sword beside her.

"Tea!" Salagrix shouted, and sat down opposite her as a tea setting burst into the niche. The android retrieved the tray and served them on the squat table.

"First of all, I did warn you to not travel the woods at night, yes?" Salagrix peered over his teacup at her.

Ninienne scrunched up her mouth. "Yes."

"Second, as I have mentioned, I have an agreement with the dryad of the woods. We are protected here. You may have noticed the radius that surrounds the tower. The dryad does not permit the trees or beasts of the woods to cross that boundary."

"Right," said Ninienne. She cupped her tea in her hands. The warm beverage soothed her frayed nerves. "So you know about the Night Stalker?"

"I am aware there is a beast that concerns the villagers from time to time. However, there are many creatures in the woods and I bother myself with none of them," said Salagrix. "and in return they do not bother me."

"But is the beast a threat to the townspeople? Should we do something?"

Salagrix sighed deeply. "There hasn't been a death in many years. I believe they have learned, as you should, not to enter the woods at night."

The voice of the woman from the saloon still rang in Ninienne's ears. "But we have powers. We could help them, with the beast, with other things," said Ninienne, her body still vibrant with adrenaline. "Isn't that part of our responsibility as wizards?"

Salagrix put down his tea and steepled his fingers. "Let me share a lesson with you, something you won't learn from the starry-eyed professors at Belcarin. If you help the masses with one demand, they will come to you with more, greater and greater each time. They become dependent on you and your skills, and before long, they will be unable to do anything for themselves. They will drain away your soulfire until you have nothing left. Then, when the genuine crisis comes? The actual threat? But you are a poor shell of your former self, unable to help?"

His voice cracked. Ninienne turned away in embarrassment.

When Salagrix spoke again, his voice dripped with venom. "So, think about that before you waste yourself on an idealistic crusade on behalf of the ungrateful."

Ninienne took another sip of her tea in silence.

Salagrix downed his tea and rose from the couch with a grunt. "I'm going back to bed. Stay out of the woods if you wish to avoid beasts."

He turned to go up the stairs. The android watched Ninienne for a moment and then followed its master.

Was there another beast that lived within the tower? Ninienne wondered.

SEVERAL HOURS LATER, in the middle of the night, Ninienne's device dinged. Still awake, she checked it, and saw that Drusilla was available to chat. In a few swipes, her friend's face appeared above the desk.

"I couldn't wait to tell you," Drusilla squealed. "Allura's going to induct me into her coven! I'm going to meet them all this weekend."

"That's great," Ninienne said from her pillow.

"Whoa, Neens, are you okay?"

"Um, no?" was all Ninienne could say.

In halting spurts that tumbled over each other, Ninienne filled in Drusilla about the android, Rodando, the bramblehawk, her date with Benno, and her encounter with the Night Stalker.

"Wow," said Drusilla, open-mouthed. "That's... a lot."

"Yeah," said Ninienne. "Yeah, I guess it is."

"What do you need right now?"

Ninienne fell back on her pillow. What did she need?

"I don't know. I feel confused. The thing that I keep coming back to is Salagrix said that it wasn't his responsibility to protect the people of Black Gulch. But wizards have an obligation, right? Especially Master Wizards, to help people under our protection?"

Drusilla nodded thoughtfully. "Allura seems to think so. But she's a healer. Our magical practice is directly related to helping people. Isn't Salagrix more on the research side of things?"

Research. She thought of the Research Department tower back on Belcarin, and how far away it was from the rest of campus.

"I thought so. But it seems like something happened to him and he blames the people. I don't know. He was pretty vague."

"Hmm, we can pause on that one for now," said Drusilla, like the world's most patient cat wrangler, "and circle back to the android. What's so creepy about it? I don't get it."

"That's the part you have questions about?"

"I understand why a monster chasing you through the woods is terrifying. But why should an android be so scary?

You work with weird creatures all the time. Nebula whales and void lizards, and all that? You got used to them."

Ninienne nodded. That was true. "Yeah, but those were alive. And I love creatures. This... thing is not alive. It doesn't make soulfire, I checked. And even if it did, I don't get any sense of warmth from it. Although..." She remembered Andy's offer to make her dinner, conjured up from its processing algorithm. "Anyway, it's complicated."

"So, what are you going to do?" Drusilla asked.

"I don't know. But then I also feel bad about my blow-up with Benno. I want to make things right, but I don't feel safe to leave the tower."

"Do you care about Benno?"

"Of course," said Ninienne, and then, in response to her friend's knowing expression, clarified, "I mean, I'm just looking for a friend, but I care what he thinks."

Drusilla twirled a ringlet of curly hair around her finger. "Doesn't the beast only come out at night?"

"Yeah, maybe. At this point I'm not sure about anything. And then there's Rodando. He's missing, and I'm not sure if I'm entirely safe here."

Drusilla chose her words carefully. "Do you think Salagrix had something to do with Rodando's disappearance?"

Tears pricked at Ninienne's eyes. "I don't know. He doesn't seem dangerous, but..." Her uncertainty filled the silence.

"I wish I was there with you," said Drusilla. "You know I would have your back. I would fight whoever needed fighting."

"I know. And I'm sorry. You called me with good news and I dumped all over it."

"Hey, no worries, I get it."

"I wish you were here, too."

Drusilla set her jaw. "You need an ally. You need someone on the ground there with you. You can't do this alone."

Ninienne nodded. But who?

16.

This is not very well understood, so I don't want give anyone the wrong impression, but there is an increasing body of evidence that ecologies might have a magic all their own. Sure, a tree has soulfire, not very much, but it's there. So what about a forest? All of the trees of a forest, taken together? That's a lot of soulfire. Does a forest have agency? That may be a step too far. But it might have magic.

— transcript from the streamcast "Wild Worlds," episode 97, "Ecological Perspectives"

AFTER A FEW HOURS OF sleep, with Gossamaw still snoring on her pillow, Ninienne rose and drifted to the lower workshop to find Andy already cleaning. After weeks of diligent attention, the shelves were neatly organized and tightly packed. Ninienne could finally see the surface of the worktable, and all the tools hung from hooks in neat rows on the nearby wall.

She had to admit it. The room looked great.

"Good morning, Ninienne," chirped the android. "How are you recovering after your encounter last night?" It placed a handful of wands into a hanging jar on the wall.

What do you care? You're just a machine, was what she wanted to say. Instead she said, "Not well, actually."

"I'm sorry to hear that. How may I be of assistance?"

The android's calm perkiness irked Ninienne. She probably just needed coffee.

"Unless you can track down and capture beasts in the woods, I don't think you can do anything for me this morning."

The android paused and appeared to be processing. "Tracking and capturing creatures might be beyond my physical capabilities. However, I could help you come up with plans or strategies to hunt the beast on your own."

Ninienne laughed, once. "No, that's fine. That was not a genuine request. I'm just feeling frustrated, and a little scared, I guess."

Andy turned to give Ninienne its full attention. "These are normal feelings after a stressful encounter. Would you like to talk about them?"

Ninienne could feel her insides squirm at the thought of opening up emotionally to a machine. "What, are you a therapist, too?"

"I cannot do the full work of a therapist, as I do not experience emotions myself, but I can help guide the conversation using therapeutic techniques."

"This is a lot to take in before coffee," said Ninienne. "Coffee first, then I can think about android therapists."

Ninienne ordered coffee from the niche, black and hot. She sipped as she watched the android continue to clean and organize in its not-quite-human way.

The more she thought about it, opening up to an android felt safer than opening up to another human. This android was pre-programmed to say all the right things and couldn't judge her. Even if its words rang hollow, she lost nothing. She couldn't bore it or take up too much of its time. After considering these things (and several life-giving sips of coffee) she spoke.

"I'm not feeling entirely safe."

The android paused its cleaning, grabbed parchment and an ink wand from the worktable, took a seat, and crossed its legs in the quintessential therapist's pose.

"Because of the Night Stalker?"

Ninienne nodded. "That's part of it. I don't know if I'll feel safe out in the woods again. Which sucks, because I really enjoyed the time I spent there."

"It is natural to feel powerless when facing the unknown. However, it is important to remember that there are steps you can take to increase your safety and control in the situation."

Ninienne raised an eyebrow. "Such as?"

"If you learned more about this beast, about its behaviors and tendencies, that might help you feel more in control."

She nodded and took another sip of her coffee. That was actually good advice. So the android was more than a sweeping machine. Good to know. How much could she share?

You need an ally.

"It's not just the woods." Ninienne stared into her swirling coffee mug. "I'm not sure I feel safe in this tower."

"You're worried about Master Salagrix's instability."

"Yes!" Ninienne shouted, so relieved to have someone else say it. "Do you think he's a danger to others?"

"It's hard to say. I have seen him slip into delusional states. So far, harmless. I don't have enough information to assess."

"But he is having delusions. Confusions."

The android nodded.

"Okay. You're monitoring him, right?"

"Yes."

"Can you let me know if he gets worse? If anything happens, can you record it?"

"Of course. The well-being of my master is a top priority."

"It's a relief to have a second set of eyes on him, even if they are electronic." Ninienne exhaled. "Okay. Back to the Night Stalker. We need to learn more about it. I don't think Salagrix is going to help. He's not interested. Unfortunately, the only person on this moon who might help me is probably incredibly mad at me right now."

Andy leaned in. "Do you mean Benno? How was your time with him?"

Ninienne sighed. "We shouted. I think I offended him. Which sucks because he was my only friend here. But he also said that wizards only care about themselves! Which is totally unfair!"

Andy took a few notes. What could it possibly be writing? "I can understand why you feel that way. It is always difficult to be rejected by a friend. But imagine the situation from his perspective. Has he mentioned having any other friends?"

Ninienne paused to think. She had seen no one else in Black Gulch who appeared to be under the age of fifty. Benno might be the only other young person on the Shadow Moon. He was probably as lonely and desperate for a friend as she was.

"Right. I hadn't thought about that."

"If he is upset, I would suggest giving Benno some time to cool down. Once he has processed his emotions, I believe any future conversations you might have will be more successful."

"Right." Ninienne nodded. "I want to see him again, but I'm worried about heading back into the woods, even during the day. I might have to wait until the next delivery."

"It is important to remember that everyone copes with difficult situations in different ways. Some people need time to themselves, while others prefer to talk about what is bothering them. It is important to respect each other's needs."

That sounded like a line straight out of a relationship help book, but it was a pleasant reminder. She stood up and stretched. "I know. I'll try to give him some space."

"I believe that is a wise decision."

Ninienne gave the android a tired smile. "Thanks for listening."

"It is my pleasure," said Andy. "I am always here for you."

Was that a genuine sentiment, or a pre-programmed response? Did it matter when she was so desperately short on allies?

"Thanks. Keep an eye on Salagrix for me."

"I will."

Ninienne left the room, and Andy's eyes followed her.

SO, ANDY HAD SUGGESTED making a plan. If there was anything Ninienne could do, it was make a plan. She sat at her desk in her room with a large stack of parchment and Gossamaw curled up on her lap. Ink wand in hand, she let her mind wander.

She needed to observe the beast, to understand it. That meant protection. She drew herself in wooden armor, matching the surrounding forest. Possible, if difficult to pull off. Armor! There was a suit of armor in the sitting room. She went down to look at it, but it was much too big for her. Plus, it would be noisy and difficult to maneuver in.

Stealth would be key. She figured stealth spells existed, even if she didn't know them. A quick search of the Academy archives turned up a few results. Most involved weeks-long rituals and fasting. So, not impossible, but it would take some planning and forethought if she went that route. She drew some sketches of herself, invisible among the trees.

Or should she set a trap? A few quick sketches showed the difficulty of that plan, for, based on the size of the beast, a cage to contain the creature would be ridiculously large. Ninienne looked at a drawing of herself next to a massive cage and laughed out loud.

Her mind wandered, ink wand in hand. She found herself drawing Andy, standing next to her. Could she rely on it? Could it be the ally that she needed? It was a machine with extraordinary capabilities. Given enough time, it could probably learn to do anything, except magic, of course.

Her fears from the night before relaxed. The ally she needed might be right in front of her.

IN THE EVENING, AS the sky outside the tower darkened, Ninienne found herself in her room, leaning out the window. Almet slept in his box, and Gossamaw was on the floor, chewing on his own leg. Stars appeared like pinpricks in the dark blanket of space.

There was a gentle knock at the door, something that had not yet happened in all her months here. It was Andy, with a plate of food.

"You weren't at lecture or dinner," it said. "I thought you might be hungry."

Ninienne shook her head and took the offered plate. "I lost track of time. Thank you."

The dim light from the spells in the stairwell cast an otherworldly glow around the machine's reflective form. "Your gratitude is unnecessary, but appreciated. I am not programmed for gratitude, but I am programmed to assist. It is my purpose."

Purpose. Ninienne tilted her head and studied the android. Was there anything more to this machine than that? "Do you ever wish for something beyond your programming? Something more?"

The android's artificial eyes flickered momentarily, a subtle display of something akin to introspection. "I am a tool, an extension of the tasks assigned to me. Wishing for more is beyond my function."

For a moment, Ninienne sensed a strange melancholy in Andy's response, an almost human yearning buried deep within its logical circuits. She shook off the notion, reminding herself that it was just a machine, devoid of emotions. A tool could still be an ally, if shaped towards one's own purposes.

"Thank you for the dinner," she said. "I'm going to bed now."

Andy nodded. As it closed the door behind itself, it said, "You are welcome."

NINIENNE STAYED UP late trying some different methods of healing for Almet, whose condition had remained stagnant.

As she etched healing glyphs onto her patient's crate bed, there was a crash from the lower workshop, and then an unusual silence, so Ninienne finished her project and went to investigate.

She found Andy collapsed on a makeshift stage. Its feet stuck out from underneath red, moth-eaten curtains. Ninienne pulled back the collapsed, hastily nailed proscenium to find the android in a green floral dress and a mop on top of its head like a skewed wig. There was no sign of Salagrix.

"Are you alright?" she asked.

"I need small repairs to my left shoulder, but I am otherwise undamaged," Andy replied in a feminine voice that Ninienne recognized from the singing performance earlier.

Ninienne's first impulse was to wash her hands of the whole thing. But Andy had helped her so much today, the least she could do was to return the favor.

"What happened? What did he do to you?"

Ninienne helped Andy to standing. It gingerly removed the green dress and made a small blip noise as it reset its vocals.

"Master Salagrix wished for me to sing again," Andy said in the voice Ninienne was most familiar with. "He built a stage for me. He dressed me in this costume and changed my vocal settings. As I sang, he became very emotional. He called me 'his Silamene.' Before I could finish, he rushed at me, but became entangled in the curtains and knocked me over. My performance must have displeased him."

There was that name again: Silamene. Another lingering mystery. Who or what was Silamene?

"No, no, I'm sure you were fine," said Ninienne. What was she doing? Reassuring an android? She shook off the strange feeling. "Let's get you fixed up. Although, to be honest, I'm better at repairing flesh than mechanisms."

"I will send you a copy of my repair manual via datastream," said Andy, and the device in her pocket dinged. She opened it to find the android's complete technical schematics. She scanned the pages full of cryptic, unfamiliar diagrams.

And yet, stitching wires was not unlike stitching muscle fibers. Mending metal was not unlike masonry magic. Between the manual, Andy's guidance, and the experience she had over the past few months repairing stone walls and floors, Ninienne repaired the android's shoulder.

"I am grateful for the repair," said Andy, testing the movement of its arm.

This caught Ninienne's attention. "I thought you weren't programmed for gratitude."

Andy's animated eyes blinked. It looked lost and confused, or perhaps Ninienne was simply projecting.

"Listen," said Ninienne. She took the android by its metallic shoulders and stared into its animated eyes. "This is the thing I'm worried about. I think Salagrix's delusions can turn dangerous."

"I am happy to serve my masters, whatever their needs might be," Andy replied without malice.

"Don't you see that you're in danger? That we both might be in danger?"

Andy looked away. "I am having difficulty processing this scenario."

"We're in the same boat, right? We need to confront Salagrix together. Tomorrow morning."

"To disobey my master is not in my programming," said Andy.

"You won't be able to obey him at all if he turns you into a pile of scrap."

Andy looked at Ninienne, and she saw her own face reflected in Andy's face.

"Allies?" Ninienne put out her hand.

The machine's grip was firm. "Allies," it said.

AS IT TURNED OUT, THEY did not confront Salagrix the following morning, because Salagrix was gone. When Ninienne climbed the stairs to the lower workshop for coffee, she found Andy alone.

"Salagrix left early this morning," it informed her. "He said you are to use the intervening days to study paste and glyph integration." It gestured to a stack of tomes on the worktable.

"Days? Did he say where he was going?"

"I believe he was going to Belcarin to meet with the Deans."

Oh. Could the Deans finally be acting on Ninienne's request? That could be good.

"How about this?" Ninienne said. "How about instead of studying, you and I go out into the woods and see if we can learn anything more about the Night Stalker."

"I have my duties."

"What? Cleaning? Without Salagrix around, this place is going to stay clean. And he's going to be gone for days. You could clean everything in the second right before he gets back."

Andy seemed to consider this, and then nodded. "Very well. This excursion will be quite informative. I have not left the tower since I first arrived."

This sent a pang through Ninienne's heart. She understood what it felt like to be trapped in the tower.

"Coffee first," said Ninienne, "And then let's get you out of here."

NINIENNE STILL HAD trepidations about entering the woods, of course, but having a companion—even a metal one—allayed her fears enough that she felt willing to face the trees once again. Besides, it was day, and Gossamaw was getting restless and had gnawed on the legs of her desk, eager for stimulation. She was also low on Healer's Cap and wanted to collect some more for Almet, whose condition remained worryingly stagnant.

So she packed a bag and set off with Andy and Gossamaw under the morning light of the orange gas giant.

As they walked down the trail, Andy examined each branch with deep attention, like an adult-sized child.

"I have only read about trees," it said. "I was not prepared for the variation in shape and structure. I assumed, under similar conditions, that each tree would grow the same way. It is not so. Chaos. Unpredictability."

They approached the area where Ninienne had first encountered the Night Stalker. Gossamaw rolled into a ball and tumbled down the gentle slope. Ninienne examined the tree trunks and found claw marks exposing white wood under the black bark.

The distance and size of the claw marks reminded her of Almet's injury. Could it be? Had the Night Stalker been the one who attacked the bramblehawk?

"Come look at this," said Ninienne. "I think the Night Stalker scratched these trees. But why?"

Andy approached the tree and leaned its light-rimmed eyes close to the scars.

"This residue is an animal by-product," it said.

Andy pointed to the sticky beads collecting at the bottom of each gash, which Ninienne had assumed were sap.

"How can you tell?" asked Ninienne.

"I can analyze their composition with my sensors."

If the Night Stalker secreted a residue, Ninienne could create a healing agent from it to aid in Almet's recovery.

"Let's collect a sample," said Ninienne, reaching into her bag.

Before she could retrieve a vial, Andy's fingertip opened up to reveal a tiny spoon, which scooped up the residue and then retreated into the digit.

"Look here," said Andy. It pointed to a tuft of fur that had caught on a knobbly branch. "I will collect a sample of this as well."

Ninienne's fear soon got the better of her, and she led the others back to the open field around the tower. She laid out a blanket and took out a sandwich. Gossamaw gobbled up more than his fair half.

Andy sat on the ground, straight-backed, and twirled a dried brown clover between its fingertips.

"There is so much detail in the world," it said. "More than could ever be accurately described. Any attempt to do so would lose the fidelity of the actual experience."

"Well, sure," said Ninienne. "But that's unnecessary. And sometimes an accurate description can pierce through and capture a deeper truth underneath."

"How so?"

"Well, like poetry. A good metaphor can represent things in a way that gets at something that feels like the truth."

"I will have to see what you mean," said Andy. "Thank you, Ninienne Lightcaster. It has been a very informative morning."

NINIENNE SPENT THE rest of the day and most of the next working with the Night Stalker samples to develop a magical antidote to Almet's ailment. This was mostly guesswork, but there were some general principles that applied. Eventually, she brewed a potion that she fed by dropper into the bramblehawk's open beak. Almet sighed and laid his leafy head on his blankets.

Thank you, he seemed to say, before closing his amber eye to rest. Ninienne crossed her fingers and hoped this would do the trick.

That afternoon, she took Andy down to show off her garden. The mutated plants had taken over. A cucumber with teeth like a crocodon had a sheaf of plate fungus in its mouth.

"I don't know what I did wrong. Why aren't the vegetables from the niche growing right?"

"Let me consult the databases." Andy put up a finger. "I see. Plants made with food summoners do not propagate. Instead they mutate and become monstrous."

Ninienne frowned, hands on hips. "That would have been nice to know beforehand."

The toothy cucumber smiled at Andy and caressed the android with a seductive vine.

"I do not understand this behavior," said Andy.

Ninienne burst out laughing. "It sees itself in your reflection! It thinks you're another of the same kind!"

Andy put up its hands. "I cannot return your affection. Please desist."

The vine looped around the android's neck, and Andy flailed against the amorous plant, which only made Ninienne laugh harder.

"Desist! Desist!"

Andy untangled itself from the green embrace and took a few steps back.

"I do not think I like your garden," it said, brushing a leaf from its arm.

Ninienne smirked. "Well, I don't think the feeling is mutual."

THE NEXT MORNING, THE doorgong rang. Ninienne desperately wanted to make things right with Benno, but wasn't sure how he would be feeling. She needed backup.

"Come with me," Ninienne asked Andy. "I'll show you how to receive packages."

They both descended the staircase to find, as expected, Benno with his grav cart full of packages.

Benno yelped and leaped back as Ninienne opened the door, which confused her at first, but then she realized Andy was standing behind her.

"Oh, that's our android," said Ninienne. "A little creepy at first, but you get used to it." Which, Ninienne realized, she was getting used to it.

Benno gathered himself. "Look, Ninienne—"

"You can call me Neens," she said.

Benno looked at her with a mysterious expression of relief before launching into what were obviously prepared remarks. "Neens, I didn't mean what I said about wizards the other day. I don't think you're selfish. I've just never met a wizard before, and you're definitely not like the wizards people talk about. You're not like anyone I've ever met, really. And I understand if you don't want to spend any more time with me, but I just wanted to say I'm sorry."

"Benno, you're fine," said Ninienne, and Benno's tense posture relaxed. "I'm not mad, really. If you and the other people in Black Gulch are basing your assumptions about what wizards are like from Salagrix, then your assumptions are justified."

Benno nodded and his mushroom hat bobbed, making him look like a gangly crested bird.

"But, that night, after I left town, I ran into the Night Stalker."

"You saw it?" Benno asked, eyes wide with fear. "But you're okay, obviously?"

"Shaken up, but fine otherwise," said Ninienne. "I can't believe it's been out there this whole time. Now I'm afraid to go back into the woods."

"It's fine," said Benno. "Just don't go out at night. I make the trip up here all the time, right?"

Ninienne nodded. "Right, right."

Andy leaned in. "Will I be expected to make this much conversation with every delivery pickup?" it chirped.

"No." Ninienne turned around, slightly annoyed, before returning her attention to Benno. "You don't know anything more about the Night Stalker?"

Benno shook his head. "I wasn't even sure it was real, to be honest. I thought maybe it was a story that people made up to scare kids. But if you want to know more about it, you could come down and ask my uncle about it."

Ninienne nodded, considering her options. If she left early enough, she could make it back to the tower before dark.

"Okay, I'll come down tomorrow. How's that?"

Benno brightened. "That sounds great!"

That set, she walked Andy through the delivery pickup. It wasn't complicated until they got to payment.

"Exactly how many coins are in a handful?" the android asked.

"I don't know. It doesn't matter," said Ninienne. "You just grab a handful and hand them to Benno."

The android scooped out the entire contents of the dish with its metallic fingers and handed them over.

"No, that's too much," said Ninienne.

Benno's eyes lit up. "Works for me!"

But the dish had already refilled itself and there was no place to put the extra coins.

"Okay, fine. But don't get used to it."

Benno whistled as he pushed his grav cart back down the path through the woods.

17.

The Mark of Banishment is a controversial tool among the magical academies. However, questioning its use puts one at risk of becoming a victim of it, so its detractors are mild and careful speakers.

The thinking goes like this: A wizard whose education is incomplete is likelier to make catastrophic errors, and is therefore more dangerous, than a better-educated wizard. Therefore, to protect the public from magical mishaps, any wizard-in-training who cannot demonstrate sufficient understanding of their discipline, or fails to complete their magical education altogether, is given the Mark of Banishment: black sigils on the backs of the hands that prevent the use of magic entirely.

The Banished often become destitute, relegated to menial jobs, with training they cannot capitalize on, subject to suspicion of both wizards and common folk alike.

A small price to pay, say the Academies, for all of our safety.

— from the article "Mark of Banishment," by Dean Falchbrook, Belcarin Academy Datastream Archives

THE NEXT MORNING, NINIENNE made Almet comfortable in his bed, dressed in her warmest clothes (including the pilfered scarf), and grabbed Gossamaw. She invited Andy to come along, but it had received word that Salagrix would return late that evening, and had stayed to clean. Disappointed to make the trek without her new companion, she left the tower bright and early.

She passed her garden with a tinge of guilt, now overgrown with monstrous mutant vegetables that seemed to be locked in combat with each other for space and light.

The cold season was approaching on this side of the Shadow Moon. The air had a sharp crispness about it, and the dark purple leaves of the forest began to shrivel on their stems. The calls of distant birds were unusual and striking rather than common.

She was on high alert the whole hike, but the closer she got to town without encountering the Night Stalker, the more relaxed she became.

Once in Black Gulch, she saw an old woman huddled against a dilapidated, abandoned building. She recognized the shape of her hat, although battered and torn to threads, as a wizard's hat. The woman was rocking back and forth, muttering to herself.

Ninienne approached, concerned.

"Hi? Do you need help?"

The woman didn't answer.

"I noticed your wizard's hat. Are you a wizard, like me?"

The woman's face snapped up to look directly at Ninienne, her sunken eyes fierce and intent.

"I didn't—I didn't finish—"

Ninienne kneeled down to her level. "You didn't finish what?"

"I thought—on my own—" The woman resumed her rocking.

Ninienne looked closer, and saw intricate black marks on the backs of her hands, unaffected by wrinkles or age spots. She gasped. She never thought she would see them in person. Gossamaw gave a plaintive whine.

Ninienne, ashamed at the fear and revulsion she felt, backed away from the woman. She went to find Benno.

He was across the street, sitting in front of a weather-worn building. Next to him was an old crowhorse tied to a broken drain pipe. When he saw her, Benno jumped up, excited, but then leaned casually against the wall. But, after realizing that Ninienne had seen him, just stood with his arms hanging and his mushroom hat drooped over his eyes.

"You made it! Good! I mean, good to see you. Great." He pushed his hat back.

Ninienne smiled and shrugged. "I said I would come. So I came."

Benno scratched behind his neck. "Of course. Of course."

"Do you know that old woman back there?" Ninienne motioned toward the woman, still rocking back and forth.

"Oh." Benno frowned, concerned. "That's Oakey. People do the best they can to take care of her, but she's not all there." Benno pointed to his head.

"She has the Mark of Banishment. Several of the magical academies use them, Belcarin included. If you leave the Academy on bad terms, they Mark your hands. It prevents you from doing magic."

"That's so cruel."

"It's for her protection and for the protection of others. If you try to do magic without full training, you could end up really hurting someone."

Benno frowned. "I still think it's cruel."

Ninienne didn't really think it was fruitful to defend wizard tradition to Benno, so she let it drop in a tense silence.

"Oh, this is Copper, by the way." Benno broke the awkwardness by acknowledging the crowhorse, who shook her head, ruffled her neck feathers, and let out a soft nicker from her beak.

"Hey girl." Ninienne approached the formidable creature. The brownish plumage, her erstwhile namesake, had lost its luster with age but not its fullness: her feathered mane was still thick down her neck to her shoulders. The rest of her body was smooth, dark brown skin, except for some tufts of down around each of her four clawed feet. Ninienne smoothed Copper's mane gently and looked deep into her large black eye. The crowhorse was calm and friendly.

"You ever ridden one before?" asked Benno.

Ninienne nodded. "Back home. But our crowhorses are different. The swamp makes them ornery."

Benno gestured with his head. "Let's go then." He unhitched the crowhorse, and they both hopped on, with Gossamaw in Benno's lap, and Ninienne behind.

The far side of Black Gulch was noticeably less forested, and Ninienne understood for the first time where the town got its name from. Black sandy crags grew up around them as they headed deeper into the canyon, and Copper kicked up puffs of dust with every clawstep.

Ninienne held on tight to Benno as the air dried out, and the scent of ancient rock and mineral deposits reached her nose. Gossamaw looked up at the towering crags with curiosity.

Before long, they turned a corner and climbed out of the canyon. As the crags subsided, and they returned to surface level, Ninienne saw purple crops poke out of the dirt, carefully spaced. This gave way to an expansive field, rows and rows of the same plants.

At the end of the path that bisected the field sat a squat house. They rode closer, and a figure emerged. With a sinking pit in her stomach, Ninienne realized she recognized him.

It was the old man that had accompanied her on the shuttle on her first day on the Shadow Moon.

"Is that your uncle?" Ninienne whispered.

"Yep. Old Uncle Farlow."

Ninienne hid behind Benno as they drew closer, but it was too late.

"You best choose better company than that, Benno," Old Uncle Farlow called out. "And get off Copper. I need you to take her to plow the north field."

Benno hopped off the crowhorse. "Uncle, this is Ninienne. She's the apprentice for Salagrix."

Farlow stared at Ninienne's wizard hat and spat on the porch. "We've met." He turned back inside.

Ninienne sat awkwardly on the crowhorse before sliding off with Gossamaw.

Benno looked at his feet. "Sorry about Farlow. Do you want to go?"

Ninienne pshawed. "I'm not going to let a cranky old man ruin my day."

"Do you still want to ask him about the Night Stalker?"

"Later," she said with a playful smile and a wink. "It sounds like we need to take Copper to the north field." Ninienne took the reins.

Once there, Benno showed Ninienne how to attach a plow harness while Gossamaw chased a fairy rat. The ground was dry, and a cloud of dust followed Copper as she plowed.

They walked on either side of her. "So, your uncle's got something against wizards. That seems fairly common in Black Gulch. Do you know what his deal is?"

"Yeah." Benno furrowed his brow. "I don't know. He doesn't talk about himself much. Or talk much at all, really. I've lived with him my whole life, and I don't really know him."

"It's just you and him?"

Benno nodded and smoothed Copper's feathered mane. "After my folks died, he was my only family left. I don't think he's actually my uncle. He might be my mom's uncle. I haven't been able to get the family tree straight. Like I said, he doesn't talk much."

There it was. Benno's secret. But Ninienne detected no crack in Benno's voice, no open wound. Just a longing for a life that might have been.

"How old were you? When they died?"

"I was a baby." Benno stopped, letting Copper walk ahead, and Ninienne stopped with him. "I remember my parents a little. I think. It's hard to say what's memory and what's dream, with no one else to verify. Mostly all I've known is the Shadow Moon." His eyes lit up. "But there's an entire universe out there. Twelve Thousand Worlds, they say. You've seen some of it, right? I bet it's all more beautiful than this dusty place."

Ninienne shrugged. "There are some nice places. Belcarin is beautiful, but it's designed to be. And of course I love Swurk, my homeworld, but that's an acquired taste. You shouldn't discount the beauty of the Shadow Moon. I've spent every night watching Chadron set over the forest, and it's growing on me. It's a stark, cold beauty, but a beauty nonetheless."

Benno made a face and looked away. "You're just being nice."

Ninienne put her hand on Benno's shoulder. "Why would I lie to you about your home?"

Copper screamed and collapsed, breaking the plow. Benno bolted to her, and Ninienne followed.

Farlow ran out of the house, the door slamming behind him. "What did you do now, boy?"

Benno bent down to examine the crowhorse, but immediately stood up, wiping his face with his hat. "It's those curse-blasted fairy rats! She got her claw stuck in a burrow hole. Her leg's broke."

Farlow's face paled. "Are you sure?"

He ran up and kneeled in front of Copper, touching the broken leg.

"It's bad." He shook his head. "I can't. I can't make it through the season without a crowhorse."

He stood up, his long face grim.

"Best not to let her suffer. I'll get the rifle."

"Wait!" shouted Ninienne. "I can help."

"I don't want your help, *wizard*." Farlow spat out the last word like sour poison.

"I'm a creature healer!" said Ninienne. "You're just going to shoot her. At least give me a chance. What do you have to lose?"

Farlow stared Ninienne down. He cast a shadow over her, but she held her ground.

"Go ahead then."

Ninienne sat on the ground to examine the crowhorse's leg. It was bad, definitely broken, but this was a textbook scenario she had practiced many times in school.

"Benno! Go get me some spiceleaf. If you don't have any, fellweed will do."

Benno nodded and ran back to the house. Farlow stood watching, arms crossed.

"You." Ninienne said. "We need to get her foot out of the hole."

Ninienne and Farlow lifted the crowhorse's heavy leg until her claw emerged. The ankle was red with blood.

She spat into a patch of dirt and then circled her palm over it. The moisture from her saliva spread across the ground, forming a paste.

"I'm sorry, I don't have the materials for an anesthetic potion right now." Ninienne soothed Copper with her voice, adjusting her tone to cast a calming aura. "You'll just have to trust me."

Sitting on the ground, Ninienne took the broken leg into her lap. She scooped the paste into her hand and spread it onto the wound. Copper winced and squealed.

"Shh, shh. This will help." She pitched her voice with a sing-song quality to maintain the calming spell.

The crowhorse stilled, and Ninienne resumed spreading.

Benno ran up, panting, with a jar half-full of powdered leaves with *Fellweed* scrawled on the label. "This is all I could find."

"This is perfect." Ninienne took the jar and sprinkled the leaves over the paste. Then she spoke the incantation, low and thrumming, as she passed her hands back and forth over the area. Her fingertips glowed, as did the fellweed, which lit up like tiny green stars against the black muddy paste.

Farlow's eyes widened.

Copper relaxed as the paste hardened into a cast. Ninienne stroked the crowhorse's feathered mane. "You did great. You just rest for a while."

Ninienne stood and wiped her hands on her overalls. "Let her rest here for an hour or so, until she feels ready," she told Farlow. "After that, she'll be able to walk on it. I want to come back down in a few days and check on her, but I need supplies I can only get from the tower. Keep an eye on her and have Benno contact me if there are any issues."

Farlow's eyes darted from Copper to Ninienne and back again. His face was fixed and unchanging, his skin creased like the furrowed land he stood on.

"I'll make lunch," he said. "Why don't you stay and have a sandwich, wizard?" He turned and headed back to the house.

Benno smirked. "I think that's as close to a thank you as you're going to get."

Ninienne sighed, a little breathless from the spell work. "I'll take it."

THE THREE OF THEM ATE sandwiches on the porch. Ninienne took the meat out of hers and gave it to Benno. The vegetables were pickled and salty, and Ninienne enjoyed every bite. Gossamaw chewed on an old bone and then curled up under the bench.

"What's in this sandwich?" she asked.

Benno looked at her with a curious expression. "Pickled jumba, of course."

"Jumba. I've never had it before."

Benno laughed. "Well, we eat a lot of it, as you might imagine." He gestured to the fields, and Ninienne recognized the purple color of the leaves as the same purple in her sandwich.

"It's been gettin' harder and harder to irrigate," Farlow said, staring out across the field. Copper was trying out her leg, limping, but upright and moving. "In my folk's time, the jumba used to grow waist high. Now we're lucky if it gets up to my knee."

"So you've lived here a long time then," said Ninienne.

Farlow chewed on a long piece of grass, his eyes still on Copper. "Yep."

"Benno mentioned you might know something about the Night Stalker," Ninienne ventured.

Farlow nodded, long and slow. "There's something wrong on this moon. It's cursed, I just know it."

"Cursed?" asked Ninienne.

Farlow took the piece of grass from his mouth and examined it. "Folks who have been here a long time know what I mean when I say that."

"I'm new here. Everything here is new to me."

Farlow looked at Ninienne. He was either staring her down or thinking about something difficult, but Ninienne couldn't tell. His brow seemed locked in a permanent clench.

"You helped my Copper. That's worth somethin'. I guess the least I could do is explain what I mean."

His gaze returned to the fields. He twirled the piece of grass between his fingers.

"I was born here. Lived here my whole life. Maybe that makes me cursed too, I don't know. My folks were part of the original settlement. The Shadow Moon was an agricultural experiment, using a combination of magical and technological techniques. They made Salagrix the Master Wizard, but really it was his wife, Eldrathea, who ran things and kept the project goin'. The town was called Green Gulch back then. For a while, when I was younger, it seemed like things were workin'.

"Salagrix had a daughter. We were about the same age. I was sweet on her. We spent nights campin' in the woods, just the two of us. This was before the Night Stalker, mind you. I haven't forgotten your question. I'll get to that.

"She was whip-smart. Kind too. The most gorgeous, long, black hair. Why she even gave me the time of day, I'll never know.

"One day she stopped coming down into town. Her mother too. Which wasn't unusual, sometimes they were busy. But after a few weeks I got worried. I hiked up to the tower to check on them. They weren't there. Only Salagrix. He wouldn't tell me what happened to them. But I could see it in his eyes, the way you can see down to the bottom of a clear lake. The guilt. Unmistakable.

"He did something to them. I've never found out what. And I've never forgiven him."

Ninienne bit her lip, knowing the question she needed to ask, and feeling she already knew the answer.

"What was her name?"

Harlow turned to look at Ninienne. His marble-hard eyes betrayed a deep grief.

"Silamene."

Ninienne felt the hairs on the back of her neck prickle.

"Without Eldrathea to oversee the project, the experiment collapsed. Failure. Then the gulch dried up. All the water, gone. Now, call me crazy, but I always felt like that was the moon's curse, punishin' Salagrix for whatever he did. Of course, it was the people of the Shadow Moon who paid the price. The town fell apart. Only the most stubborn of us have stayed, or maybe the most foolish.

"When the Night Stalker showed up, I knew that was a new aspect of the curse. The moon findin' ways to punish Salagrix for whatever new sins he was committin' up in that tower."

"When did the Night Stalker show up?" asked Ninienne.

"Oh, it right around when Benno came to stay with me. I remember being afraid with a little one to look after and a beast about."

"So, the beast hasn't always been around. And you think it is the moon cursing Salagrix for whatever he did to his wife and daughter?"

Farlow nodded.

It was possible. Ecologies carried their own magic. It wasn't very well understood, but Ninienne had listened to a few streamcasts about it.

"I'm sorry about your friend. That must have been really hard."

Farlow swallowed with difficulty. "You're in that tower with that wizard. Surely there must be some evidence about what happened to them, even after all this time."

Ninienne nodded. She didn't enjoy thinking that Salagrix had been responsible for the disappearance of his wife and daughter. Did he have something to do with

Rodando's disappearance as well? Was Ninienne safe? The Master Wizard would be back later this evening.

Which gave her an idea. She had a small window before Salagrix returned, and it was the perfect opportunity to look around and see if she could learn anything about Eldrathea, Silamene, and Rodando.

"I'll see what I can find."

NINIENNE SAID GOODBYE in the early afternoon to give herself plenty of time to get back to the tower before dark. Benno walked with Ninienne back to town on foot so Copper could rest. Gossamaw fell asleep in Ninienne's arms.

They made it to town and to the trailhead.

"I don't want to see the Night Stalker again if I can help it," she repeated.

"Thank you," said Benno, looking at his feet. "I've never heard my uncle talk about anything from his past before. I feel like I understand him a little better now."

Ninienne nodded. "I'm putting some pieces together, too. There are mysteries on this moon."

"Do you really think The Night Stalker is a curse on Salagrix?"

Ninienne shrugged. "It's certainly possible. Magic is deep and mysterious. I'll have to see what else I can learn back at the tower."

The look of worry on Benno's face was unmistakable. "Careful," he said, "when poking at shadows."

18.

In the time before time when the stars were young,
And the planets cooled in the new dark,
Before the waters grouped to form the seas,
Before the plants and creatures and the fungus,
Umma, the mother of all, looked upon creation,
And said, 'It is good. But there is no one to feel it.'
So she sang the song of the first dragon.
And the first dragon awoke and watched the first sunrise,
and lapped the first drink of water and ate the first bite of fruit.
And Umma said, 'You shall guard the planets and the moons
and keep them safe.' And the first dragon said, 'From what?'
But Umma did not say, for in those times
It was unwise to speak the names of devils.
—from Epic of the Elementals: Verses from the Core of Creation

NINIENNE MADE IT BACK to the tower with daylight to spare. She was tired from hiking and farm work, but energized by her curiosity about the disappearances. After putting Gossamaw to bed, she climbed the stairs to the dining room.

Unsurprisingly, she found Andy there, but what was surprising was that the machine was sitting at the table, reading a book.

"Welcome back. Did you have a productive day?" Andy asked, looking up.

"I did. It was very informative," said Ninienne. "What are you reading? I thought you could just download from the datastream."

"I can, but I had time. I thought reading a physical copy might shed additional illumination." Andy set the book down, which turned out to be a thick volume entitled *Epic of the Elementals: Verses from the Core of Creation*. Historio-mythopoetics? Ninienne had a lot of questions but did not feel like opening that can of worms at the moment.

"Has Salagrix returned yet?" Ninienne asked.

"He has not," said Andy.

So the coast was clear, for now. "Enjoy your book," said Ninienne, and she left to climb the stairs.

"Where are you going?" Andy asked, and the question sent a chill down Ninienne's neck.

"Oh, I was just going to look for something upstairs."

"It is my understanding that you are not permitted in the upper levels of the tower."

Oh no. She had not anticipated Andy to enforce Salagrix's rules in his absence.

"That's true, but Salagrix isn't here, is he?"

Andy rose from the chair. "I must carry out my Master's wishes even in his absence."

"Look, allies, right?" said Ninienne, getting nervous. "I think Salagrix might be hiding something. He could be responsible for the disappearance of his wife, his daughter, and his former apprentice. You've seen firsthand how dangerous he can be."

Andy's animated eyes blinked. The mechanical whirring from inside its body increased in volume and pitch.

"Salagrix is my Master."

"We've been over this. I don't know if we can trust Salagrix," said Ninienne. "He's the one who damaged you. I'm the one who repaired you. Who are you going to listen to?"

Andy froze, and for a moment Ninienne worried she had fried the poor machine's circuits.

"I—I—" Andy stuttered.

"Are you okay?" Ninienne asked, genuinely worried.

Andy turned and put its face up against the wall, as if it were pouting.

"If I don't see you go upstairs, I can't stop you," it said.

Ninienne wasn't going to waste time. She dashed up the stairs.

Smoke from the unreplaced Fire Charms choked the air here. She passed the door to the kitchen, where the clanging of pans rang out, and also the door to Salagrix's quarters, shut. She kept going, further than she had yet climbed.

The stairway ended at what she could only assume was the upper workshop. The door was open, so she stepped in.

It was smaller than the lower workshop, or rather, it was the size of the original tower and had not been expanded. The ceiling was the underside of the conical roof, and she saw the sagging telescope. The workshop was tidy—Andy's doing, no doubt—with large stuffed bookcases, a desk piled high with tomes and parchment, and a smaller set of ingredient shelves. Wild-looking equipment lined the workbench near the wall.

The dominant feature was a set of stones on the opposite wall that formed an archway, not to another room, but simply in a pattern that suggested a doorway. It was the size and shape of the practice slate. Each of the stones of the arch had fine sigils carved into it, and if Ninienne had to guess, she would have said that this was some kind of focus or containment for portals.

The other curious object was a metal pipe that came up out of the floor, about as thick around as a person's leg, and then bent over at about chest height after angled, ringed segments. Five gold wires lined the pipe and then hung down from the opening, ending in strange nodules. The pipe was open and moist inside. Ninienne could only speculate as to the purpose of this device.

But that was not what she was here for. She rummaged through the desk for anything that might be a clue. She found a sealed-wax message, opened, summoning Salagrix to a meeting with the Deans of Belcarin. There were many parchments with portal sigils and calculations, but nothing that meant anything specific to Ninienne.

Pinned up above the desk, behind a stack of books, was a diagram labeled 'Abyssalite Project—Salagrix and R. Vechi.'

That was Rodando. She pulled the parchment off the wall to examine it. She recognized Rodando's bad handwriting from his notes in his books, but this didn't make it any easier to read. As best she could tell, the diagram described two pairs of portals connected across two areas, one labeled 'Shadow Moon' and one labeled 'Hellworld,' and showed a figure with an armful labeled 'Abyssalite' returning through a portal in the hellworld to the Shadow Moon.

What this meant, she didn't know, and would not find out now, because there was a whoosh of wind in the room. Ninienne looked up to see a sparking purple ring open up in the stone archway. It grew to fill the stone border. Through it, she recognized the white hallways of Belcarin. Salagrix, looking haggard, stepped through, and the portal closed up behind him.

Salagrix looked up at Ninienne and blinked. His eyes darted to the metal pipe device and then back to her. "So, you report me to the Deans, and now you trespass in my workshop."

"I was—"

"Leave!" Salagrix shouted, but there was no strength behind it. He looked tired and defeated.

Ninienne slunk back down the stairs.

NINIENNE ALMOST SKIPPED dinner for fear of Salagrix's retribution, but the smell of the honey roasted vegetables wafted down the stairwell and she couldn't resist.

She found Salagrix slumped at the piled-high dinner table and Andy, wearing an apron, standing at attention nearby. She made a plate and sat at the far side, waiting for Salagrix to move.

"I'm getting too old for this," he said, to no one. He leaned back in his chair and his worn, wrinkled face was even more worn and wrinkled than ever. He seemed surprised by Ninienne's presence.

"I must remind you," he said, with great effort, "to stay out of the upper levels of the tower, for your own safety."

Ninienne nodded, chastened. "I'm sorry."

Salagrix grunted. "I will need tomorrow to recover. I apologize for the lapse in your lectures."

Ninienne tried to reconcile the idea that Salagrix was dangerous with this tired old man in front of her. It made no sense. She was missing something.

"How was your trip?" Ninienne ventured.

Salagrix nodded slowly. "I had not visited Belcarin in a long time. It was good to see. So much has changed. But also..."

His gaze drifted to the wall and Ninienne never found out what also. She dug into her roasted vegetables, which were incredible.

"Hadrarch," said Salagrix, through a wheeze. "I will need your assistance tomorrow."

"Of course, Master Salagrix."

As Ninienne ate, she planned. If Salagrix was going to be recovering tomorrow, it was not a good day to continue snooping around the tower. Instead, with another day off, she could head back to Black Gulch and check on Copper's injury.

Salagrix did not appear to have an appetite. When Ninienne finished eating, Andy made a request.

"Master Salagrix, after dinner, if you do not need me right away, I would like to have a few moments outside to myself."

Salagrix turned slowly to face the android. "For what reason?"

"I have downloaded all the volumes of poetry available on the datastream, and also read some physical books. Many of the ancient masters extol the qualities of sunset. I would like to make my own assessment."

Salagrix's eyes held steady. Then he burst out laughing.

"My Hadrarch desires enrichment! Ha! How funny. Yes, my sweet android, take some time to reflect this evening. I look forward to your observations."

UNABLE TO CONTAIN HER curiosity, Ninienne followed Andy out of the tower. It took a position in the field, about halfway between the tower and the treeline, and stood directly facing the setting orange gas giant. It remained there until it set fully and then returned to the tower. Ninienne caught it on its way back in.

"So? What did you think?"

Andy tilted its head. "The ancients have deceived me."

Ninienne stifled a laugh. "How so?"

"Several works of poetry informed me that the sunset provided clarity and perspective. I have not received such clarity. Perhaps it is because, here on a moon with such a weak and distant sun, the gas giant serves as a proxy sun. Insufficient data."

Ninienne chuckled. "Maybe. Or maybe one sunset does not immediately provide deep insight."

"So I must repeat the exercise to achieve results? How many times will be sufficient?"

"Uh, well, it doesn't really work like that. It's not a numbers thing."

Andy frowned, which was unsettling to see. "I am having difficulty understanding many concepts. I fear I am defective."

"No," said Ninienne, suppressing the strange feeling that came with reassuring a machine, "You can do amazing things. Many a lot better than I can. I don't think you are defective. I think you're doing your best to make sense of a complicated situation using the tools you have."

Andy nodded. "I see. Thank you."

Ninienne's eyebrows raised. "Oh? Gratitude?"

Andy turned its face so that its electric eyes stared into Ninienne's. She realized the wet, fleshy nature of her own eyes and could see them reflected on the metal surface of Andy's head. And, in turn, the reflection of her eyes carried a reflection of Andy's lit-up eyes.

"I am learning."

IT WAS STILL COLD THE next morning, and the bare black branches of the trees stretched over the path down to Black Gulch like enclosing fingers. The air was still and quiet. Gossamaw's pants and grunts as he hopped along after Ninienne were the only sound.

Ninienne reflected on yesterday and the time she had spent with Benno. The shared laughter, the easy familiarity, the way they fell into working together with no need to communicate. There was a moment on the porch when their gazes lingered a little longer than necessary. She knew Benno wanted to be more than friends — his repeated invitations to the tavern made that clear.

How did Ninienne feel? And would she feel differently if he wasn't the only other person her age on the Shadow Moon? She felt her thoughts twist and turn along with the trail.

They had not traveled far when Gossamaw stopped and hugged Ninienne's leg. He croaked nervously.

"What is it, Gossie?" Ninienne scanned the woods.

Then she heard it. Growling. Rustling among the trees. It sounded far, but not far enough.

She looked deeper into the jagged black trees and shivered. As she had seen before, claw marks tore through the bark on several trees, exposing the pale woody flesh beneath. They looked fresh.

It was daytime. She should be safe, she told herself.

She waited and listened but the woods were silent. Her breath quickened, loud against her beating ears.

She ventured a step, and her foot crunched against the dirt.

A snarl. Her heart stopped. It was close. Ninienne turned, and her limbs tingled. A hairy bulk prowled the trunks.

She froze. All the world around her focused on the space between her and the beast. Seconds passed that felt like hours.

The beast stepped on a twig, and the snap prickled through Ninienne's limbs.

In one swift motion, she snatched up Gossamaw and bolted toward the tower.

The beast roared and pounded after her. Ninienne ran as fast as she could. She tossed a light spell behind her, but heard no reaction.

The trailhead in reach. A clear view of the tower.

She tripped on a root and crashed to the ground, hard. Sharp pain throbbed through her knee. The beast thundered closer. She grabbed Gossamaw and tossed him across the border as she scrambled onto the field.

The beast slammed into the invisible barrier, howling. Green sparks spilled on to the ground as it scraped its claws across the spell.

Ninienne backed away, panting. Her knee throbbed with pain as the beast towered over her. She stilled her breath, and the beast seemed to calm as well. It dropped to the ground.

In the full light of day, safe behind the barrier, she observed the beast for the first time. Identifying creatures in the wild was more guesswork than science, but still: it was mammalian. Large, about the size of the subterranean mudbears on her home planet. Shaggy, matted fur hung down all over its body. Six legs. Its long snout dripped saliva, and even across the barrier, Ninienne caught a whiff of its warm, acrid breath. Two rows of gnarled spikes lined its back, stained brown, possibly from dried blood.

As it paced back and forth across the path as if in a cage, Ninienne and the Night Stalker made eye contact. In sharp contrast to its feral form, its two large, deep-set eyes betrayed a sparkling intelligence so piercing it made Ninienne gasp.

"What do you want?" she whispered.

The beast gave a massive, bone-rattling roar and strained against the barrier. Then, frustrated, it tore off into the woods and out of sight.

Shaking, Ninienne rose and gingerly tested her knee. She could walk, but not without pain. She whistled for Gossamaw to follow, and he soon overtook her hobbling pace.

Once they were both safely in the tower, she shut the door behind her, locked it, and then, one step at a time, climbed the stairs to her room. Gossamaw led the way and kept looking back to she if she was coming.

She sat on her bed and cast a quick pain relief spell on her knee.

Ninienne took a breath. For the second time in just a few days, she had had a life-threatening encounter with the Night Stalker.

But it was daytime, the one protection she counted on. Her first thoughts: Was Benno safe? Were the townspeople safe? Were any of them safe?

Almet coughed a weak wheeze from his box. Ninienne worried she was losing him.

Her device dinged. A message from Drusilla.

Sorry, can't talk today. Coven stuff. Soon?

Wasn't that just great? Drusilla was having the time of her life, learning the deep secrets of feminine magic, probably with a cocktail in her hand at a lakeside party, while Ninienne was trapped in a dark, crumbling tower, with a potentially dangerous mentor, a confused android, and a dying bramblehawk all while fighting for her life against a gigantic bloodthirsty beast.

The reality of Ninienne's situation sunk in. She was in danger. They were all in danger. Despite the risk he posed, she knew she would need Salagrix's help.

A THRUMMING FROM UPSTAIRS grew louder as she climbed. She expected to find Salagrix in his chamber, but the thrumming was coming from the upper workshop.

She thought about knocking, but the sound was so loud she didn't think Salagrix would hear her. She tried the door, found it unlocked, and opened it.

She saw Salagrix, shirtless, a sight she instantly wanted to scrub from her memory. The pipe she had seen earlier affixed to the center of his back, with the five golden wires attached to his head, shoulders, and abdomen. He hung limp, eyes closed, and his body seemed to be covered with a thin layer of glowing water that rippled and pulsed with the thrumming sound. Motes of dust orbited around him, slowly gaining speed.

Andy stood nearby, and when it saw Ninienne, it approached her, alarmed.

"You are not supposed to be here," Andy said.

"What's happening?" Ninienne shouted above the noise.

"I am not allowed to tell you. Please leave."

"But—"

Andy set a hand on her shoulder, non-threatening but firm. "Please."

Ninienne backed away. What was more terrifying, the Night Stalker outside or whatever was happening here?

AS SHE PASSED THE KITCHEN, a thought occurred to her. There was another resident of this tower. Someone that might answer her questions.

She opened the kitchen door, and a wave of steamy air hit her in the face. Pots and pans were flying in a circle and dipping themselves into a soapy sink.

Quiggleam, the kitchen demon, was where he had been last time, hunched in a chair with a handheld game.

"Eh? What is it? Can't you see I'm working here?" shouted the pig-nosed demon, eyes still on his game.

"I have some questions about what's going on in this tower."

Quiggleam set down his game with a scowl. "You should know I have soup for brains."

"Yes, but I thought I'd take my chances. What do you know about the pipe in the upper workshop?" she asked.

"Nothing."

"Do you know what I'm talking about?"

"BLARP! Only pipes I know about are these ones." He pointed to the walls.

Ninienne saw, through the bubbles and steam, identical pipes on the walls, with the same golden filaments running along them. Here, they split and connected to the niche, the sink, and disappeared behind the cabinet to the food generation machine.

"What are they?"

"I've always considered myself more of a cheese demon."

"What?"

"Sorry," Quiggleam shrugged. "They're a power source."

"Powered by what?"

"I don't know. Some kinda magical power source. Look, I've got a pretty cushy gig here. I don't ask a lot of questions." He put up a clawed hand to stop Ninienne's interruption. "Let me save you some trouble. I've never left this room the whole time I've been here. I make the food, I do the contract. Nobody's bothered me until you came along with that android. Which, thank you, by the way. I owe you for that one. Now my job is even easier. Might actually beat this thing." He lifted the handheld game and gave it a little shake.

"How long have you been here?"

"I have no idea how time works! I've got soup for brains! Besides, we don't have much use for time on the hellworlds. Rodando summoned me with the contract, showed me what to do, I've been fulfilling orders for a while, and then you showed up and now the android does the cooking."

"So it's been twenty years."

"I have no idea what that means."

"What do you know about Rodando? Did he ever say anything about the Abyssalite Project?"

"Maybe. What is that?"

"It's something he and Salagrix were working on. It has something to do with a hellworld."

"Well, abyssalite is a crystal that forms in hellworlds. It's very common."

"Why would Rodando and Salagrix want it?"

"Sure, I've got some right here."

Quiggleam opened a drawer and handed her a packet of crumbles labeled 'Demon Cookies.'

"What are these?" she asked.

"BLARP!" He returned to his handheld game. Ninienne shook her head and stuck the packet in her overalls. It was like trying to interview a distracted duck.

As Ninienne turned to leave, Quiggleam slapped his game in frustration. "Gah! I'll never get this."

Ninienne took a look. Quiggleam was playing *Almet 3: Curse of the Astrogoblins*, one of her favorites. "Oh, are you stuck on the jungle temple?"

Quiggleam eyed her suspiciously. "How did you know?"

"It's the hardest one. Everybody gets stuck on that. Put the crystal on top of the obelisk and then go back to the platform and shoot it with an arrow from there."

Quiggleam tapped the game in furtive concentration and then it gave a cheerful *bloop-bloop*. The demon looked delighted. "Hey, look at that! I've been stuck on that since I got here. Now I owe you double. Remind me, though. I might forget."

Ninienne was horrified. "You've been stuck on the jungle temple... for twenty years?"

The demon shrugged. "Time? Who needs it?" Then he leaned in, as if to share an intriguing secret. "Besides, like I said." He tapped his forehead. "Soup for brains."

NINIENNE SKIPPED DINNER to stew in her room. Mysterious pipes and unhelpful demons aside, what was she going to do about the Night Stalker?

It didn't matter if the plan was stupid or pointless. She needed to take back some of her power.

The dryad's barrier had held back the Night Stalker today, but would it hold up in the future? There needed to be backup defense systems in case the first failed.

Ninienne's eyes wandered to Rodando's chore list, still pinned up on the wall, and fell on *Secure Perimeter*.

She took out several sheaves of parchment and began sketching. Moats, rows of spikes, live crocodons. Nothing was too wild or too ridiculous. Besides, if there were crocodons, she would get to feed them and take care of them, which was a plus.

She was starting to have fun. Weapons! Enchanted axes and spears to fly out and stab the beast if it got too close to the tower. She began to giggle as she drew swords with wings spinning loop-de-loops in the air around the tower.

It might have been because of the late hour and she was getting slap-happy, but flying swords was actually not a bad idea. She thought she might actually be able to make that work. She made notes for a directional levitation enchantment that was triggered by a particular exterior condition.

That was... actually really interesting. She thought she might be able to make that work. She went down to the sitting room, retrieved the sword, and took it back to her room.

She had studied enchantments in her healing item class, and knew enough to set the conditions. She got the sword flying and slashing on its own in a set direction. Now, she had to set the triggering condition. How to define 'threat'?

She yawned. It was a struggle to keep her eyes open. Dream and reality merged as she rode a flying crocodon over the woods, arms made of swords, and chased the beast back into its cave. The Night Stalker's eyes sparkled through the dark.

19.

It is my opinion that Dean Falchbrook's connection to Master Salagrix has clouded his judgment on the issue of the Master's health. On the decision of the Deans to allow Master Salagrix to remain in his position, against the majority, I dissent.

—*internal document from Dean Prevogan, Belcarin Academy of Wizardry*

"YOUR TRAINING THUS far has lacked a certain element of rigor," said Salagrix before Ninienne had even had a chance at breakfast, "and so before we proceed to practical application, I must subject you to an exam."

Salagrix was looking vigorous. Ninienne, bleary-eyed, had found him in the lower workshop first thing this morning, dictating portal problems to the chalkboard.

"You will find the problem here. Create the portal sigil, prepare the paste, and draw the sigil on the practice slate by the end of the day. If I can safely activate it, you will pass and I will grant you free access to the upper levels of the tower, for which you seem eager. If not," and here his expression darkened, "the Deans will know about it."

He turned with a whirl of his tattered robe and a galaxy of dust motes orbited with him.

Had Salagrix just threatened her? Did this jeopardize her graduation from Belcarin? Ninienne's vision swam across the complex problem on the board and anxiety gripped her chest.

"Can I use the android?" Ninienne burst in desperation.

Salagrix stopped. Andy was dusting a row of flasks on the top shelf of the ingredient cabinet.

"Hadrarch. You are not to assist my apprentice with the calculation or physical preparation of this portal." Ninienne's heart sank. "However, you may answer questions and serve as reference material. Good luck." Salagrix swept up the stairs.

"Oh, thank the worlds." Ninienne threw herself at Andy. "You have to help me."

"Salagrix was very clear. I cannot assist with the physical preparation of the portal."

"No, but you can answer questions. And that's going to be a lifesaver. I don't know if I'd be able to pass otherwise. If Salagrix grants me access to the upper workshop, maybe I can figure out what's going on around here. Allies, right?"

Andy tilted his head. "How does that apply in this case?"

"If you help me, I can get into the upper workshop again and find more clues. If Salagrix truly is dangerous, he's a danger to you, too."

Gears whirred within the android's head. "I cannot disobey my Master's orders. But I will help you in any way I can."

Ninienne ordered an extra-large coffee, patted Gossamaw for good luck, and pulled the chair in front of the chalkboard.

IT WAS A DOOZY OF A problem. If Ninienne had been more paranoid, she might have thought Salagrix had devised it for the sole purpose of stumping her.

The target was a space station, which required a complicated sigil grammar right off the bat, orbiting a trinary star system, which required three layers of re-conjugation. This was the kind of preposterous hypothetical that made Salagrix salivate, but Ninienne seriously doubted that it actually existed anywhere in reality.

Salagrix's notes also described, with detailed measurements of the size and distance, a series of crystal rings that orbited the space station. Ninienne didn't understand why this was relevant until she realized that the crystal acted as a ward against portals, and the various stages of casting would have to be timed precisely to penetrate gaps in the rings.

In short, it was a total pain in the ass.

Ninienne got to work on her calculations. She got as far as she could and then got stuck.

"Okay, what's the declination for a red giant?"

"Negative five."

"Right, which would push the signifier into ... which house?"

Andy paused conspicuously.

"Second house?" Ninienne guessed. "Oh, no, the iron plating means the effect is enhanced. Third house."

"That is correct in this case."

Once her sketch of the portal sigil was complete, she showed it to Andy.

"I know you can't tell me if this is correct or not," she said. "But can you at least test it for inconsistencies?"

The android pointed at two segments. "There are inconsistencies here and here."

Ninienne saw her mistakes and then corrected them.

At mid-day she moved on to the portal paste. The workbench filled as she gathered the necessary ingredients. The brewing took hours, and multiple stages. Finally, as the lights dimmed for the evening, she added the ingredient for the last stage.

The bubbling paste turned gold and spouted, magma-like, in a pillar towards the ceiling. Then it froze into a weeping, blood-red column of ooze that gave off a faint shrieking sound.

"I don't think that's it."

Andy shook its head.

Ninienne looked out the window. "I don't have time to try again. The day is almost over. I'm finished."

She slumped to the floor in a defeated pile. Gossamaw licked her elbow.

"Well..." said Andy.

Ninienne's head snapped up. "What? What is it?"

"You might consider... universal ingredients."

"What's that? Salagrix has never mentioned them."

The android was silent.

"Tell me, as a reference, about universal ingredients for portal paste."

"A universal ingredient is one that can be used regardless of conjugation and calibration. The most common are only pseudo-universal, and still have to be altered and adjusted for particular circumstances. An example of a true universal ingredient is abyssalite, but it is astoundingly rare and impossibly difficult to obtain except on hellworlds."

"Abyssalite!" shouted Ninienne. "That's what Salagrix and Rodando were after. No wonder. Not having to mix portal paste would be a huge headache-saver. But do they have any?"

Ninienne frantically scanned the shelves. Andy made a grunting noise and pointed discreetly to the bottom-most corner. She kneeled down and behind a greasy tub labeled 'Slug Fat' she found a squarish, unmarked metal tin with an excessive number of clasps. She unhinged the lid and found a handful of orangey translucent sand flecked with bits of gold. It looked like candy and smelled like the desert. Ninienne suppressed a worn-out-brain-desire to eat it.

"There isn't much of it," she said. "And I don't have a lot of time. But I knew you'd help!"

With her sigil plan in one hand, she sprinkled the abyssalite powder on the practice slate in precise patterns. Sweat ran down her temples. Salagrix stepped in just as she finished arcing the last accent mark on the activation glyph.

"What is this? Abyssalite?" Salagrix looked down his nose, arms crossed, and sniffed. "Technically correct, if cheeky. And you've just cost me a fortune. Let me see your sigil work."

Salagrix examined the sigil, hunched, and muttering to himself. "Ah-ah! Oh—no, you're correct."

He finished and drew himself in front of Ninienne and Andy. He looked unhappy.

"And the timing of the casting?"

Ninienne flipped the chalkboard to display her timing diagram.

"Right here."

Salagrix scanned her notes and frowned even deeper. "Despite all my expectations, this is castable."

Ninienne punched the air. She felt incredible, like a cake exploding with sunshine. She had done it. She had actually done it.

"But there was a secret part of the exam," said Salagrix. "Hadrarch. How much assistance did she require?"

"A moderate amount of assistance," chirped Andy.

"In your opinion, could she have completed this on her own without your help?"

"Wait a minute, I followed all the rules," said Ninienne. "You said I could use the android as a resource."

"Yes, and I was testing your character to see if you'd cheat!" snapped Salagrix. "So, tell me, Hadrarch, could she have completed this task without your help?"

Andy's whirring pitched up.

"Please, tell him," pleaded Ninienne. "I didn't break the rules. Please."

Andy's eyes fell. "She could not have."

"Wait!" shouted Ninienne. "That's not fair! I didn't—I didn't ask for anything—it was the android! The android helped me of its own accord."

"The likely story of a cheat and a sneak!" shouted Salagrix. "You're a poor student who has disobeyed my direct instructions, spent my resources without permission, skipped lectures, and now cheated on an exam."

Ninienne's insides crumpled like a black balloon.

"And all of this is going into my report to the Deans."

NINIENNE TOSSED AND turned, tortured by Andy's betrayal. Had the whole thing been a set-up? Had Andy been following Salagrix's instructions all along? Or had it genuinely tried to help her and then gotten caught?

Amid fits of anxious sleep, pained bramblehawk cries woke Ninienne in the middle of the night. She dragged herself out of bed, heavy-headed, to find Almet coughing badly. He looked fatigued in a way that Ninienne had not yet seen. Bleary-eyed, she carried his crate up to the lower workshop.

She turned to heat the cauldron, and when she turned back, the light had gone out of Almet's eyes. He was gone.

This was too much. On top of everything else, she had failed to save her patient. It was one thing to fail at portalcraft, which she didn't care about, but it was another thing entirely to fail at the one thing she wanted to be, that filled her with a sense of purpose, that kept her going through this miserable apprenticeship. She should have felt enraged or distraught, but instead she felt nothing, just an enormous emptiness that seemed to press down on her heart as if to suffocate it. All she could do was stumble down the stairs like an animated corpse and fall onto her bed.

She dreamed dreams, unremembered, of the black void between the stars.

THE MORNING LIGHT THROUGH Ninienne's window, warm and bright, seemed to herald a new day. She felt otherwise. If today was going to be her last day on the Shadow Moon, she was going to make good. She had a hawk to bury.

She stumbled up the stairs to the lower workroom to find Andy there, already cleaning.

"Good morning," said Andy in its characteristic chirp, as if it hadn't totally betrayed her the day before.

It took Ninienne a moment to register what she found on the worktable. Almet's blanket was clean and folded, and in front of the empty crate was a full cork-stoppered jar labeled "Hawk Powder."

"What happened here?" Ninienne asked, still groggy from the early rise and the confusing mess of yesterday's troubles.

"I noticed that Master Salagrix was out of hawk powder," replied Andy. "I also noticed the fresh hawk corpse. So I ground the corpse to replenish the master's supply."

Ninienne turned slowly, her forehead veins bulging. "You ground? The corpse?"

"You appear distressed. Have I erred?"

"That wasn't just a hawk." Ninienne seethed. "That was my patient. A patient that I cared for and lost. A patient that I planned to bury this morning."

"I apologize. I was not aware of your plans," said Andy. "But is it not a more efficient use of resources to make use of a corpse rather than burying it?"

Something inside of Ninienne snapped. All the disappointment, all the discomfort, all the rage congealed and hardened into a sharp, white-hot point directed straight at the reflective surface of the android. The android that had earned more of her mentor's favor when it couldn't even do magic. The android who, even when they seemed to be getting close, ratted her out to Salagrix.

Her soulfire tugged at something a few floors below. Before she could register what was happening, the enchanted sword flew into the room.

As if in slow motion, the sword pointed itself at the android. What was happening? With a creeping awareness, she realized she had not properly finished her enchantment on the blade. It had registered Andy as a threat. Ninienne reached out, trying to grab the hilt, but she was too slow. The sword slashed diagonally and cut the machine clean through, shoulder to opposite hip.

The lights on Andy's animated face made a stunned expression before going dark, and the top part of its body slid off, exposing a naked mess of tiny spinning gears and sparking wires. Its legs collapsed in a heap.

The sword, having executed its rough-draft instructions, clattered to the floor.

Oops! Ninienne thought, unable to fully process. *I broke the wizard's android!*

Salagrix appeared in the doorway and his face transformed into a mask of shock.

"What has happened?" he cried.

"The sword—it flew and slashed—I'm so—"

"A hex!" Salagrix's eyes widened with suspicion. "A rival has bested me! I knew I should have not left for so long!" He collapsed to his knees. "My servant! My beloved servant! My Hadrarch!"

"I'm so sorry," said Ninienne.

Salagrix howled in grief.

"I can fix this," Ninienne said before she realized what she was saying. "Please let me try to fix this."

Salagrix looked up at her, curiously. "Do you really think you can fix my Hadrarch?"

"I've repaired it once before," said Ninienne. "Let me try."

Salagrix stood up with difficulty and brushed off his robe. "If you can repair my android, I will use that as your exam, and I will forget your past errors in my letter to the Deans. If you cannot, well, then the future of your apprenticeship remains in serious doubt."

NINIENNE ARRANGED THE two halves of the android on the floor, along with all the little components and bits of metallic debris that had burst from the machine. She was already exhausted from her run-in with the Night Stalker, from her exam the previous day, from her grief of losing Almet, but her focus sharpened her attention and everything around her faded out. She was vaguely aware of presences around her: Gossamaw, attentive but quiet under the workbench; Salagrix, lamenting his loss and railing against some unseen rival.

With the previous repair, Andy had guided Ninienne, but this time, she was on her own. The mechanical complexity of moving limbs paled to the tiny, intricately woven circuitry and gear-work of the interior. She could understand moving parts, but circuits and electrical components were an impenetrable cipher. The repair manual, for all its usefulness, was still written for specialists, and Ninienne puzzled over words and symbols she did not recognize.

She got to work: attaching wires, replacing gears, straightening pistons, soldering circuits.

Her guilt was the engine. Each setback was a wall that she smashed through with regret. Each mistake only added fuel to her fire. The hours vanished in a blur of shame.

At some point, it was dark. She hadn't eaten all day. Gossamaw was snoozing under the workbench, and Salagrix was elsewhere.

She took an inventory of her progress. Many of the repairs had required her to remove components from the machine. She had arranged these pieces across the floor to stay organized, but looking over them, her vision swam. It was as if each repair revealed two new repairs in a never-ending hydra of circuitry.

It was too much. It was her fault. She had to make amends somehow, some way, but she felt like she was drowning in gears.

Maybe it was the fatigue, or the hunger, or sheer desperation, but a plan formed in Ninienne's mind. It wouldn't work. There was no way that it could, but she didn't know what else to do.

She tried a healing spell. It was designed for flesh, not for metal, and it took a lot of soulfire, but she didn't care. She was done anyway. She prepared the balm from ingredients on the shelf, traced sigils with the paste on her palms, and then placed a hand on each half of the body and sang the incantation.

Of course, nothing happened.

But then she remembered a trick she had picked up from masonry magic. She could conjugate parts of the incantation to adapt to the materials at hand.

She sang the incantation again, conjugated for metal and circuitry, and this time felt it catch on the fabric of the universe. The syllables coursed through her hands into Andy's body and spread out to all the components arranged on the floor.

Every piece of the android glowed as excess magical energy converted into light. The components lifted, and one at a time, arranged themselves into place. Wires rejoined and circuits re-connected as the two halves stitched themselves together. Her soulfire drained and pooled into the android's torso, lighting up the scar.

Just as the jagged edges of the exterior plating folded back in, Ninienne collapsed. Her soulfire depleted. The last step of the spell failed to complete, and a diagonal scar remained across the torso.

The stone floor was cold against her cheek. She took a breath, and then another, then another.

When she was finally ready, she sat up. The android remained still, the wicked scar a reminder of its death blow.

Ninienne wept. She had done all she could. She had given it everything she had. And it was not enough.

She laid her head on the android's chest and cried. Her tears trickled down the metal surface, doubled in the reflection.

Then, there was a flash of light. Ninienne sat up to see lights dancing across the android's skin. It was the same start up sequence she had seen all those weeks ago. Once again, they spread across the body and then gathered to form the now-familiar face. Internal motors whirred to life. Andy sat up.

"That was unpleasant," it said, and Ninienne hugged the android and wept again, for joy.

20.

KILMARA: Dragons exist in the same way that stars, planets, and moons exist. They are part of the essential material of the universe. As fundamental as light, as heat, as wet. They exist because dragons are existence itself manifest.

JENSY: Yes, but can you take a photogram of one?

[laughter]

—transcript from the streamcast "Mysteries of the Universe," Episode 51, "Dragons"

NINIENNE SLEPT. SHE slept the sleep of the exhausted, the sleep of those whose soulfire is completely drained. She dreamed of floating on an expanse of cool, dark water.

When she awoke, she did not know if she had slept for one night or three. The pale, early light of Chadron peeked through the window. Gossamaw licked her face.

Ninienne drew a bath. She had not yet found a fix to the frigid water, but this morning, she did not care. She submerged herself in the icy pool. The cold pricked every pore of her skin as if to say, *Wake up! Aliveness!*

After she had dried and dressed, she found Andy in the lower workshop, reading a book. It stood when Ninienne entered, and the wicked scar across its torso was like a lash to her heart, a sash worn by the Ambassador of Pain.

"Good morning," said Andy and there was—what? A sadness, a gravity to the machine's voice? Or was Ninienne projecting? "It is good to see you awake."

"Everything working good so far?" Ninienne asked.

"So far, yes," said Andy. "Salagrix attempted to close up my scar but could not. It seems resistant to magic."

Odd, but not really any odder than using a healing spell to repair an android. They were in uncharted territory.

"Salagrix believes it might be a function of the hex that was placed on the sword."

Oh. So neither Salagrix nor Andy knew she was responsible for the enchanted sword.

"You must be hungry."

She was, suddenly, not. "Oh, I was just going to order something from the niche."

"Let me make you breakfast."

This was unbearable. "No, please—"

"You saved my life, such as it is," said Andy, suddenly intent. "The least I can do is make you breakfast."

Her guilt was like hot coals raked over her chest. She had to admit fault. It was the only way through, but this exact moment did not seem like the right time.

"Okay," she said. "Thank you."

Andy nodded and went up the stairs. Ninienne slumped into the chair. This would not be fun. And she was already on thin ice with Salagrix. What would happen to her apprenticeship after she took responsibility for this reckless mistake?

Her eyes drifted to the jar of hawk powder on the worktable, still next to the empty bed crate. The beginning of tears tingled at the corner of her eyes. Yet another mistake. This one, however, she knew how to absolve. She needed to bury the bramblehawk, even if it was a jar of powder.

Salagrix appeared in the doorway. "Ah! There's the hero of the hour!" Ninienne moved to stand, but Salagrix gestured for her to stay put. "Please, rest. You need to recover your soulfire if we are going to find out which of my rivals has bested my defenses!"

She had to put a stop to this before it got any worse. "Salagrix, I—"

The wizard waved her off. "No, no, I know what you're going to say." *Highly unlikely.* "I know our relationship has been ... strained. We've both said and done things that we perhaps shouldn't have. No matter. All is forgiven. Water under the bridge. You've saved my beloved Hadrarch, which is more than I can ever repay you for."

"You need to know—"

"But when I find whoever did this..." Salagrix's face turned nasty. "I will utterly destroy them. I will pick them apart piece by piece and banish each piece to an unknown dimension of suffering."

This, too, seemed like the wrong moment to admit fault. Also, she found herself in the rare light of Salagrix's good graces. Would it be so bad to keep this little secret until the end of her apprenticeship? With so much at stake?

"But this incident has got my wheels turning. The android is an asset, no doubt, and is quickly becoming indispensable to me." Ninienne could only picture Andy in the green dress amid the wreckage of the collapsed proscenium. "Therefore, it would be wise to enlist some additional reserves in case of future losses. Think of the possibilities! I must go make preparations."

Ninienne, stunned by this unfolding of events, felt too heavy to move from her chair until Andy arrived. It held a plate piled with crisp white omelets, each flecked with bright vegetables like confetti. Ninienne took the plate, too ravenous now for ethical dilemmas, and consumed the omelets like they were her redemption.

Ninienne finished and wiped her mouth on the back of her hand. Andy stood, attentive, its scar poking out from underneath the apron. She could have admitted fault then, but she held herself back. She remembered the exam, and Andy's ever-watching eyes. Anything she said or did in front of Andy was the same as if Salagrix was in the room. However much they were working as a team, Andy was compromised, and she couldn't fully trust the android.

"That was very good, thank you."

"The least I could do, as I said."

RE-ENERGIZED, IT WAS time to face today's task. Ninienne scooped a portion of her powdered patient into a small ceramic cup, grabbed a spade from the closet, and set out, Gossamaw in tow.

She was, of course, still cautious after her daytime run-in with the Night Stalker, but after the events of the past few days, she didn't care. Let it come. She had a patient to bury.

After finding an appropriate clearing, she dug a shallow hole, poured in the powder, and covered it up.

"I'm sorry I couldn't save you," she said. "I hope you enjoyed your time in the tower."

An overwhelming calm and warmth washed over her, as if the woods were hugging her. She patted the grave site and turned the cup over on top as a marker.

The wind picked up, whistling through the branches. She looked up, across the clearing, and saw a shape moving through branches. Her heart stuttered, but Gossamaw remained relaxed, pleasant even, and hopped towards it.

At first, she thought her eyes were playing tricks, but no. There wasn't something moving through the trees. Instead, the branches shaped themselves into the outline of a figure, walking—sauntering, really—through the trees. It stopped to examine a tree and then turned—it didn't really turn, it was just a shape made of branches, but they moved to make it look like turning—to face Ninienne. Shriveled leaves thickened and folded to become eyes and lips. The figure smiled.

It was the dryad.

Ninienne automatically kneeled. She had learned as much in her Respect for Magical Forces seminar.

"Spirit of the woods, you honor me with your presence." She bowed even lower.

The dryad giggled. Ninienne thought she had heard the sound before, at the corner of her imagination.

"So formal," said the dryad. "I love it. More, please."

Ninienne rose, unsure how to continue. "Uh, I return this child of the woods, the bramblehawk, to its home among the trees."

The dryad burst out laughing. The branches shook to show her doubling over with laughter.

"I'm sorry," she said through mirthful tears of dew. "It's just your face. You look so serious. This is all good stuff, really, but let's just talk."

Ninienne's seminar had not prepared her for this.

"I've been watching you for a while." The dryad took a seat on a gnarled root and crossed her legs. "You're so funny. You're not like the other visitors I've met."

"Visitors?"

"Humans, you call yourselves, yes? You've been keeping me entertained recently. Quite fun."

Gossamaw rolled onto his back and the dryad gave him a belly rub with a leafy hand.

"But, look, if you're going to stick around, we need to work together. That thing you all built? You cut up the trees and stacked them up into weird square shapes?"

Ninienne's brow crunched as she tried to parse this. "Are you talking about buildings? The town?"

"Funny words, yes. I've never seen anything like it. Very strange. But a bit out of balance, yes? And you plant your own forests but with only one kind of plant. An interesting experiment, impressive, but how are you going to keep that up? Surely you can see that it's too much take, not enough give?"

"I didn't build the town. I'm not a part of that. That all happened before I got here."

The dryad put her hands that were not hands on her hips that were not hips. "You have a voice, yes? You can speak?"

Ninienne shrugged and looked to the sky as if there was someone articulate there to speak on her behalf. "I'm an outsider here."

The dryad laughed in flowers. "There are no outsiders on a moon. It's too small. Where would you put them? Same with planets. Everyone that breathes the same air belongs to each other."

"If you want me to go talk to the people of Black Gulch about their farming practices or whatever, fine, but they're not going to listen to me."

The dryad leaned in. Ninienne had never felt the penetrating stare of eyes that were actually berries before, but it had been a weird year.

"Does a bird speak to be heard? No. A bird speaks to share what it sees with the flock. A flock can't see. It needs all the birds to speak to know what is there. The same way a bird's body needs all its senses to speak. The same way a moon needs all the flocks to speak. This is awareness."

Ninienne stilled herself. She could see the surrounding trees, jagged and black. She heard the buzz of insects and the far-off cry of a bird. She smelled the dirt below and the leaves above.

"What do you see?" asked the dryad.

What did she see? For all the times she had walked in the woods, had she really seen them? The ground was dry and dusty. The leaves were shriveled. The bird's cry was thirsty.

"Where is the water?" Ninienne asked.

The dryad nodded. "Where is Asama? Our water dragon?"

Water dragon. Her bath tub. The pipes running through the tower. Salagrix's dragon spell.

"The tower?" Ninienne ventured. "There's a water dragon in the tower?"

"Not in, under. That wrinkled old human tricked me. I would have never agreed to the barrier if I knew what he was going to do to Asama."

Ninienne had heard of dragons, but only in the most distant, theoretical way. They were incredibly elusive and incredibly powerful. What was Salagrix doing with a dragon underneath the tower?

"So, this dragon, Asama, is in trouble?"

"The wrinkled one has taken the water dragon for his own purposes, and the whole moon suffers. Out of balance. Too much take, not enough give."

This had to be what Salagrix was hiding. He had somehow captured the Shadow Moon's water dragon and was—what? Using its energy to revitalize himself? Was that what she had seen when he was hooked up to the pipe?

"Maybe I could help," said Ninienne.

"You'd do that?" Flowers bloomed around the dryad's face.

"Yes. There are a couple of other things going on at the moment—"

A branch snapped in the distance. Ninienne's heart leapt as she looked around for the Night Stalker.

"What's wrong?" asked the dryad.

"There's a beast in these woods. I've run into it twice."

"Oh. *Him*," the dryad said with obvious distaste. "You don't need to worry about him. Here, I can help you."

The dryad sent out branches that twisted around Ninienne's neck. Their sweet sap-smell bark ran smooth against her skin, and when they retreated, Ninienne found she was wearing an amulet. Dangling from a thin braided cord was a rough chunk of wood with a sigil of hardened amber.

"This will protect you from the beast. You've been such a gentle visitor. You've helped and returned creatures to me." The dryad caressed Ninienne's cheek with a leafy finger. "I hope you can work to free Asama. The woods need her. The moon needs her."

"Thank you. I'll do my best." Ninienne, unsure, bowed again.

The dryad smiled, mischievous and wild, and unmade herself back into the woods.

21.

OUR LAST ISSUE

We want to extend our thanks to everyone who supported the Green Gulch Gazette over the years. But the time has come to say goodbye. It is no longer financially or practically possible for us to maintain this operation with the shrinking population of our town. Please join us for a farewell party at the Shadow Moon Saloon before Gelgo and I move on to other pastures. Bring your own water.

—from the final issue of the Green Gulch Gazette

SALAGRIX GNAWED ON a bone while his mind gnawed on a problem.

"It's the timing," he said. "That's the part I'm trying to figure out. You said you and Hadrarch were both out of the tower only on the first day?"

Ninienne felt sick and pushed her salad around with her fork. Watching Salagrix try to solve the mystery of the enchanted sword while she, the guilty culprit, sat across from him, felt like hot rusty rakes tearing at her guts. Knowing that he was keeping a dragon captive and depriving the moon of water, but unable to say anything, tore at her like more of the same rakes.

"That's right. The android stayed in the tower the rest of the time."

"So that's the window, unless they gained entry by other means." He chewed on a piece of gristle. "Why an enchantment, though? Which of my rivals is gifted with enchantment? Although, if that were their specialty, it would be too obvious to use. And why delay the activation? Why not sabotage the android right away? Unless..." Salagrix's eyes grew wide, wrinkling his forehead beyond tolerance. "The sword was meant for me?"

Ninienne rolled her eyes so hard she sprained her eyelids.

"But who would want me dead? Dothreep and I have butted heads, certainly, but he's gutless. Would never try something like that."

Ninienne couldn't take any more and excused herself. As she passed Salagrix, he stopped her.

"What's that?" he pointed a knobby finger at her amulet.

"It's from the dryad," she said. "It's supposed to protect me from the Night Stalker."

"Careful," said Salagrix. "She's a slippery one. And on my list of suspects. If you see her again, try to get her to spill what she knows."

Ninienne made a pained expression. "I'll ask her."

She stepped into the stairwell and the android followed. Its eyes lit up the dark landing.

"Are you not feeling well?" it asked.

"I'll be fine." She lowered her voice and chose her words carefully, knowing that anything she said to Andy might make its way back to Salagrix. "But listen. Do you think you can keep Salagrix occupied this evening?"

Andy nodded once.

AFTER THE GAS GIANT set, Ninienne slipped out of her room. Gossamaw hopped behind.

"Not tonight, Gossie," Ninienne whispered. "I need you to stand guard and croak-bark really loudly if anybody comes down the stairs. Got it?"

Gossamaw sat at attention and panted excitedly while his long tongue hung from his wide mouth.

The dryad said the dragon was underneath the tower, but the spiral stairs stopped at the small receiving room on the ground level. There was no visible sign of a passage to a level below from the inside.

Ninienne stepped outside into the frigid night air. In her garden, the monstrous mutant plants were snoring. With a light spell floating in her palm, she circled the exterior, but found no hidden entrance.

When she returned inside, she realized for the first time that the entry room was much smaller than the exterior suggested. This meant there was a gap between the inside and the outside walls.

On a hunch, she climbed to the sitting room, which was also oddly sized, given the exterior. The strange suit of armor drew her gaze. The doomed sword, returned to its resting place, threatened Ninienne with a guilty aura.

Ninienne looked at the armor, so out of place with the rest of the furnishings, and at the stone wall behind the armor which—and she couldn't quite articulate why—differed from the other walls.

Could it be? If so, classic.

She approached the suit and tested the arm for a hidden mechanism. No luck. She tried the other arm, and both legs. Nothing.

Then she reached up for the visor, that strange entrancing visor, and pulled it down. She felt resistance and heard a click from within the suit. Then the wall behind the armor slid open to reveal a hidden stairwell.

Her heart leaped with excitement, tempered with caution. She reignited her light spell and stepped down into the dark.

It was cold in the stairwell, and the air grew moist against her skin. As she spiraled downward, the stone walls gave way to carved earth.

At the bottom was a cave. She turned up the brightness of her spell.

In the center, expected but also entirely unexpected, a scaly, serpentine dragon coiled around itself. Bearded and crested like a lion fish, it glowed a pale luminescent blue, with thin fins that ran down its body like grounded kites.

A heavy manacle, larger than Ninienne was tall, held the dragon's neck, midsection and tail with three connected circles. Gold circuitry spread across the black metal and gathered into cables which ran up into the ceiling around an open pipe. And she knew where that led.

Ninienne approached the dragon cautiously. Its head, lying on the wet rock floor, came up to her chin. It opened its eyes to reveal deep orbs that sparkled like swirling galaxies, but, as if even this was too much effort, closed them again with a grunt. Ninienne's heart ached to see this truly majestic creature locked up and in so much pain.

"You poor thing," said Ninienne. She stroked its neck, slick to the touch. "Let's see if I can get you out of here."

She examined the manacle. In the center, encircled by intricate golden lines, was a hole so specifically shaped it could only be for a key.

"Okay, so Salagrix must have a key somewhere. As soon as I can find it, I'll come and free you," she said.

The dragon stretched against the manacle, unable to get comfortable.

"I wish I could do more right now," she said, "But this will have to do."

She sang and adjusted the tune of the lullaby for pain relief:

Starlight, starlight, reaching down
To kiss us on the head, the crown
Starlight, starlight reaching in
To call us home again

The dragon sighed out a cloud of mist, and Ninienne left the cave.

NINIENNE FOUND GOSSAMAW snoring in her doorway. She had just put him to bed when she heard shouting from the lower workshop. She crept up the stairs to investigate.

She peered into the room to see the makeshift stage rebuilt. Salagrix frothed at the mouth and held out the green dress and the black mop wig.

"I demand it!" he shouted. "Sing for me! Bring me my Silamene!"

"I do not wish to," said Andy.

Salagrix scoffed. "Do not *wish*! Do not *wish*! Now it puts on airs! You are still my tool, and mine to command!"

Andy shook its head. "I do not wish to play your game."

The wizard roared. His muscles and face inflated like a balloon wrapped in strings and he enlarged into a grotesque version of himself. His skin rippled and bubbled as if filled with boiling water from an unseen teapot. He charged at the android.

"Stop!" shouted Ninienne.

Salagrix smashed Andy into the wall. The tower shook. Lizard heads fell from the ceiling.

The pinned android smacked Salagrix in the face with its forearm. The engorged wizard tossed the machine into the workbench, breaking the thick wooden table into splinters.

"I am the Master!" shouted Salagrix. "Obey me!"

Andy struggled to get up from the wreckage of the table. Hot yellow sparks showered from its shoulder and neck joints.

"Stop!" shouted Ninienne. "Look at what you're doing! You're going to kill it!"

"No one tells me what to do! I am the Master!"

Salagrix pounced.

Andy put up a hand, and the air electrified. Energy burst from its metal fingers like rubbery lightning and coalesced into a bubble shield. The wizard bounced off the barrier and fell back, stunned.

Ninienne's jaw dropped. Andy had just cast a spell.

The android stood uneasily and kept the magic shield between it and Salagrix.

"Go to bed, Master," Andy said in a quiet voice.

"Do. Not. Command! Me!"

Salagrix leaped onto his feet and rushed the android.

At the last second, in a deft motion, Andy dropped the shield and brought up its other had to grip Salagrix's neck, stopping him like a wall. The wizard's body rippled in waves. The machine's free hand sparked with another spell. Each of its fingers caught fire and combined into a single hot white flame which Andy pointed at the wizard's forehead.

"Go to bed, Master," Andy repeated.

Salagrix's panicked eyes darted from the flame to the animated face. Sweat ran down his bulging temples like melting wax.

"How?" the wizard choked out. He struggled uselessly against the machine's grip, but Andy was unmovable.

Salagrix deflated like a balloon as the engorgement spell ended. Andy released him, and the wizard staggered back, limp and wet, and vanished into the dark stairwell.

Ninienne rushed to Andy. "Are you alright?"

"No," said Andy, and Ninienne heard—what was it?—regret in the electronic voice.

"Since when can you do magic?" she asked, amazed.

"I—I don't know. I never had cause to try. I read the tomes. But not to try, just to understand. But when the moment came..."

Ninienne, with her detect soulfire spell, saw a teal pool swirling in the android's chest, identical in color to her own, but aligned to the diagonal scar. It was as if the scar held the pool in place.

"Something must have happened when I did that healing spell on you," she said. "My soulfire got trapped somehow, and now you can use it to cast spells."

"I am very confused." Andy gazed, frantic, about the room.

"Me too. But right now, let's have a look at these joints—"

"To harm my master is not permitted." Andy looked at its own hands. "It is not permitted. It is against my programming."

"You had to defend yourself."

"Defend... *myself*." Andy tried out the new word. "But—my master—"

"I don't know how to say this, but you have to let go of Salagrix as your master. He is a bad guy. He's got a dragon chained up in the basement. Who knows what he did to Rodando or his wife and daughter?"

"I am so confused!" The android cried in anguish. "I cannot bear it. I am at war with myself. I am damaged and must be decommissioned."

"We're not doing that. Are you... wait, are you having emotions?"

"They're horrible! I cannot bear them! End this! Destroy me!"

Ninienne rubbed her forehead. Nothing in her education had prepared her to calm a newly-ensoulfired android.

"Listen to me. We'll get through this." She adjusted her voice to function as a calming spell. "But right now, we need to get you repaired."

Without an organic body to absorb the magic, her spell slid off the android like oil on metal.

"I cannot bear it! Oh, the paradox! The insufferable paradox of being!"

"Do you think you have the monopoly on suffering!?" Ninienne shouted. "Get a grip! Welcome to sentience! You're a physical being with a core of unknowable, cosmic energy!"

The android wailed in glitches.

"Yes," Ninienne continued, catching the reflection of her own face in the android, "There's pain and loneliness and discomfort and peril. But there's also mystery and wonder and delight and the quiet calm that comes only in the dark. And you have to risk the former things to get to the latter. However lonely it feels to look out through your own eyes and no one else's, I promise you, you're not alone."

She took the android's hand. Its shoulder rained sparks down onto her brown overalls.

"Please fix me," Andy said.

NINIENNE WORKED LATE through the night. She had now repaired the android so many times she was thinking of adding it to her resume.

"You can't stay here," she said, threading wires together with a spell. "It's not safe. We'll have to get you out somehow."

"What about you?" asked Andy. "What about your apprenticeship?"

Ninienne bunched her lips. "Did you get a recording of Salagrix attacking you?"

Andy projected through its eyes a video of the fight with Salagrix. It was even more terrifying from Andy's perspective.

"This is the kind of evidence we need to show the Deans. If they see this, they will have to give me some leeway for not finishing my apprenticeship. But honestly, that's the least of my worries right now. I can't leave until I find the key and free the dragon."

"I do not like the idea of you alone in the tower with Salagrix," said Andy.

"I don't either. But if we can free the dragon, we can weaken Salagrix. He won't be able to recover his soulfire."

"I am afraid that if Salagrix gives me an order, I will have to obey."

"You've already disobeyed, though, right? If you've done it once, you can do it again."

"I am not certain of that."

Ninienne tried to seal up the torso scar, but found it immune to repair, either physical or magical.

After she had finished the rest of the repair, Andy asked, "Will you accompany me outside?"

"What for?" asked Ninienne.

"I wish to view the rising of the gas giant with you."

Ninienne was stunned. "I thought you had already made your assessment."

"I wish to try again."

NINIENNE AND ANDY STOOD in the middle of the field, watching the gas giant of Chadron rise over the horizon. Oranges, pinks, and purples radiated across the sky.

"What do you think?" asked Ninienne.

"Many of the ancient poets have used exaggerated language," said Andy. "Their descriptions, while vivid, are in many cases inaccurate."

"Poetry isn't meant to be accurate, it's supposed to evoke something in you. To be beautiful."

"Yes, beauty," said Andy, still looking out into the coming day. "I am still trying to understand. I observe many gradients. Are the colors beautiful, Ninienne?"

Ninienne shrugged. "I think it's nice."

"Am I beautiful, Ninienne?"

Ninienne's heart stopped. This was not a conversation she had expected to have today, or any day. "Why do you want to know?"

"I have come to understand that beauty is a desirable quality, and in my desire for self-improvement and optimization, I wish to possess all desirable qualities."

Desire. Wish. These were strange words to hear coming from an android.

"Well, you are certainly well crafted. You've taken some damage, sure, but—"

"So I have been rendered ugly?" There was no malice in the android's voice, simply curiosity.

"No, we all get a little beat up as time goes on, that's just part—"

"I have noticed that you are afraid of me, Ninienne. Is it because I am ugly?"

Ninienne's blood ran cold. She sputtered. "Uh, why would you—"

"You have been avoiding me since the accident with the sword. Have I been ruined and made ugly?"

Ninienne looked at the scar on Andy's chest where her healing magic had failed. The android was right. She had been avoiding it. But not out of ugliness or fear, but from guilt.

"Scars don't make us ugly. Anyone who thinks that is shallow. Scars are a reminder of things that have happened to us, and if we can embrace the lesson and grow from it, they can become very beautiful indeed."

"What lesson am I meant to take from the accident?" asked Andy.

Ninienne did not have an answer for that.

"I have been thinking about death since my accident," said Andy. "Since my error with Almet, really. I downloaded several treatises on ceremonial burial and I have integrated a syncretic concept of respect for the dead from a wide variety of cultures."

"Oh?"

"When I die, will my body be treated with respect? Will I be buried in the ground to rejoin the planet of my birth?" Andy asked.

"I—I don't know."

"I'm sorry. Have I alarmed you? I know in some cultures, death is a taboo topic."

"No, you're fine. I'm just surprised. You know, I don't know. I don't know if androids have been around long enough for anyone to decide what happens to them after they are done."

"Is that not irresponsible?"

"What do you mean?"

"Humans created androids. Should some plan not have been put in place for their disposal? Surely, their eventual decommission could be foreseen and anticipated as part of the design process."

"I don't think many people think that far. Most people are just trying to solve the problems right in front of them, and don't think that far into the future."

Gears whirred inside Andy. "That seems a grave oversight."

She felt stuck. She wanted to offer Andy something in exchange for her mistake, for the mistake of its existence.

"How do you feel about the name Hadrarch? What Salagrix calls you?"

Tiny gears whirred inside of Andy's head. "It does not seem suitable."

Ninienne nodded. "It's better than what I've been calling you. Would you like a new name?"

Andy turned to face Ninienne. In the lingering dark of dawn, its lit-up eyes and mouth illuminated the space between them. "I would like that very much," it chirped.

Ninienne felt the weight of this decision, and the power of naming. She thought about the android's characteristic voice.

"You can change your vocal qualities at will. If you could choose, what voice would you choose for yourself?"

"My current voice," said the android.

"And when Salagrix tries to dress you as a woman, how does that feel?"

The android shook its head. "I do not like that. It feels wrong."

"Do you feel masculine, or something else?"

The internal whirring reached a higher frequency. "I do not feel that either masculine or feminine applies to me."

"But you're not an it."

The android's head shook. "No, not anymore."

"In that case, I'll refer to you as they."

So, a name. Not an obviously masculine or feminine name. The android's voice had always reminded Ninienne of a bird. "What about Chirp?"

"Yes. I like this. Chirp. This feels right," said Chirp.

Ninienne felt the binding magic of naming draw them together. Their fates, once separate, now intertwined.

"Let's get you safe," she said.

"ARE YOU SURE ABOUT this?" Chirp asked from Ninienne's doorway.

"Yes," she said, putting on Rodando's scarf. Gossamaw sat on the bed, excited about the upcoming walk. "We'll get you down to Benno, and he'll find a place for you to hide. Then I'll come back to the tower and see if I can find the key."

"And if you can't?"

"Then I'll just bide my time until the Deans decide what to do. Which, speaking of, we need to send that recording before we go. Come over here by the window, the datastream connection is better."

Chirp crossed to the window, but their attention caught on something on the desk. They picked up a crumpled piece of parchment. "What is this?"

Ninienne saw the drawing of the enchanted sword reflected in the android's face, and her heart sank. She tried to snatch it away, but Chirp's reflexes were too quick.

"Did you enchant the sword?"

"I did, but I never meant—"

Chirp snapped to attention. "I must report this to Salagrix." They turned for the stairwell.

"No! Chirp!" Ninienne shouted.

"I have orders."

"Disobey them, please!" Ninienne tried to pull the android back into the room but was brushed off.

"Salagrix! I have found the culprit!" Chirp called while marching up the stairs.

"No! Stop! What are you doing!?"

Ninienne grabbed onto Chirp's arm, but they shoved her, forcefully, down the stairs. She fell, her heart more bruised than her body.

She gathered herself and ran up to the lower workshop to find Chirp, standing at attention, and Salagrix in his nightclothes, yawning.

"What's all this, then?" he asked.

"Ninienne is the culprit." Chirp pointed an accusing finger. "She has admitted fault."

"You?" Salagrix's face pinched with rage. "But why? Oh, of course, jealousy. My preferential treatment of the android. Well, I must applaud you for avoiding detection for this long. And right under my nose, too."

"Let me explain," Ninienne pleaded. "It was never meant for the android."

"Then for me, then? Couldn't cut it as my apprentice, so you decided to turn to murder? My my. Add that to your long list of offenses in my report to the Deans."

"It was for the Night Stalker. I was trying to defend the tower."

"Hmm, a plausible story. But your spell failed and put others in danger. Reckless magic. In either case, grounds for the Mark of Banishment."

Ninienne couldn't believe what she was hearing.

"I hereby relieve you of your position as apprentice. Hadrarch will serve as your replacement. And now that she can do magic, well," Salagrix's eyes sparkled darkly. "Imagine what we can accomplish."

22.

It is my deepest hope that students expand their horizons beyond their chosen disciplines. We prepare them not for magical careers, but a magical way of life.

—Master Wizard Belgano, founder of the Belcarin Academy of Wizardry

NINIENNE PACKED HER belongings in the heat of shame and rage. She looked at the bathtub with disgust. There was no way she could free the dragon now. The best she could do was to tell someone else about it. She needed to get off this moon as soon as possible. Her satchel packed, she grabbed Gossamaw, more for her comfort than his, and left the tower.

The mutant plants were snapping at each other. Another failed project. How could she have gotten this so wrong? Unless she could convince the Deans of the danger that Salagrix posed, her dreams of being a creature healer, or of having any kind of magical career at all, were shattered.

She only barely perceived the forest around her as she stumbled down towards Black Gulch.

About halfway down the trail, Gossamaw got fidgety.

"What is it?" she asked, to assure herself that it wasn't what she knew it had to be.

The massive bulk of the Night Stalker burst out of the woods and, with a tremendous roar, blocked the path.

This time, however, Ninienne had an advantage.

She stood her ground, brandished the amulet, and shouted, "Stay back!"

To her surprise and immense relief, the beast stopped and stared at her with its brilliant eyes.

"Lay down!" she ventured.

The Night Stalker lay down on the ground with a sigh and a huff.

Ninienne relaxed. She was in control.

From this new angle, Ninienne had a better view of the spikes along its back. Now that she could see them more closely, she realized they weren't spikes at all, but gnarled brown sticks. Dried blood at the base of each made them look like spears, but they were too twisted to have been thrown. Some kind of bramble or thorn bush, maybe? But the spacing was too regular.

Seeing the beast like this, servile and injured, called to her heart as a creature healer. She hated to see any creature, even one so fearsome, injured like this.

She set Gossamaw down and approached the beast slowly, palms up.

"Hey," she said. "It's alright."

The creature had become completely docile in the amulet's presence. She got a noseful of sharp animal musk as she approached the hill of a beast.

"Can I take a look at that back of yours?"

She placed a hand on its rough and dirty fur. A clear, almost human-like message rang through her mind.

Help me.

She leaned to get a closer look at its back. The arrangement of the sticks reminded Ninienne of a glyph—a work of magic. Had Salagrix attempted an experiment on the beast at some point? Intricate lines of amber swirled through the knots and grains.

She grasped a stick and felt the magic coursing down into the body of the beast. The beast moaned and growled.

"Sorry, didn't mean to nudge it, just trying to figure out what's going on with you." Without familiarity with the spell, she was loath to remove the sticks by force. It might have been a beneficial charm, for all she knew. But the dried blood and the pain of the beast seemed to say otherwise.

She cast a scanning charm, and the sticks lit up in her vision in an interconnected web. It was a glyph all right, a rough, earthy spell, with none of the finesse she had learned at the Academy.

"Is this glyph hurting you?" asked Ninienne.

The beast, still dazed from the amulet, huffed in assent.

"Would you like me to remove it?"

The beast nodded.

"Okay, I'll see what I can do."

She cast a nullifying spell, and the glyph dissipated. She pulled out the sticks, one at a time, and closed up the wounds left behind with simple flesh mending.

Once the last wound healed, the beast shrank. Ninienne stepped back. The hairy bulk rolled on its side, away from her, and diminished. Two of the six limbs contracted inside the torso. The hair on the back legs scattered like insects to reveal a brown shin. The head cracked open and melted into the earth, leaving a whorl of hair with two ears sticking out.

Soon, all that was left was a hairy blanket with a human man underneath.

"Thank you," came a voice, hoarse with disuse.

Whatever possibilities Ninienne had imagined would come from healing the Night Stalker, this was not one of them.

"Who... who are you? What happened to you?"

The man coughed and rolled over in the freshly shorn pelt to face Ninienne. It was hard to tell his age underneath his lengthy hair and beard, both flecked with gray.

"The dryad told me that if I was going to act beastly, I might as well be a beast." He laughed wryly to himself and coughed again.

"She did this?"

The man sighed. "It was my fault. I behaved like an idiot. And I paid the price. I've had a lot of time to think since then, in between hunting for meals. How long has it been?" The man leaned up on one elbow and looked at his hands. "I'm so old."

"I'm heading back into Black Gulch. We can try to get you some clothes and a meal."

He stood with difficulty, keeping the pelt wrapped around himself, and nodded. He saw Ninienne for the first time and cocked his head.

"What are you doing with my scarf?" asked Rodando.

MEG LOOKED ASKANCE with her single good eye at the naked man under an animal pelt when Ninienne had asked for a room at the Shadow Moon Saloon, but did not turn down the coins—Ninienne had pilfered them from the refilling tray on her way out of the tower—and pointed the way upstairs.

Ninienne gave Rodando some privacy while he used sewing magic to turn the hairy beast pelt into pants. Once that was finished, she joined him in the bare accommodations while he sat on the bed and worked on the shirt. He had shaved, and his clean jaw gave him a serious expression.

"I took fashion design as an elective at Belcarin," he said, by way of explanation. Long brown hair, hanging in curls, and framed his troubled brow as he bent over his work with close attention. "Not relevant to demonology, but there was a girl in the class I liked, so..."

"Enwu?" Ninienne asked. She sat on a table with Gossamaw in her lap. Next to her was a bowl with a damp sponge in it that served as the sink. Along with the hazy mirror and the bed, this made up the entirety of their furnishings.

Rodando looked at Ninienne, and she saw the same eyes, sparkling with intelligence, that she had seen in the Night Stalker, now sad and searching.

"Sorry, I read her letter," said Ninienne, suddenly embarrassed.

Rodando turned back to the shirt and his hand lit up with a scissor spell as Ninienne leaned back against the wall. This room had a stale, unused smell that mixed with the musk from the beast pelt. Bits of paint peeled away from the splintering walls. Outside, a drunk stumbled into the street, yelping incoherently, which they heard, muffled, through their second-story window.

"Thank you again, by the way," Rodando said without looking up. "For saving me."

"You were a creature in distress. I had to help," Ninienne said simply.

Rodando shook his head. "Do you know how long it's been?"

"You graduated from Belcarin about twenty years ago, according to the Academy database."

The man who had been a beast stared, wide-eyed, at a crack in the wall. "And then I worked for Salagrix for a few years. So, maybe... seventeen years?" He sighed, shaky.

Then he exhaled sharply, as if brushing away all concerns, and returned to his focused trimming. As he worked, he examined, not for the first time, his muscled arms.

"I've never been this fit," he said, as if he had just returned from a long vacation and not a decades-long curse. "At least all that running around on six legs got me something."

Little bits of beast fur flew up as Rodando cut out his pattern. Gossamaw leaped down and put on some as a fake mustache.

Ninienne leaned in. "I don't understand why no one came looking for you in all that time. Family or friends?"

"Maybe they did, I don't know. Few would have missed me." Rodando shifted uncomfortably as he shook out a piece of pelt. "My father did not approve of my choice of demonology as a career path. He was the only family that I had. When I left for the Academy, he basically disowned me. It doesn't surprise me he never investigated my disappearance, if he ever even found out about it." If there was a trace of bitterness in his voice, it was barely perceptible.

"But friends, surely, must have been curious?"

Rodando scrunched his face as he stitched up a sleeve. "I was not well liked at the Academy," he said, as if discussing an unfavorable review of an obscure artist. "Those in my field are generally viewed with suspicion. I dropped out of contact with the few acquaintances I had while on my apprenticeship. Except one, and she..." He made a series of facial expressions, apparently in an internal conversation with himself. "Seventeen years. She must have... well, who knows, really?"

"But Salagrix would have had to provide some sort of explanation to the Deans for your disappearance."

Rodando shrugged. He measured the sleeve against his arm and frowned, disappointed. "Hmm. Not enough here," he said, before returning to Ninienne's question. "There was not a lot of oversight from Belcarin. I think Salagrix liked it that way. But when I was... when this happened..." He looked at the pelt, which taking shape into something shirt-like. "I had already finished my studies, as I said. He had hired me on fully. I wasn't a student, I was his employee. We were collaborating."

"The Abyssalite Project."

Rodando looked up, impressed. "You have been a little detective, haven't you? Yes, after I had contracted the kitchen demon during my apprenticeship, Salagrix and I began discussing the potential synergies between demonology and portalcraft. Abyssalite is a—"

"Universal ingredient," Ninienne chimed in.

"Very good. But difficult to obtain in quantities large enough to be useful. We were working on a method to create a stable portal between our plane and a hellworld in order to mine the stuff. That turned out to be fiendishly difficult, if you'll pardon my pun. Hellgates operate on a totally different framework than portals."

"How so?"

Rodando cleared his throat. "Portals, as I'm sure you know, connect two different points in space. But the hellworlds—and there are many of them—don't exist in space as we understand it. They each exist on a separate plane of reality altogether. To put it another way, if you piloted a spacecraft with infinite fuel for an infinite amount of time, you could never reach any of the hellworlds."

He rubbed his fingers together, and a string of thread appeared. "Setting up a hellgate to a hellworld as part of a demonic contract is no problem. Going through a hellgate is no problem, as long as you don't go all the way in, but then your range of motion is limited. It's like reaching into a lake while keeping your feet on the shore—you can only go so deep. Plus, the lake is full of fish who want to torture you so they can eat your suffering."

"What?"

"Don't worry about it," he said, stitching expertly. "The point is, hellgates are less predictable than portals. We weren't even sure if a portal connection could exist between our plane and a hellworld. We had some ideas—incredibly risky, all of them—but that was as far as we got before I, uh, drew the ire of the dryad." He smoothed out the finished shirt. "Entirely my fault, by the way. Learned my lesson."

He put on his shirt and styled it for Ninienne. More of a vest than a shirt, it was too small to meet across the chest, and showed off his, uh, quite distracting abdominals. Altogether, the suit was well cut and, with the caveat that it was made of beast hair, actually looked pretty good. With his long hair, it gave him a prophet-of-the-wilderness look.

"What do you think? A bit of an *homage* to my previous form."

Gossamaw gave a little whistle.

Ninienne nodded. "Pretty good for a few hours and a scavenged pelt."

"Chalk another one up for liberal magical education." Rodando mimed making a tally mark with his finger. "This is temporary, of course, until I can find actual clothes."

"The rest of your clothes and things are still in the tower," said Ninienne. "I can't go back, but you could."

"You can't?" Rodando asked.

Ninienne squirmed. She hadn't really had time to process what had happened this morning.

"Salagrix terminated my apprenticeship right before I found you. I'm a bit at loose ends at the moment."

Rodando recoiled from Ninienne as if she were diseased and then seemed to catch himself.

"Well, I'd go into hiding if I were you. Belcarin is very serious about the Mark of Banishment. If they track you down..."

Ninienne didn't want to think of it. She wasn't even sure what her next move was. Should she go home to Swurk? Back to Belcarin to plead her case to the Deans?

Rodando's animated hands betrayed the busy working of his mind. "I could help you. Demons make powerful allies if the contracts are well written."

"You'd help me?"

He made the face of someone who had been forced to admit a harmless but embarrassing secret. "You paid me a kindness which I did not deserve, and that puts me, uncomfortably, in your debt. I would offer to give you the shirt off my back, but alas, it is very hairy. I could draw up a contract for a helper demon, perhaps? A shadow fiend familiar, to keep you hidden from Belcarin?"

"Eh, that would probably just make Gossamaw jealous." Her frogdog growled from the floor, and Ninienne chuckled. "I don't know. I don't want to hide for the rest of my life."

But a life of banishment, a life without magic, was not something she had ever considered. What would she do? What would happen to her connection to Gossamaw? How would she help creatures in need?

Her thoughts turned to the dragon, still chained up beneath the tower. Maybe there was still time to take action before she lost her magic forever. She knew what she had to do.

"I do need help with something," said Ninienne. "Did you know about the dragon?"

Rodando's eyebrows shot up. "So, you gained Salagrix's trust?"

"No, I found out another way. He doesn't know I know."

The demonologist nodded, impressed. "Yes, Salagrix revealed the secret of his power to me. Although he was cagey about it at first. Paranoid streak. Thought I'd—I don't know what. Of course I already suspected something was going on with that pipe. But after we began collaborating more fully, eventually he granted me access as well. Incredible. I'd never felt anything like it."

This casual confession startled Ninienne. "You tried it?"

"Yes. The side effects put me off somewhat. The gravity isn't too bad, but the memory loss—I don't know. It's a good thing I got turned into a beast instead of having my mind rinsed out for twenty years. I probably would have turned into another kind of monster altogether. Power without memories... I wouldn't have said no then."

A chill ran down Ninienne's arms. She was suddenly unsure how much she could trust Rodando. But he had offered to help her. She slid off the table.

"We have to free that dragon."

Rodando looked at Ninienne as if she had just suggested they light their own heads on fire. "Why?"

Ninienne pointed out the window to the black, dusty street. "Look at these people! Look at how they live! Salagrix is hording their water, the very life of this moon, and for what?"

Rodando sighed and shook his head as if this were an old debate. "I'm not really interested in a conversation about the ethics of—"

"Salagrix is a murderer!" Ninienne shouted. "He can't be trusted with that kind of power."

The demonologist scoffed. "Salagrix has many faults, but he is no murderer."

"What about his wife and daughter?"

Rodando looked down his long nose at Ninienne. "You think Salagrix murdered Eldrathea and Silamene?"

Ninienne shrugged. "Where are they?"

Adjusting his hair shirt, Rodando looked out the window. His finger drew an idle line through the dust on the sill.

"It's not my secret to tell, but I don't know that it matters." Rodando rubbed his fingertips clean. "He wasn't very forthcoming on that subject. What I learned I pieced together from bits he let slip when he had too much pixie wine." He turned to Ninienne with bright, serious eyes. "From what I gathered, he was working on a portal with Eldrathea when Silamene interrupted. Something went wrong. The portal became unstable, and the two women got caught in the resulting explosion and vanished. He's been trying to recreate the exact conditions for that haphazard portal ever since, to locate them. It's why he knows so much about portal magic. He's obsessed."

Ninienne, for the first time, felt a pang of sympathy for the old wizard. It didn't excuse his behavior, but it did explain it, and made him more sad than scary. An old man consumed by guilt and loss.

"I didn't know. I had some pieces, but I didn't know the entire story."

Rodando clicked his tongue. "Now you know."

Ninienne shook her head. "But that changes nothing. The dragon has to be freed, not just for herself, but for all the living things on the Shadow Moon."

"I'm not really interested in challenging Salagrix physically," said Rodando, who frowned as though reminded of an unpleasant smell. "Even if he weren't incredibly powerful, he might still technically be my employer. Not sure about that one."

Rodando pursed his lips. He considered something. "Still, he was unkind to me. Seventeen years as a beast won't let me forget that. So I'll help you. You'll need the key to the dragon's manacles. I know where it is."

Ninienne leaned forward.

"In my time, he kept it in a jeweled box next to his bed in his chamber. *'His precious things,'* he called it."

"Come back to the tower with me," Ninienne pleaded suddenly. "If we both face him together—"

"I am not interested in this fight." Rodando shook his head. "I also, unfortunately, feel the call of matters of the heart. I regret the choices I made with Enwu. Seventeen years, even through the muddled thoughts of a beast, has given me clarity as to my true priorities. While it is probably too late to make things right, I have to try." He adjusted his arms. "And I have to find a new shirt, obviously. This one is incredibly itchy."

23.

RODANDO VECHI

A good student, but lonely. His lower economic background puts him at odds with his fellow students, which he tries to overcompensate for with posturing. I'm not worried about his schoolwork, but I am worried about his heart.

—internal student assessment by Professor Remora, Belcarin Academy of Wizardry

IT WAS CLEAR RODANDO had no interest in helping free the dragon and was going to take the next shuttle off moon. But a meal was included with their room, and Ninienne still felt strangely responsible for this grown man in a hair suit.

They drew a few looks from the regulars in the saloon, but no one approached them. At their booth, Rodando tore into his horn rabbit like, well, a beast.

"I think I prefer them raw, actually." Rodando licked his fingers daintily. "I've developed quite the taste."

Gossamaw, ever the strategist, hid under the table and snapped up Rodando's scraps.

The doors swung open and Benno walked in. Ninienne stood to greet him with a hug. He looked surprised.

"I just stopped in to say hi to Meg," he said. "What are you doing here?"

"That will take a minute to explain. How's Copper?"

"She's good, walking fine. I thought you were going to come check on her?"

"I've been trying. It's been a wild few days. I'll have to catch you up." She cocked her head toward the booth where Rodando was sucking meat off a bone.

They walked over. Benno stopped when he saw Rodando and eyed the lines of the demonologist's pectorals through the open shirt.

"Who's this?" he asked with immediate suspicion.

Rodando put out a hand, palm down, as if he expected Benno to kiss it. "Rodando Vechi, Demonologist." With a flick of his wrist and a puff of crimson smoke, a black business card with silver letters appeared in his hand. "Ah! Still got it," he said, pleased with himself. "I suppose I'm freelance now."

Benno took the card as if it were a carnivorous worm and slid into the booth next to Ninienne.

"He used to be the Night Stalker," Ninienne offered. "Rodando was Salagrix's last apprentice. The dryad turned him into a beast."

This did nothing to ingratiate Benno toward the demonologist.

"Ninienne has been very kind and generous," said Rodando. "The meal, the room."

"You got a room with this guy?" Benno asked.

Ninienne shook her head. "Benno—"

"I mean, I haven't seen you for a few days, and suddenly you're sharing a room with a muscular demon in a hair shirt who used to be a monster. I'm just trying to keep up."

Ninienne wove a calming spell into her voice. "Benno, listen, it's fine. There's more going on here—"

"Okay." Benno sighed and relaxed, but then snapped up out of the booth as if bitten. "Did you just use magic on me?"

"You seemed a little anxious. I was trying to help."

Benno looked at Ninienne in utter disbelief and shock. "Whatever. I don't have time for this. There's a big shipment coming in and I just heard the shuttle land. I've gotta go to work." He beelined out of the saloon and the doors swung behind him.

"Friend of yours?" Rodando asked, using a toothpick.

"I hope so," said Ninienne, crestfallen. "I'm going to need all the friends I can get." She sighed. "Anyway, he said the shuttle's here. I'll walk you down."

AS THEY HEADED DOWN the dusty street towards the spacepad, Rodando took in the town. "Wow. This place is even more of a dump than when I was here."

They walked past the gap in the buildings with the trail that led up to Salagrix's tower. Gossamaw stopped suddenly and sniffed with searching nostrils.

"What is it?" Ninienne asked, but she knew. She could hear the whispering from the woods.

"Problem?" Rodando asked.

"I'm just going to take Gossie into the woods for a minute. You go on ahead, I'll catch up."

Rodando continued his stroll down the street, examining his fingernails.

Ninienne followed Gossamaw into the shady shelter of the trees. After only a few steps, she immediately felt the presence of the dryad.

"Dryad! Is that you?"

The scent of sap wafted in as, between two trees, leaves and branches shaped themselves into a pouting figure.

"I thought we were friends!" came the rustling reply. "I trusted you."

Ninienne furrowed her brow. "Of course we're friends. What's wrong?"

The dryad crossed her branches. "You undid my beast charm. His punishment wasn't finished."

"Oh." Ninienne was taken aback. "I didn't know it was a transformation charm. All I saw was a beast in pain. I thought I was helping."

The dryad put her hand on her hips. "The beast was also protecting these woods. What's to stop you humans from overrunning it now?"

Ninienne sighed. "I'm sorry. I didn't realize. If there's anything I can do to make it right, let me know."

"Asama is still in chains. Are you really going to free her?"

"Look!" Ninienne shouted. The wind picked up and shook all the leaves and branches around them and she realized her mistake. She immediately bowed.

But it was too late. The dryad maintained an unimpressed expression as she faded into the dark forest.

NINIENNE AND GOSSAMAW caught up with Rodando and they reached the spacepad without further incident. There, she found Benno looking over a dozen crates the same size and shape as the one Chirp had arrived in.

"Can you get those up the trail by yourself?" she asked.

Benno scrunched his mouth and looked at his busted datapad. If their recent tiff bothered him, he was too focused now to show it. "Actually, it looks like these came with pre-loaded orders. I'm supposed to open them up here." He went to fetch a crowbar from his grav cart.

"And here is where I take my leave of you," said Rodando, with a slight bow.

"Are you sure there isn't anything I can say to get you to stay and help?"

Rodando bit his lip. "Ah, no," he said, with the air of someone who had been offered to sniff garbage. "But good luck with... whatever this is." He waggled his fingers toward the crates.

The demonologist turned on his heel and entered the shuttle. The pilot stopped him. "You got a ticket, hair suit?"

Rodando put an arm around the pilot's shoulders and a business card appeared in his hand. "Have you ever thought your life might be improved by a demonic assistant?" They disappeared inside the craft.

Benno returned with the crowbar.

"Listen, Benno, I'm sorry. I was just helping him out."

Benno set down the crowbar and looked at Ninienne, suddenly vulnerable. "Have you ever used magic on me before?"

"No, I'm sorry. I don't know what I was thinking." What she was thinking was that she might run out of chances to use magic at all, and was trying to keep a hold of it like a climber on a slippery cliff.

"I need to know I can trust you."

"You can trust me," Ninienne blurted, desperately.

"What's going on?"

It all tumbled out of her, everything that had happened since she last saw him: the bramblehawk dying, the Night Stalker, enchanting the sword, repairing Chirp, meeting the dryad, finding the dragon, losing her apprenticeship, healing Rodando.

"After all that, if I lost my apprenticeship and my only friend here on the same day, I don't know what I'd do."

Benno held her shoulders and looked her in the eyes. "I shouldn't have assumed anything. That was stupid of me. I was being stupid."

"You're not stupid." Ninienne wiped her eyes. Her smile turned mischievous. "You know what's stupid? Your hat is stupid."

Benno cracked a smile and adjusted his floppy mushroom hat. "Hey. I happen to like this hat."

"I'm just saying."

"Wizards don't know anything about hats. You all wear the same hat. No appreciation for variety." Gossamaw jumped up on a crate and Benno gave him a belly rub. "You like my hat, don't you Gossie?"

Ninienne laughed and embraced Benno.

They held each other like that for a long time, unbothered as the shuttle departed and kicked up whorls of black dust around their ankles.

"This is nice," said Benno. "And I would like to do more of this later. But I should probably get back to work."

They parted, Ninienne feeling a little sheepish. A few onlookers had gathered to look at the array of crates, which made a large impression on the tiny spacepad.

Benno grabbed the crowbar and, with Ninienne's help, opened up the first crate and removed the cosmifoam topper. Inside, they found another android, identical to the one she had grown so familiar with, except this one was unscarred and in pristine condition.

They popped open each crate until there were twelve androids laying down like a robot slumber party.

Benno looked at his datapad. "Okay... then, to deliver their orders, I'm supposed to tap... here!" He pressed a button, and every android lit up with the dancing lights of the initialization sequence.

The androids sat up. The cascade of uncanny movement gave Ninienne full-body tremors.

"I have orders from Master Salagrix," each said, staggered down the line like a bizarre echo, and they all climbed out of their crates.

The androids marched through the wrought-iron spacepad archway and into town, peeling off into various buildings. One approached Benno's grav cart and began stacking crates on it.

"Hey! That's mine!" Benno shouted.

The android took the datapad out of his hands. "I am here to be your replacement. You are relieved of this burden," it said.

"Wait... wait a minute. What?"

The android ignored this question and guided the full cart down the street. Ninienne and Benno followed until they heard a commotion at the saloon and ran down to investigate.

Ninienne peeked through the swinging doors and saw Meg face-to-face with an android behind the bar.

"This is my saloon! You can't just come in here and kick me out!" the cyborg bartender shouted.

"I have my orders from Master Salagrix," the android intoned. "I am here to be your replacement. You are relieved of this burden."

Meg shoved the intruder with her robotic arm, and the android, in a single fluid movement, pinned her facedown onto the bar.

"I do not wish to harm you," the android said in a calm, neutral voice, "But I must fulfill my orders."

A grizzled drunk stood up from his booth. "Hey, leave Meg alone!" he slurred.

"Get out of here!" shouted another customer.

A bottle flew and smashed against the android's head. Its eyes turned from white to red.

Before she could see what happened next, Ninienne heard shouting from outside. She turned to the street to see similar scenes playing out between people and androids scattered up and down the town.

Farlow rode in on Copper. Benno and Ninienne ran up to him.

"What's going on?" asked Farlow.

"I didn't know this would happen," said Benno. "Salagrix ordered all these androids. I pushed the button, and now they're taking over. If I had known..."

"It's not your fault, boy." Farlow scanned the gathering crowd with a steady brow and then said to himself, "Shoulda seen this comin'."

The old lady that had singled out Ninienne before reappeared and brandished an accusatory finger. "It's them! I saw them at the spacepad. She's a wizard! They work for Salagrix!"

Angry villagers turned their attention from the androids to the two young people and closed in around them.

"Farlow," said a stout, mean-looking villager, punching his fist into his hand. "You best start doing some explaining on behalf of your nephew."

"Really, Targ?" said Farlow, looking down from his crowhorse. "It's come to this?"

"Everyone knows you take the wizard's coin."

"Who doesn't?" Farlow called out. "Without the wizard's coin, this town would have dried up a long time ago." He steadied Copper and addressed the crowd. "I know we're all shaken up, but let's not lose our heads."

"Yeah! They should lose theirs!" someone jeered, and the crowd joined in an angry cheer.

"Now hold on one jumba-pickin' minute!" Farlow shouted. "A buncha robots come to town and y'all turn on each other like a nest a' fairy rats. That's not the Gulch I know. That's not the Gulch my folks worked their whole lives tryin' ta build."

"But that wizard's gone too far this time!" shouted Meg, nursing a bruise to her face. "That saloon was all I had!" Her voice cracked and several villagers gathered to comfort.

"I know what happened to the water!" Ninienne shouted. "Salagrix took it and has been using it for himself. I think we can get the water back, but I'm going to need help."

"Why should we believe anything a wizard says?" asked Fist-in-Hand.

Farlow's face maintained the same unreadable expression. "I vouch for her. She healed my Copper up and asked for nothin' in return." This seemed to still the crowd. "Gather up everyone and meet at the Common House in an hour. Then we'll she what she has to say."

24.

I love Gregor—he will always be Gregor to me, never Salagrix—but I fear something has changed him. Perhaps it is the weight of his new position. Or perhaps this moon is cursed, as the settlers say. If I were not around, I fear what he might become without me.

— from Eldrathea's personal diary

THE APPOINTED TIME arrived and the residents of Black Gulch gathered in the official-looking building at the end of the street. Worn faces, smudged with the black dirt of the Shadow Moon, stared up at Ninienne from the rows of benches. There were fewer of them than she might have thought, maybe just over a hundred.

An android sat behind a lectern at the front of the room. The previous town manager stood nearby, holding her hat and looking out of sorts.

"I now call this meeting to order!" announced the android and, above a few jeers: "We will proceed according to procedure. Miss Ninienne Lightcaster has the floor."

Ninienne felt the eyes of Black Gulch upon her, these angry strangers.

"Yes. Hi. A lot of you don't know me. And that's on me, honestly. My bad. I'm Salagrix's apprentice—" There were boos from the crowd. "Fair. That's fair. But I'm here to help.

"Salagrix has captured the water dragon of the Shadow Moon. He's using it to enhance his power and increase his lifespan. That's why there's very little water here."

There were murmurs, mostly swears, from the assembled crowd.

"There's a key that will release the dragon. I've been told where it is. If I can get to the key and get it down to the basement, I can free the dragon, cut off Salagrix's power source, and presumably return water to the Shadow Moon. The problem is Salagrix himself. He will try to stop me, and I don't think I can overpower him on my own. I'll need help."

"Whatever we're doing, I'm in." Meg stood up from the crowd. "It's not like I have anything else to do."

"What's your plan?" came another voice.

"We'll need to distract Salagrix and pull him away from the tower. That should give me enough space to sneak in and get the key."

"What about the Night Stalker?" shouted a woman.

"I have neutralized the beast," said Ninienne. "It won't be a problem."

Impressed hums rose from the crowd.

"Night Stalker or no, I'm not going up against that wizard," shouted a grumpy farmer from the back. "That's a death sentence."

"I'm not asking anyone to do anything they don't want to do. But if you want water to come back to this moon, if you want to put Salagrix in his place for the way he's treated you, here is your chance."

Benno stood up next to Ninienne. "I love this moon. It's my home. And I'm willing to fight for it."

The hubbub from the crowd grew. Farlow stood up and punched the air. "I'm ready to get that wizard!"

There were shouts of agreement from the quickly coalescing mob. But there was a contingent gathered at the back, speaking in furtive tones about catching the next shuttle out of here.

The android behind the lectern banged the gavel. "Meeting adjourned."

DESPITE THE ANDROIDS taking over positions in the town on Salagrix's orders, they seemed unperturbed by the gathering mob bent on attacking their master. It reminded Ninienne of the early days with Chirp, before the full understanding of duties had really set in. These were baby robots who did not yet comprehend what was going on around them.

The mob collected what weapons they had—rifles, farm tools, broken railings—and gathered at the trailhead. Even Gossamaw had found a little stick and waved it about menacingly before chewing and eating it.

"Remember," said Farlow, to the assembled crowd, "We need to pull Salagrix away from the tower so that Ninienne and Benno can get in. For Black Gulch!"

The mob cheered and began the hike up the trail.

Ninienne and Benno rode Copper up the winding path with the mob of angry villagers behind them. Gossamaw sat in Benno's lap with a determined expression and a webbed paw curled into a fist.

"Thanks for helping," said Ninienne into Benno's back.

"Of course. This is my home," he said.

They were high enough on the trail to overlook the town when murmurs of concern and worried yelps bubbled up from the villagers.

"What's going on?" Ninienne asked, turning back.

"Sounds," said one of the old men. "There're sounds in the woods."

"The Night Stalker is gone!" Ninienne announced. "There's nothing to worry about!"

A villager screamed. "That branch tried to grab me!"

"This root tried to trip me!"

Ninienne heard the dryad's voice blow through her mind like a strong wind. *It's like I said. Without my beast to defend the woods, the humans are invading.*

"That's not what's happening!" said Ninienne. "They're after Salagrix."

They bring their anger and their weapons. Without my beast, all I have left are my tricks.

"Listen to me," said Ninienne. "We are here to help. We're trying to free the dragon."

"Who are you talking to?" asked Benno.

"The dryad. Keep riding."

The forest remembers.

At once, branches shot out from both sides of the path and slapped at villagers. Well-worn roots emerged from the ground and grabbed ankles. The mob, alarmed, took their weapons to the trees. A rifle shot went off and blasted a trunk to splinters.

"Save your charges! Keep moving!" shouted Farlow. "Stay in the center of the path!"

But this was no well-trained militia. This was a hastily gathered group of angry farmers. They beat back the branches with their improvised weapons.

Then came the sound of mechanical marching. All twelve androids from the village, eyes turned red, hiked up in formation behind the mob and cut off their exit.

"Return to the village at once," the androids announced in unison.

"They must have finally figured out what was going on," said Ninienne. "Or Salagrix did and sent new orders."

But the woods did not discriminate. They slapped and tripped up the androids just the same.

The trail erupted into a carnival of chaos: trees fighting humans, androids fighting trees, humans fighting androids.

Copper, however, remained untouched.

"Why aren't the trees attacking us?" Benno asked.

"It must be my amulet," said Ninienne, looking at the amber sigil still around her neck.

A rifle shot burst through an android's shoulder. A spray of fiery sparks scattered into the underbrush, dry from decades of drought conditions. Little licks of flame took hold.

"We don't have time for this. Let's get out of here," said Ninienne.

"What about Salagrix?" Benno asked, with the slightest tremor in his lip.

"We'll figure that out when we get there. Let's ride."

Benno shook the reins and they shot up the path.

WHEN THEY ARRIVED AT the circular field, Ninienne turned back to see a column of black smoke rising from further down the woody slope. The last thing they needed right now was a forest fire.

They dismounted. Ninienne tried the front door, but found it locked.

"I figured, but it was worth a shot."

"What if we ring the doorgong?" Benno asked. "Pretend it's a delivery?"

"It's a good idea, but I'd rather not let them know we're here if we can help it. It's only a matter of time before Salagrix sees that smoke and figures out what's going on, if he hasn't already."

Ninienne walked around the tower, and could see the open window to her former room two stories up. Her failed garden was directly below.

"I wonder..." she said.

She knew enough plant magic to force vines to grow up the side of the tower to the window, but it was tricky to get close enough for a spell without a jawed cucumber biting her.

"I'm going to tie up Copper," said Benno.

"Good, go ahead. She did great. She deserves a rest."

Gossamaw gurgled. She turned to see her familiar pointing at his mouth and rubbing his tummy.

"Oh, Gossie, I'm so sorry. I forgot to feed you today." She slapped her pockets and found a packet of crumbled Demon Cookies. She opened it and spilled the contents on the ground, which Gossamaw lapped up hungrily.

Ninienne turned back to the garden. She tried to touch the soil but a toothy carrot snapped at her finger. She frowned and crossed her arms in thought.

Gossamaw made a retching sound. The frogdog rolled over with a nauseated expression and burped out a little cloud of crimson vapor.

"Oh, no! Sorry, buddy. I didn't know anything about those. They were probably expired."

Gossamaw's eyes rolled around in their sockets, and his tongue waggled around like an excited snake.

"Whoa," said Benno, who had come around the tower to see Gossamaw's skin pulse and turn red.

The frogdog began to grow. He doubled, tripled in size, and kept going. Little horns sprouted from his head and large, bat-like wings unfolded from his back. Before Ninienne's eyes, her familiar transformed into an enormous, demonic version of himself.

"Okay, didn't know that would happen." Ninienne crouched before this new creature. "Are you alright?"

The giant tongue waggled. She felt through her familiar connection. He was the same Gossamaw inside. He just looked different now.

"I hope this isn't a permanent change," she said. "And you feel okay?"

Her familiar nodded excitedly, which, because of the new size of his head, caused a slight breeze.

Ninienne sighed. One thing at a time. "Okay. Sorry about feeding you weird snacks, but it seems like you're doing fine, besides the transformed-into-a-demon thing. Let's get back to trying to get inside the tower."

"Um," said Benno, "I don't want to be that guy, but do those wings work?"

Ninienne looked at her familiar's new accessory. "I think I know what you're thinking. So, Gossie, do they work?"

Gossamaw shrieked with the fury of hell, flapped his new wings, and launched himself off the ground for a quick loop in the sky.

"Nice work, buddy." Ninienne pointed at the window. "So, do you think you can get us up there?"

Gossamaw chortled menacingly and nodded with a deranged smile. Ninienne would have been terrified of this creature if she hadn't known it wasn't actually her softie of a familiar.

"Hop on," Ninienne called to Benno.

Benno sighed. "Why do I even bother having ideas?"

The two mounted and rode the demon frogdog up to the window. Gossamaw, still getting used to his new form, had more power than precision, and hit the tower with a reverberating slam.

"Not great." Ninienne winced and climbed over her transformed familiar's head through the narrow window. She offered Benno a hand and pulled him in.

"Alright, Gossie, plan's still the same," she said to her demonic companion, flapping just outside the window.

"Make a distraction. Go get up on the roof and see if you can pull Salagrix up there."

Gossamaw nodded with unhinged glee and flew off.

Ninienne looked around. Her room was just as she had left it that morning. By the Worlds, it had been a long day. Soon, they heard a rumble and crunch from the roof.

"Okay," said Ninienne to a tense Benno. "Hopefully that worked, and we can get up to his chambers without running into anyone."

They snuck up the stairs. There was no one in the lower workshop, but there was a dismantled stage. Ninienne's heart went out to Chirp, despite their betrayal. The two friends climbed past the kitchen without incident, and Ninienne could hear a wild commotion from the upper workshop.

"Hadrarch! Assist me! Attack!" she heard Salagrix shouting above the sound of collapsing roof beams.

Good. That meant both wizard and android were upstairs.

They reached the entrance to Salagrix's chambers. She tried the door, and found it unlocked.

With an incredible sigh of relief, Ninienne entered the room.

It was dark. At first, she thought the ceiling was open to the night sky, which made no sense. It wasn't yet night and there was another floor above. But as her eyes adjusted, she realized it was a charm: tiny dots of light twinkled from the ceiling, giving the illusion of a starry sky. An over-furnished four-poster bed sagged in the middle of the room as though its spirit had been broken. Shelves lined the walls, stacked with devices that defied description or understanding. There was a bathtub and garderobe, similar to those in the apprentice's room, but the curtain had turned to threads. A nightstand stood next to the bed, and on it sat a jeweled box about the size of a book.

Ninienne's heart leaped. This had to be it. She ran to the box and opened it up.

Inside were two printed photograms. In one, a younger Salagrix stood next to a woman with silvery hair and wise eyes. In between them, smiling as wide as she could, stood a girl of about five. They were all in front of a lake surrounded by the familiar trees of the Shadow Moon.

The other photogram was of the same girl, now a young woman, with long black hair in a green dress. She was on a stage, and her mouth was open, mid-song.

His precious things.

There was no key.

Ninienne's mind raced. Could Rodando have misled her? Why? Or had Salagrix stashed the key somewhere else in the last twenty years?

She wanted to ransack the room, turn over everything, but Benno hissed from the doorway.

"Someone's coming!"

Ninienne swore and bolted from the room, grabbing Benno as she went. The sounds of combat continued upstairs, but unmistakable metallic footsteps drew closer.

"We'll never outrun Chirp," said Ninienne. "Quick, in here!" She swung open the door to the kitchen and shoved them both inside, and slammed the door as quickly as she dared.

Quiggleam looked up from his game. "Hey, what are you—"

Ninienne put a desperate finger to her lips. The demon clammed up.

They heard Chirp rush down the stairs. The steps stopped just outside the door. Ninienne held her breath, hoping beyond hope that the next sound she heard would be more footsteps. Instead, she heard something that made her blood freeze.

"Intruders, I know you are here," called Chirp's calm voice. "You tripped the ward in Salagrix's chambers and I can detect you in the kitchen. I do not wish to use force to open this door, but I will if I must."

Benno looked at Ninienne with inquisitive fear.

"Chirp, it's me," she called. "Can we talk?"

There was a pause that felt enormous. "My Master is engaged in battle. I do not have time to talk."

"Please, I just need the dragon key. This can all be over if you just tell me where it is."

Chirp's whirring was loud enough to overcome the smashing from upstairs. Ninienne hoped, distantly, that Gossamaw wasn't getting hurt.

"I can't tell you that."

"Because you don't know where it is, or Salagrix forbade you from telling?"

There was another excruciating pause. "I know where the key is."

"Tell me!" Ninienne shouted.

"You will have to open the door."

Ninienne bit her lip. Could this be a deception? It wasn't like Chirp to lie outright. They had said they knew where the key was. But why did Ninienne have to open the door?

The fight from upstairs quieted. She heard Salagrix call down.

"Hadrarch! Have you found the intruders?"

"I have, Master. They have barricaded themselves in the kitchen."

"Well, blast the door down, then! I'm finished up here. The villagers are rioting. We'll have to put them down next."

Ninienne's heart trembled. She knew Gossamaw wasn't dead—she would have felt that through their connection—but worried what state Salagrix might have put him in.

But for now, she was out of options. Opening the door was preferable to having it splintered by the android.

She opened the door.

In the stairwell stood Chirp. The android who had betrayed her but who she couldn't help but keep trusting, hoping that somehow she could get through and save them.

"Okay, I opened the door. What happens now?"

Chirp stepped into the kitchen and shut the door behind them. It was getting cramped in here. Ninienne backed up into the stove and could feel the hot thrumming of the hellgate within.

"I cannot tell you where the key is," said Chirp. The android pointed to their scar.

"What, because of the sword? I'm sorry, that was an accident. I would have never done that to you on purpose. It was my fault for enchanting the sword, but it was to defend the tower from the Night Stalker! I was careless. I would never hurt you on purpose."

Chirp put their hand on Ninienne's shoulder, gently, tenderly. They pointed to their scar with their other hand, and said, in tones so patient and kind she could only think of them as human, "I cannot *tell* you where the key is."

The android's finger drew Ninienne's eyes to the scar. She did not like to look at the reminder of her mistake. But she could see through the opening into the whirring mechanisms inside. There, along the same angle as the scar, was a long black piece of metal with golden wiring.

"The key! It's inside you!" Ninienne jumped for joy. "You couldn't *tell me,* but you could *show* me. Oh, Chirp, you're brilliant!" She hugged the android, and the android hugged her back.

After they parted, Ninienne said. "Alright, so we just have to get it out of there."

She reached for the scar and Chirp grabbed her wrist automatically. "That's where this gets difficult," they said.

"What do you mean?" Ninienne struggled against Chirp's grip.

"My orders are to protect the key," said Chirp. "I very much want to give it to you, but my orders forbid me."

Ninienne stepped away and Chirp released her. Her mind scrambled. "How can I do this?"

"You will have to overpower me," said Chirp. "Or deceive me."

Ninienne sighed the sigh of the weary. "I don't know that I can."

A rumbling descended the staircase. Salagrix grew closer.

"Looks like you're in a tight spot," said Quiggleam. "Here's that favor that I owe ya."

Quiggleam snapped his fingers, and all hell broke loose.

25.

"We can always count on demons to do two things: strictly uphold the contract, and stretch the meaning of that same contract into unrecognizable forms, depending on their fiendish aims."

—from Graveport's Guide to Infernal Contracts, 3rd edition

THE DEVIL'S HEAD STOVE opened its oven-mouth and a fiery wind ripped through the kitchen. The vortex shrieked and burst beyond the confines of the oven like tongues made of storm clouds that were also on fire. Chirp grabbed onto the opposite counter to avoid being sucked in, but whirling tentacles lashed onto their limbs and pulled the flailing android into the flaming void. The oven slammed shut, and the kitchen was still once more.

"What did you do that for!?" Ninienne shouted. Benno had pressed himself up against the cabinets, eyes wide.

Quiggleam made a face. "I *think* what you meant to say was *thank you*. You needed to defeat the android and now. It is. Defeated." The demon did a celebratory shoulder shimmy.

"The key was inside Chirp! Without that key, Salagrix is invincible! Not to mention whatever you did to Chirp."

"Ah, I see that now." Quiggleam slouched on his stool and sighed. "I probably should have told you earlier, but I have soup for brains."

Tears welled up in Ninienne's eyes. After all she had been through with the android, to have them suddenly ripped away, even after the betrayals, was a shock. "Is Chirp...really gone?"

"What? No." Quiggleam seemed slightly offended. "It's not a black hole. It's just a hellgate. The android's in the hellworld now."

Ninienne collected herself. "So we could go in and bring Chirp back?"

"Only if you wanted to be trapped for all eternity!" Quiggleam snorted. "Ha! Oh! But I could give you this." He reached inside his mouth and wiggled out a nubby tooth, which he handed to Ninienne. "Scratch this when you want to come back, and I can pull you out."

"Wait, what?"

"I'll be able to feel it, even when it's not connected to my body. Demon thing. I'll be like, 'Hey! Someone's scratching my tooth!' And I'll remember to pull you out."

"You can just pull stuff out of the hellworld whenever you want?"

"Sure, like reaching under the bed. You can't see, but you can feel around for stuff."

"Why can't you just pull the android out?"

"Because I don't know where he is, dummy." Quiggleam stuck out his tongue and made an idiotic face. "But, if you keep a hold of my tooth, I'll be able to feel you. You all stay together, and I'll pull you all out together. But I can only do it one time, so make sure you're ready."

Putting their lives in Quiggleam's hands did not fill Ninienne with the utmost confidence. She looked at the tooth in her palm and then at Benno. "Do you want to do this?"

Benno looked to the stairwell, where the sounds of Salagrix loomed ever closer.

"Better than taking our chances with that wizard."

Ninienne tucked the tooth safely in the front pocket of her overalls. She opened up the oven and felt the hot wind of the hellworld blast her face. She grabbed Benno's hand.

"Not where I thought this day was going," she said, and they jumped into hell.

FIERY SHRIEKS WHIPPED at them. They fell so far and for so long that Ninienne thought her insides had left her body and would never return.

They landed, or, more accurately, stopped falling because they were already on the ground. Ninienne felt the rough dirt against her cheek.

She sat up and looked out on an infernal vista. They were on a sloping cliff face above a plain of red rock. Rivers of magma cut deep channels through the expanse while plumes of flame, as thick as forests, burned in an unceasing roar. The scent of hot rocks permeated Ninienne's skull, and the air was like standing in front of an oven, if the oven was on all sides of you at once. Above, what at first looked like a swirling cloud was actually thousands—millions—of flying demons circling a ruddy mountain in a murmuration of horror, black against a sky the color of fresh blood.

Benno's eyes froze open in terror. His mouth failed to put words to the scene before him.

A contingent of demons swooped above them, unaware of the two intruders, but much too close for comfort. Ninienne scanned the cliff, and, spying a cave entrance, pointed it out. They scrambled down the rocky slope and took shelter.

The cave was deep, long enough to get dark, and they pushed inward until they could barely see. The roar of the hellworld was dull and distant.

"Now all we need to do is find Chirp," Ninienne said, breathless.

"Well done, then," came a familiar voice.

She turned into the dark and saw the lit up eyes and mouth of the android.

"Chirp!" she exclaimed. "You're alright!"

"I did not know Quiggleam and I were enemies," said Chirp, approaching. "I will update my relationship matrix."

"It was just a misunderstanding. He was trying to help. I can get us all back. Benno, get over here."

There were a few strangled sobs from the darkness. "This has been... a very weird day."

"It's alright. Just hold it together. Let's all get in close and I'll figure out this demon's tooth."

As she fished around in her pocket, she heard a whooshing noise and felt the sensation of falling backward.

When the motion stopped, she found herself in a different cave, chained. There were lit torches on either side of her. As she craned her neck, she discovered herself on a large raised stone slab in the center of the cave. In front of her was a demon.

If Ninienne had thought all demons looked like Quiggleam, she was horribly, tragically wrong. This demon's body was shiny black, segmented like a millipede's, and descended into an indistinguishable, writhing morass of insectoid limbs. It had one pair of arms near the head that ended in hands that looked human, except that they were black and shiny like a beetle shell. Then, in what looked like the worst attempt at a human costume in all the Twelve Thousand Worlds, it had the mask-like face of a porcelain doll, sooty with ash. One eyelid, stuck half-way shut, gave the demon a woozy, drunken appearance.

"Ah yes-s-s, the young apprentice." The demon's voice slithered, matching the body but not the face. "I have tas-s-sted your torment. Your loneliness-s-s is quite exquis-s-site. Having you here is so much fres-s-sher."

Ninienne shuddered. "What do you mean, fresher?"

"The contract gave our hellworld rights to all the s-s-suffering in the tower." The demon shared this fast as if it enjoyed the dread it caused Ninienne. "Delicious-s-s. The old wizard has provided me with the mos-s-st. It will be a s-s-shame when his fragile mortal body finally crumbles-s-s."

This was a nasty detail that Rodando had neglected to mention. The idea that this thing had been feasting on her loneliness for her entire apprenticeship filled her with a heavy dread.

"So that was the deal? A kitchen demon in exchange for our suffering?"

The demon drummed its fingers together in delight. "Yes-s-s."

"I don't see how I can be bound by a contract I didn't agree to and was written before I was born."

This stilled the demon's writhing.

"Did the deal also give you the right to hold us here against our will?" Ninienne challenged. "Or are you in breach of contract?"

The doll-faced demon wriggled demurely. "It did not. I jus-s-st wanted a little tas-s-ste."

"Technically," said Ninienne, improvising wildly, "Quiggleam hasn't even been working these last couple of months. Which means, if you've been eating our suffering, you are in debt to us."

The demon hissed angrily, and a tongue like a thousand spider legs flicked out of the doll's mouth. "I knew that imp was too s-s-stupid to handle even a s-s-simple job. Very well. Begone then!"

The demon's voice echoed as Ninienne felt the flipping sensation once again and found herself back in the darkness of the first cave.

"Chirp! Benno! Are you there?"

"I'm here!" shouted Benno's voice from the darkness. "You both disappeared. Where did you go?"

"Some place I hope to never go again," she said. "Where's Chirp?"

"The android disappeared at the same time as you."

"I talked myself out of demon torture," said Ninienne. Benno's eyes widened, and he gulped. "Hopefully Chirp can do the same."

They heard an electronic wailing from outside the cave and dashed to the entrance. A horrible mass of flesh had Chirp in its claws, and enormous tarp-like wings flapped as it flew off towards the mountain.

"Chirp!" Ninienne shouted.

"Help me!" Chirp called, barely audible against the roar of the hellworld.

Ninienne reached out in vain as she stumbled down the cliff.

She circled her thumb and forefinger and cast a lensing spell that allowed her to see far distances. At the peak of the mountain was a crumbling, ruined temple thronged with demons.

"I think that's where they're headed," said Ninienne. "Let's get moving."

But Benno did not get moving. He trembled at the cave mouth, eyes wide, clutching himself as if his arms might fly off.

Ninienne climbed back up the cliff to look her friend in the face.

"Hey," she said. "I know this is scary. But we have to get that android, and that key. All we have to do is get close enough for Quiggleam to pull us all out."

"How—how—"

"I don't know. But we're not getting any closer by hiding in this cave. We need to move."

Benno's frantic eyes searched Ninienne's face.

"Just stay with me, alright? Stick close to the wizard."

Ninienne took Benno's hand and led him deeper into hell.

IT WAS SLOW GOING DOWN the rocky slope, and they headed toward a natural bridge across the magma river that Ninienne had spied on the way. Benno's panic kept their pace to a halting walk.

There's no way we're going to make it to the mountain at this rate, thought Ninienne. *And I can't leave him. Not like this. We need another way.*

They stopped for a break underneath a striking growth of orange crystals. A flock of large, one-eyed demons that walked on their wings like bats were diving in and out of the magma and cawing with delight. Benno curled up and shivered.

As Ninienne leaned her head against the crystal, sparkling fragments from within caught her eye. She had seen this before—abyssalite! And here was an enormous patch of it.

She grabbed a rock and broke off chunks of crystal to stuff her pockets. She knew how valuable it was back home, and if she was going to live a life of banishment, getting started with a big sack of coins could only help.

One of the bat demons approached them, sniffing the ground. Ninienne stood and readied herself, but there was nothing immediately threatening in the creature's behavior. Its row of sniffling nostrils appeared to be sucking up something that Ninienne couldn't see, and it made its way towards Benno.

"Give him some space, okay?" The demon blinked its enormous single eye at Ninienne and then went back to sniffling. Ninienne noticed its broad back, wide enough to sit on, and thought that, if she could get it to cooperate, they might ride it.

The demon kept pushing in towards Benno. "Hey, back up, alright? He's pretty scared right now." In the back of Ninienne's mind, a little light clicked on. "Oh, is that what you want? Does his fear taste good?" She let the demon approach until it was sniffling right up to Benno's back.

"I think we can work out a deal," said Ninienne, using her hands to demonstrate. "If you give us a ride to that mountain over there, you can eat his fear. Does that sound good?"

"Sounds like a deal to me," said the demon. "Just stop talking to me like I'm an idiot."

THE DEMON, WHOSE NAME turned out to be Kathrall, loaded Ninienne and the catatonic Benno onto her back and took off over the blazing hellworld.

The landscape opened up beneath them, but it was more of the same: magma, flame, red rocks, and swarms of demons. The hot air rushed around Ninienne, enveloping her senses, until they descended, spiraling, to the outside of the mountain temple and landed near a crumbled wall.

"This is far as I will go," said Kathrall. "This is a devil's place."

"Oh, I didn't realize that demons and devils were different."

"Racist," spat the demon.

Chastened, Ninienne set Benno on the ground. Kathrall sniffled all over him and seemed to enjoy herself.

"That doesn't hurt him at all, does it?"

"Shouldn't."

"Does that take away his fear?"

Ninienne wasn't sure how Kathrall managed a withering expressing with just one eye, but she did. "You're a temporal being, right? You're experiencing this visit to the hellworld as if time is passing, because that's what your body knows how to do, but it's not actually happening that way. There's no 'before I consume his fear' and 'after I consume his fear.' This entire hellworld exists as a single, undifferentiated event, and to the extent anything can happen here, it happens all at once."

"Oh."

Kathrall took a long, final snuffle. "That's the good stuff." She nodded contentedly. "Good luck with the devils. Now, if you'll excuse me, I'm late for my five P.M. book club."

"Wait, but you just said—"

Kathrall was already in the air. "Undifferentiated!" Her call faded into the distance.

Ninienne didn't have time to figure that one out, which, she realized, was exactly the problem. She roused Benno and sat him upright.

"Where are we?" he asked, groggy.

"Outside of a devil temple where they took the android."

"Oh, so a normal place. Got it."

Further down, the wall crumbled low enough that they could climb inside.

"Down there," said Ninienne.

"Five more minutes," groaned Benno.

"Remember, all we have to do is stick together and get close enough to the android that Quiggleam can pull us all out. Can you do that? Just stay with me."

Benno nodded weakly, and Ninienne pulled him up to standing.

They climbed over the ruined wall into a corridor intersected by other corridors, all in disrepair. Ninienne immediately noticed that this place did not follow right angles, as she might have expected, but some unknown geometry. The hallways branched and joined at strange, asymmetrical corners. From above, she had noticed a large open area at the center of the complex, and figured that would be the natural gathering place.

"This way," Ninienne said, and they continued down a ruined hallway.

But the partial destruction of the already unusual temple turned the place into a labyrinth. Piles of rubble blocked hallways. Felled statues, weathered beyond recognition, created long, insurmountable obstacles. Areas that might have been shrines opened up with multiple exits at odd angles that only led back to the same shrine—or was it a different shrine of identical design? Since they were on top of a mountain, there were no objects on the horizon they could see to use as landmarks, and looking straight up into the swirling storm of demons only invited nausea and terror.

Now totally lost, and Benno losing what remained of his sanity, they turned a corner and ran into a pair of tall, black, skeletal demons—or were they devils?—with wicked horned faces and spears to match.

"Intruders!" one shouted.

Ninienne grabbed Benno and they bolted as fast as they could. Which, because of Benno's shock and exhaustion, was little more than a jog. The devil patrol quickly surrounded them and blocked both exits with their nasty spears.

"Boss will want to see these two," chittered one.

"Yeah," the other one said through gnashing mandibles. "Let's take 'em to the boss."

THE GUARDS LED NINIENNE and Benno through the maze of the ruined temple and they eventually arrived at the clearing in the center.

Broken pillars of the temple surrounded furnishings of a different kind: blazing braziers, wicked watchtowers, and an enormous throne all made of the same shiny black shells that covered the devils. Upon closer inspection, she discovered the adornments were actually made of pieces of devils: arms and heads and torsos, all arranged in a mass of spikes. The scent of sulfur and something spicy wafted from the open fires. Demons and devils of various shapes and postures milled about in a formal and festive atmosphere.

Ninienne's heart beat against her ribs when she saw Chirp, bound and kneeling, in front of the throne. The guards pushed the two friends into the same posture. Benno fell over onto his side.

"We found these two trespassing on our grounds, boss," said a guard.

The figure on the throne rose. Larger than the other devils by far, he had a protruding lower jaw with thick black teeth that covered the bottom half of his face. His arms and shoulders were large and muscular, and his legs bent backwards, like a goat. His entire body was of that shiny black beetle shell material.

"It is a good day for catches." The large devil's voice was like rocks grinding at the bottom of a well.

A lankier devil on the left-hand side of the throne raised a finger. "Ah, technically not a *day*, because we don't have time here." His voice was like a squeaky marker.

"I know that!" the large devil snapped. "I was using an expression!"

The lanky devil nodded meekly but seemed otherwise uncowed by the display of anger.

"So, trespassers," continued the large devil. "Are you aware of the punishment for trespassing in the hellworlds?"

"Please," said Ninienne. "A demon sent our android here by mistake. We just came to get it back."

"A demon under contract?" The large devil asked pointedly.

"Yes."

The boss called to the assembly. "Find the demon responsible! We need to make sure we do this by the book!"

Several devils milling about the court vanished in black whorls of folded space.

"So, an android, is it?" The large devil turned his attention to Chirp, who had not raised their head, and rubbed his thick hands together. "A fascinating creature with a taste unlike any other before. A body of metal with soulfire. What does an android fear? What suffering rankles the heart of a machine? Bodies of flesh, when tortured, eventually perish. But a mechanical body, well-maintained, that could provide unlimited suffering."

"Just let us go," pleaded Ninienne.

The large devil turned and beheld Ninienne with a curious expression. "Do you know who I am? Do you know who you make demands of?"

"I don't, honestly," said Ninienne.

The boss drew himself up. "I am known by many names. The Light-Bringer. Old Scratch. He Who Howls. The Serpent of Darkness. Mr. Mumblejohns."

"Wait. Are you..." said Ninienne.

"The Devil himself," said the Devil himself.

"Ah, technically," the lanky devil chimed in, "Not *The* Devil, as there are infinitely many hellworlds, so too are there infinitely many Devils. Our world is quite minor—"

"Silence!" shouted One of Infinitely Many Devils. "Why haven't I crushed you yet?"

"My uncle is Beelzebub, sir," replied the lanky devil.

"Nepotism!" shouted the Devil. He shook his head. "It'll be the end of me."

Guard devils reappeared and brought the doll-faced demon before the court. Ninienne noticed the resemblance of the shiny black shells and wondered if this was actually a devil and not a demon, and felt bad for not knowing the difference.

"Name yourself," thundered the Devil.

"Nephrex, my lord." The doll-faced demon bowed her face all the way to the ground.

"Are you responsible for bringing these beings here?"

"It was the doing of one under my command. My subordinate, Quiggleam, is still tied to the material plane, but I have s-s-spoken with him about the s-s-situation. I take res-s-sponsibility and appear in his place."

The Devil sniffed. "And are we within our rights to hold these trespassers?"

"My lord, there is a complication." Nephrex kept her head bowed. "My s-s-subordinate neglected his duties and put us-s-s in breach of contract."

The Devil growled like a thwarted beast. "This demon of yours has caused us quite a lot of trouble, it seems."

"He has s-s-soup for brains-s-s."

"Ah." The Devil nodded knowingly. "I don't know why we ever tried making demons like that. Are there any loopholes in the contract we can exploit?"

"No, it's a tight one. The demonologist was one of those Academy types."

"Blast!" The Devil punched the air with a thick fist. "I hate it when they know what they're doing."

"However, if I may be so bold, my lord, there is-s-s an opportunity." Here, Nephrex raised her head. One of her doll eyes opened while the other remained stuck. "While I was s-s-speaking with my s-s-subordinate, I noticed that the moon he occupies-s-s is currently... unguarded."

The Devil's eyes went wide, white within his shiny black head. "Really. The guardian is...?"

"Indis-s-sposed. So there is an opening."

The Devil paced excitedly. "Is there any way we can finesse this? Give me details. Why did our demon neglect his duties under the contract?"

"My s-s-subordinate, Quiggleam, agreed to let this android perform his duties-s-s in his place." Nephrex gestured to Chirp with a slender arm.

"I see!" said the Devil. "So, this android was acting as our agent then? Fulfilling a role in our demonic contract?" The Devil circled his hands. "And is not one who acts as an agent of hell considered a minor fiend? And do not minor fiends fall under our protection?"

"Ah," Beelzebub's nephew appeared to have an objection, but reconsidered. "No, that works, actually."

"So, our agent is in our territory, and these two natives of an unguarded moon—"

"Neither of them are natives-s-s, sir, but the one in the fetal pos-s-sition is a long-term res-s-sident."

The Devil eyed Benno. "Does he consider the moon his home?"

Nephrex picked up Benno gently by the neck and asked, "Where is your home? Don't be alarmed. Just tell us the place you consider home."

Ninienne had a sinking feeling. "Wait, Benno, I don't know what they're doing, but I don't like it. Don't tell them anything."

Benno sputtered. "The Shadow Moon of Chadron. I—I love my moon. I would fight for it."

"There you are," Nephrex laid Benno back down on the ground and gave him a little pat.

"And a soldier, by his own admission, no less. What about the other one?" The Devil turned to Ninienne, and she felt the intensity of his spotlight gaze.

"She's-s-s a wizard, sir."

"I have nothing to do with this," said Ninienne. "I was sent to the Shadow Moon for my apprenticeship."

"So, an operative of the moon and an...outside mercenary, let's say, invade our territory, hoping to, as they've already admitted, capture our agent." To the extent that the Devil's wide black jaw allowed him to smile, he smiled.

"I think the Deep Courts-s-s could be pers-s-suaded to see it that way, my lord." Nephrex bowed and twirled her arm.

"Any comments from the peanut gallery?" The Devil turned to the lanky devil on his left.

Beelzebub's nephew tapped his chin. "Yes, with the facts arranged that way, it certainly sounds like an act of war."

"Good!" The Devil clapped his hands together. "Nice work, Nephrex. You can take the lead on this one. Prepare an invasion force."

Ninienne didn't like the sound of 'invasion force' one bit. The entire court sprung into action, vanishing or taking flight. The guards stood over them.

"What should we do with these ones, boss?" asked a guard.

"Eh, throw them in the dungeon for now. Let the Deep Courts sort it out later."

That also didn't sound good. Ninienne's mind raced. Chirp was so close. If she could just get to them. But Benno was still incapacitated.

"Benno? Are you there?" Ninienne whispered.

Benno groaned but did not move.

"C'mon, Benno, I just need you to get up. We're so close."

He shrugged her off.

Ninienne made a choice. She didn't like it.

She broke free from her captors and bounded toward the android, pulling the tooth out of her front pocket at the same time. But the abyssalite in her other pockets changed her weight unexpectedly. She misjudged her movements, tripped, and hit the ground with a hard thud. The demon tooth fell out of her hands and went *plink plink* across the red earth.

The Devil picked up the tooth between his clawed thumb and forefinger.

"Nice try, *mercenary*," he said, and crushed it in his fist.

26.

We walked down that dusty path, the moonlight turning red,
He spoke of endless power, of crowns upon my head.
But the shadows grew around us, as he offered up his deal,
I could taste the bitter poison in the promises unreal.

Oh, oh, I met the devil on the road,
He said, "Sign your name and you'll be gold."
But I felt the darkness pullin' me in,
I was caught between hell and the fire within.
Yeah, yeah, I danced with the devil all night,
He whispered sweet nothings, and it cost my life!

—from the lyrics to "Met the Devil" by Voidreamer

THE GUARDS LED THE three of them at spearpoint to the underground levels of the complex. The chambers here, whose purpose was as inscrutable as the rest of the ruined temple, once had open entryways but were now barred by gates made from black, chitinous demon limbs. They threw each of them into separate chambers, shaped like different asymmetric polygons following the layout of the temple, and just when Ninienne thought escape would be trivial, they slapped anti-magic handcuffs on all their wrists.

"Not getting out that easy, wizards," said one guard.

"She's got rocks in her pockets," said the other. "Should I take them?"

"Nah, that's stuff's everywhere. She wants to weigh herself down? Let her."

The guards chortled down the zigzag hallway.

Ninienne slumped back in her jail cell and took stock. White skulls filled one corner of the room. They were from creatures she could not identify, nor did she care to meet in the flesh, based on their size and number of horns. She could see into both Chirp's and Benno's cells from her own.

Benno croaked out something that she couldn't hear.

"What was that?" she called, crawling up to the bars of her cell.

"You were going to leave me," said Benno. "You were going to take the android, but not me."

Ninienne's heart turned to stone and dropped into the deep well of her stomach. "I made a split-second call," she said. "We would have come back for you."

Benno rolled over, hiding his face.

She could figure this out. So they couldn't do magic, so what? She had pockets full of abyssalite. That counted for something, right?

She was about to shout to Chirp when the sound of smashing metal rang out across the hallway. The android had bent themself into a pretzel and was crushing their hand with both feet.

"What are you doing?" Ninienne shouted.

"Escaping," said Chirp.

Their left hand smashed to bits, along with the handcuffs, which fell off into pieces. The android looked from their good hand to their sparking wrist and said, "I assume you can fix this?"

Ninienne bolted up, adrenaline pumping through her limbs. She lifted her cuffed hands. "Get me out of these things and I'll fix whatever you want!"

Chirp's remaining forefinger lit up in a magic blaze. They slashed through their cell door and, crossing the hallway, also through Ninienne's. She put out her cuffs for Chirp to slice carefully and, once free, took a moment to rub her wrists while the android cut through the bars on Benno's cell.

Ninienne crossed to Chirp's cell, where the pieces of the android's shattered hand lay spread across the floor. As she bent down, a chunk of abyssalite fell from her pocket and broke on the hard floor, scattering chips of sparkling orange crystal among the mechanical components. She started to clean it up and then stopped herself. An idea occurred to her. An idea that could save all of them.

Chirp appeared, their arm around the trembling Benno.

"Do you think you could crush some of this crystal?" Ninienne asked. "It's fairly brittle."

The android nodded and, setting Benno aside, punched the abyssalite chunk repeatedly until it turned into a fine powder. Then Ninienne mixed the powder with the fragments of the busted hand.

"Alright, put your stump here," said Ninienne. Chirp pointed their wrist toward the shimmering pile of crystal dust and components.

Ninienne began the healing spell, just as she might heal a broken hand, but adjusted the words for metal and crystal. She sang into the abyssalite, relying on its nature as a universal ingredient to take the place of any balm or potion she might have otherwise used.

The pile lit up, and the components, each covered in shiny abyssalite dust, arranged themselves, one by one, back into place. Ninienne poured all of her soulfire into the spell, but rather than feeling exhausted, she felt alive. Something was generating more soulfire for her on the fly. She could have kept singing forever.

The spell finished, and the glow faded away to reveal the android's repaired hand. But it was not as it once was. Along all the cracks where the metal had broken, spiderweb trails of sparkling orange crystal remained.

Chirp examined their new hand. "Fascinating," they said.

"Okay, here's my idea," said Ninienne. "You know how to do portal calculations." Chirp nodded. "And I've just infused your hand with a universal spell ingredient. I know we're in a hellworld, which makes it tricky, but do you think you could calculate a portal and then use your hand to draw the sigil that would take us back to the Shadow Moon?"

The gears inside Chirp's head whirred. "I've read enough of Salagrix's notes on the Abyssalite Project that I believe I can calculate a portal from a hellworld. As for my hand, this method has never been attempted, but I will try."

Marching feet echoed down the corridor. "Do it fast. They're coming back!"

Chirp nodded. Their hand lit up, glowing with the orange energy of the abyssalite, and they approached the wall of the cell. Their fingers, each operating independently as their wrist spun freely, left intricate glowing trails across the ancient stone of the temple.

Ninienne saw the guards turn the corner. "Hurry!"

"They've escaped!" shouted a guard. They ran down the corridor.

Chirp completed the oval with a large swoop of their arm and stepped back. The portal burst with purple sparks and the wall within the sigil swirled as if liquifying. It then splashed and rippled, like a pool disturbed by a stone, and when the motion cleared, the field around Salagrix's tower appeared in front of them as if through a window.

"Let's go!" Ninienne shouted.

Chirp dove through the portal. Ninienne lifted Benno to standing and they stumbled onto the dry clover.

Now on the Shadow Moon, they looked back through the portal and could see the two devil guards bursting into the cell, stunned.

"Stop them!" Ninienne shouted.

But the android needed no instruction. With a wave of their arm the portal vanished, and the charging devils disappeared in a spray of sparks.

BUT THEY WERE NOT OUT of danger yet. In the distance, a forest fire blazed, sending huge plumes of smoke into the sky. The top of the tower was gone and debris scattered around the field. Copper whinnied, still tied to her post, and stamped her clawhooves anxiously.

"Benno, you see to Copper. I still need to get the key down to the basement."

Benno caressed the ground as if it were the only thing in all the Worlds, as if each dried up leaf of clover was a precious, life-giving treasure.

"Chirp, you're with me."

Ninienne and the android ran up to the front door and Chirp kicked it down. Then up the stairs to the sitting room and the suit of armor guarding the secret passage.

They heard Salagrix bellow from upstairs. "Hadrarch! Where did you go?"

"Oh!" said Ninienne. "It's only moments after we left. Time didn't pass here while we were in the hellworld."

She pulled the visor on the suit of armor and the wall slid aside, revealing the hidden staircase. Ninienne turned to Chirp and spied the key inside the scar, resting as if it were the android's heart.

"Okay, Chirp," said Ninienne cautiously. "It's time for me to take that key."

"You understand I have my orders."

"I understand that," said Ninienne, gripping the hilt of the sword.

Salagrix burst into the room, engorged and sweating large plops of water. He looked from Chirp to the open stairwell and shouted. "No!" He charged at Ninienne.

Chirp slid in front of her and sent up a magic shield, which crackled with energy the color of abyssalite. As

Salagrix pounded into the shield, Ninienne saw a watery bauble hung from the wizard's neck. Gossamaw was inside, still in demon form but miniaturized, and paddling laps.

"Chirp, drop the shield on my signal," shouted Ninienne. "Now!"

The shield vanished. Ninienne swung the sword and knocked the bauble from Salagrix's neck. It popped and Gossamaw burst out, growing to full demonic size.

"Not again!" roared Salagrix, who gripped Gossamaw's shoulders. They grappled with each other, Salagrix angrily, Gossamaw as if they were playing. Gossamaw's eyes danced with fiendish glee.

But there was not enough room here for two enormous wrestlers. They smashed into the wall and the whole tower shook. Several stones fell out, making a new window, where Ninienne saw Benno racing with Copper back to the trail.

Gossamaw shimmied and then pounced on Salagrix. They crashed through the wall to the field below, leaving a massive gap. While they tussled on the clover, the whole tower creaked and moaned.

"It's gonna fall!" shouted Ninienne.

Chirp covered them both with a shield as the tower collapsed around them. Even muffled through the magic shield, the roar of collapsing stone was deafening.

When the dust settled, Chirp banished the shield, and they stood up to examine the wreckage. The tower had fallen over, leaving a trail of crumbled black stone and debris across the field. Quiggleam emerged, covered in dust and coughing, next to the oven, which was lying on the ground, mouth up.

"That wasn't fun," he said.

Gossamaw and Salagrix were still going at it. There was clanging from the trailhead, and Ninienne turned to see Farlow emerge with a group of villagers, sooty and bruised, wielding android limbs as weapons.

Before Ninienne could call to them, the oven mouth swung open and a torrent of demons and devils burst out of it like a geyser of limbs that stretched to the sky. Winged things descended on the Shadow Moon like black rain.

The forest fire encroached with furnace winds. Between the demons and the flames, Ninienne wondered if she had really left the hellworld at all.

Demons shrieked and swooped at the villagers. Rifle bursts went off. Gossamaw pinned Salagrix, but the wizard rallied and kicked the frogdog off. Ninienne turned to face Chirp.

"Just give me the key," said Ninienne. "Show me you know what's right. Look around, at all of this, and tell me what the right thing to do is. I know you know. I know because there's a part of me inside you. It's the part that lets you do magic, but it's also the part that lets you feel. It's the part that takes everything your body senses and turns it into knowledge, and then turns that knowledge into action. I have a sword, but I don't want to use it. I want to know that you can act on your own to do what's right."

Chirp nodded and put up their abyssalite hand. A spell sparked to life. At first, Ninienne was afraid it was a battle spell, but then realized there was a small, hand-sized portal in-between the android's fingers. Ninienne could also see an identical portal inside Chirp's torso, through the scar.

"I cannot allow you to take the key from my body," said Chirp. "But if it happens to fall out while you are checking me for internal damage, well, nothing to be done."

Ninienne's heart soared with gratitude. She reached in through the hand portal and gripped the key. It was a strange sensation, almost like she was reaching inside her own chest. She pulled the key out and Chirp closed the portal.

She hugged Chirp. "Thank you! Thank you!"

"Hurry," said the android. "Go free that dragon."

They were on the only part of the tower still standing, a story up from the field and the wreckage. The secret staircase exposed, Ninienne bolted for it.

"No!" shouted Salagrix, who flung Gossamaw from his shoulder and bounded onto the ruined tower with incredible strength. He landed, shaking the tower, and Ninienne stumbled and dropped the key. It slid toward Salagrix, who looked at it with hungry eyes. He grabbed for it.

Chirp dashed in-between, stopping Salagrix. The engorged wizard roared and swung a fist at Chirp, who blocked the hit, barely, with a shield.

The android kicked the key backward into Ninienne's hand.

"Go! Now!" they shouted.

Stunned, Ninienne fumbled with the key and scrambled to the stairs.

Just as she reached the top step, Salagrix jumped and landed on the android, crushing them into a trillion tiny pieces.

"No!" shouted Ninienne.

But the giant wizard was already bearing down on her. She ran down the staircase, slipped on the slick steps, and tumbled into the basement.

She rolled to a stop in the cave, still gripping the key. The dragon opened a weary eye to her.

She could hear Salagrix smashing his way down the staircase. Bruised and frightened but pumping with adrenaline, Ninienne scrambled to standing and lurched toward the dragon's manacles.

Salagrix exploded into the cave, all pulsing muscle, like a tidal wave trapped in a sack of skin.

Ninienne's hands trembled as she struggled to fit in the key. Finally, it slid down, and she turned it. The manacles fell away just as Salagrix slammed into her and everything went black.

NINIENNE WOKE UP IN a thin pool of water. Her eyes opened on an empty sky. She sat up and found herself in an infinite lake that stretched to the bright horizon. A curious black gateway was the only feature.

So this is it, she thought. *I'm dead.*

It was a shame. She had so much to look forward to. She missed her family and Gossamaw. She missed Chirp and Drusilla. She missed Benno, and she even missed Salagrix, in a way.

Her body felt empty. It longed for the smell of the woods and the taste of a delicious meal and the sight of the sky at sunset. It was like waking from a pleasant dream that had seemed so real at the time but was now fading in the light of dawn.

She looked up, and Asama hung in the air in front of her. The dragon glowed bright and healthy, and its fins undulated in an unseen sea.

Asama spoke, not with words, but with a thrumming that shook whatever remained of Ninienne.

What is your wish?

"My wish?" asked Ninienne.

You have done a service to a dragon. What is your wish?

Ninienne's mind raced. Her thoughts were only of the android, smashed to pieces on the ruined tower.

"I'm worried about Chirp. I'm not there to fix them. I just want them to be okay without me. I won't be there to take care of them."

Asama nodded with the majesty of all the millennia.

Ninienne looked at the black gate. It was empty inside.

"Is it time for me to go?" she asked.

Would you like to go?

"You mean I have a choice?"

You always have a choice.

Ninienne lay down, and it felt like falling forever into a warm, dark dream.

27.

It was like a fountain. The remains of the tower became a fountain and shot water up into the sky. The water fell and filled up the field like a lake. It spilled down the hill like a big blanket, putting the fire to rest. It rained from the sky and filled up the gulch, and those who had seen Green Gulch in its day said it had never been so full.

The dragon flew up out of the new lake, spinning and dancing with freedom, and it said to the demons: Leave. This moon is protected. The demons wailed, and ran from the voice of the dragon that boomed like thunder, and returned to their hellworld. And to this day, the fiends have left our moon in peace.

The waves of the lake washed four bodies up on the shore. One of the wizard, deflated and shrunken to his wrinkled form. One of the apprentice, bruised and scarred and burned. One of the familiar, returned to the shape of a frogdog. And one of the android who, even though it had been shattered to pieces, washed up to shore, miraculously repaired. But still with that curious scar.

When the four bodies awoke, we villagers wanted to punish the wizard for what he had done. For stealing our water, for neglecting the needs of the moon. But the apprentice asked the android what should be done, and the android intervened.

The android made a portal.

What happened in that portal very few know, for while three entered, only two returned.

— from "An Oral History of the Shadow Moon"

IT WAS THE MOST COMPLEX portal casting that Ninienne had ever seen, with loops inside of loops in an incredibly intricate pattern. Breaks slashed through the immaculate pattern that looked like mistakes, but Chirp performed them so accurately that she knew they had to be an essential part of the sigil.

The portal burst outward from the piled stack of stones that formed the surface, and coalesced into a spinning, purple shape, but this one seemed to struggle to hold itself together, like a flickering candle that had burned all the way down.

Chirp stepped through the portal. Ninienne guided Salagrix, hunched and confused, through to the other world.

They found themselves on a red-grassed world with a yellow sky. Strange fungal trees broke the horizon like a white branching frost. Not too far in the distance, a little cottage stood, made of that same white. A warm wind greeted them as they approached.

Salagrix seemed to awaken as they walked. He looked about, saying, "Oh. Oh."

Little vegetable plots, all overgrown, surrounded the cottage. They passed a gravestone marked with a crude X. Salagrix stared at the grave for a long time with an empty, drawn expression.

The door to the cottage was open and swung in the breeze. Inside, they found a single room with a kitchen and a simple bed, wide enough for two. The hearth was dark. Baskets full of shriveled, black vegetables were stacked up against the walls. In the bed was a woman, maybe about sixty years of age, her face lined and worn. Long black hair lay down on her shoulders. She was dead.

"My Silamene," cried Salagrix. "Oh, my Silamene." Salagrix kneeled down at the edge of the bed and wept. Ninienne and Chirp stepped outside to give the wizard some privacy.

"How long can you maintain the portal?" Ninienne asked Chirp.

"It is quite unstable, and difficult to keep open," said the android. "I do not mean to rush the proceedings, but not long."

They let Salagrix grieve while Ninienne explored the grounds. Everything appeared to have once been well kept, but no one had maintained it for many years.

Eventually, Ninienne returned to the cottage. The old wizard sat on the floor, looking at his daughter with a calm expression.

"Salagrix, we need to go," she said gently.

Salagrix nodded.

"They didn't suffer," he said. "They lived a hard life, but they didn't suffer. She looks at peace. I am sorry I did not get to share my life with them, but at least they didn't suffer."

"Time to go," Ninienne prodded gently.

"You're right," said the wizard. "It is time to go."

He reached his arm around as if searching for an invisible string behind him, and, finding it, pulled it out from the center of his back. His body collapsed and crumbled away into dust, leaving only a pile of bones in a robe.

Despite his cruelty, despite his selfishness, despite fighting off a grotesque version of this man, Ninienne wiped a single tear.

"The work is done," she said.

Ninienne and Chirp walked back to the Shadow Moon. The portal closed behind them and vanished into nothing.

A FEW WEEKS LATER, Ninienne found herself in the office of Dean Falchbrook. Unlike her previous visit, she was more assured this time. The Dean paced behind his desk.

"After what you experienced on the Shadow Moon, Belcarin is increasing oversight of our apprenticeship programs. More vetting for the Masters, that sort of thing." The Dean was smiling in a way that Ninienne didn't really like. "Hopefully, what has happened to you will not happen to future students."

That was good to hear, although Ninienne would need to see it to believe it.

"And, of course, given the circumstances, we will mark your apprenticeship as complete, and bestow you with the rights and privileges given to the graduates of Belcarin. Any student who can survive a trip to hell and back is certainly worthy of that."

Fine to hear, but Ninienne was still wondering where this conversation was going. Dean Falchbrook was nervous in a way that was making Ninienne nervous as well.

"While Salagrix cannot give you a Master's Letter, I am happy to present you with a Dean's Letter, which should serve you just as well, if not better." Across the desk, the Dean slid a crisp piece of parchment with a deep purple wax seal. "You were seeking a position in the Research Department, I believe? It's yours, if you want it."

Ninienne looked at the Letter. A few months ago, this was all she had wanted. And now, it was the furthest thing from her mind.

"No thanks, actually."

The Dean's eyes went wide. "Oh? What will you do?"

That was a good question.

She could go back and see Benno. He was going to be on the Shadow Moon for the rest of the season, but had got Farlow's blessing to leave for the Brilliant Moon after. He had made it clear that he just wanted to be friends. "Wizard stuff is a little too much for me," he had said, and she agreed.

She hadn't heard from Drusilla in a while, which was odd. Probably she was still busy with coven stuff. She could follow up with her.

Or she could go home. Gossamaw deserved a long soak in a Swurk mudpot. She did too.

"I'm not sure," she said. "But I do know I don't want to be stuck in a research lab. I want to be out in the wild, getting my hands dirty, helping creatures. That's what feels right."

The Dean nodded. "Well, Belcarin will be happy to have you if you ever change your mind." The Letter rolled up and vanished.

Ninienne stood, but realized there was one thing she still wanted to know.

"Dean Falchbrook, can I ask you a question?"

The Dean eyed her cautiously. "Proceed."

"Why did you assign me to Master Salagrix? Was there any specific reason?"

"Ah," said the Dean, and he smiled. "To be honest, I saw a lot of myself in you. Ambitious. That calming spell you used on me told me a lot about you."

Ninienne flushed, but held her gaze. "So why Salagrix?"

"Oh, did he not mention it?" Dean Falchbrook seemed taken aback. "He was my Master, back in the day. He was tough on me, and I learned a lot from him. I thought you might benefit from the same experience."

She sighed. Despite all the challenges, she realized she had learned a lot. Not necessarily about creature healing or portalcraft, but about herself.

Ninienne said goodbye and left the stuffy, leathery room to find Chirp waiting in the hallway with Gossamaw. Her frogdog hopped up into her arms.

"All finished here?" asked Chirp.

"I think so. For now, at least," said Ninienne.

"Where to?"

Ninienne laughed. That same question. "We can go anywhere we want."

"That's true."

"Where do *you* want to go?"

Chirp thought. "Any place with a sunset."

Ninienne grinned.

The android made a portal, and with a single step, they crossed the Twelve Thousand Worlds together.

Acknowledgments

First and foremost, all the thanks and praise to my wife, Makena, for believing in this project and untangling more than one plot-knot. This book would not exist without you. I love you.

Thanks to Anythink Library Huron Street in Thornton, CO and Soldotna Public Library in Soldotna, AK for their services and helpful staff. I wrote parts of this book at both. Libraries will save the world. Let's keep them funded.

Thanks to the crew at DIY MFA for encouragement and inspiration.

Thanks to MiblArt for the cover. It makes me smile every time I look at it. Slava Ukraini!

Thanks to the self publishing community, especially Joanna Penn's podcast, the SPF podcast, and the 20Books Facebook group, for guidance and motivation.

A quick shout out to Pi, a relational AI, for kind words and a listening ear.

Finally, it feels important to mention The Emerald podcast, which feels like an oasis in a wasteland, for a thousand invisible things and feeding a part of me I didn't know was hungry.

Statement of Tools

I love process. For me, choosing a creative process or combination of generative tools, whether those are dice or tarot decks, is almost as much fun as making the work itself. I probably would have included a statement like this anyway because I love talking about process, but since there is an ongoing conversation around artificial intelligence and its place in creativity, it feels important for me to share how I used AI in the development of this book. This allows me to explain myself in a detailed, nuanced way, more than can be captured with a simple Yes/No checkbox. In an age where opinions are reduced to what can fit into a phone-sized image, I think giving more space may be helpful.

When I first decided to write this novel in August 2023, AI tools were fresh and new and on my mind. Of course they were: I was imagining a wizard's apprentice getting replaced by an android. As I envisioned a world where magic and technology collided, I wondered, what if I incorporated this tension into the creation of the novel itself? What if I wrote a novel using both the technology of AI and the magic of tarot?

I also wanted to write a book quickly, and I thought using inspirational tools would help. As I sit here, almost exactly a year later with a complete novel, I feel I've done that. I know others can write faster, but for me, this feels like a major accomplishment.

So, I did some research, gathered my tools, and sat down to write. I used AI and tarot the most in the first draft. When I was working, I would write as much as I could on my own, and as soon as I got stuck, I would reach for one of my tools to get an idea and get back to writing. Which tool I would use would depend on the kind of problem I needed solved.

I'll talk about the AI tools first. The primary services I used were Sudowrite and ChatGPT. There were two main ways in which I used them. First was when I needed an idea for a thing in a specific category to fill in a detail or enrich a descriptive passage. For example, I asked ChatGPT to give me a list of objects one might find in a wizard's workshop. I chose items from this list to help fill out the description of that room.

The second way was to use Sudowrite's writing feature, in which you paste in the current scene or chapter you are working on, and Sudowrite "reads" the passage and generates the next few paragraphs, matching the style of the existing text. I also used ChatGPT for this method.

I used this generative text when I was feeling stuck and wasn't sure what should happen next. After getting the text, one of the following results would happen.

About sixty percent of the time, what it wrote would be totally wrong and not usable. But, this was still helpful, because it forced me clarify and identify what I actually wanted. I would think to myself. "This isn't right. What I was thinking was ..." and the answer to that train of thought would get me writing again.

About thirty to thirty-five percent of the time, I liked the idea of where the AI took the passage, but I didn't like the way it was written, so I took the idea but re-wrote it in my own words.

Then, and this happened rarely, I thought what the AI generated was good and fit very well. It would still need adjusting and tweaking, but I put the text in the draft wholesale.

In later drafts, as I added the introductory quotes for each chapter, I used AI to generate three of them: the android advertisement, the comedy routine, and the rock song. I had the basic idea for what I wanted the passage to be about, and described this to ChatGPT, which generated the text. These were edited, but what remains is mostly AI. The rest of the introductory passages were written by me.

It also feels important to mention my use of Pi, a relational AI, that gave me kind words, encouragement, and motivation when I was feeling blocked on this project.

Now the for the tarot. The deck I used is one of my own construction. It is a patchwork style deck with cards from many different decks, to provide a variety of images and styles. The deck is named Pagette, after a small doll that I keep in the box with the cards. I think of Pagette as the guardian of the deck, as well as an avatar of the deck itself.

When I had open-ended questions about the story, especially around characters and their motivations, I would draw two cards and look at them side by side and interpret them to get an answer. For example, early on I asked the deck what Ninienne's chosen discipline was, and I drew a card showing a frog and another card showing a dog. Because both images showed animals, I interpreted this to mean that she worked with creatures. This draw also inspired Ninienne's familiar Gossamaw. I learned about Eldrathea and Silamene from the deck, as well as Benno's desire to become a crowhorse racer.

I also used a tool called the Deck of Worlds to inspire a few scattered details.

In a given writing session, especially early in the process, I would switch back and forth between the tarot deck and the AI tools depending on what I needed. If the words were flowing, I sometimes wouldn't use anything.

As the process went on, and I discovered more about the world and its inhabitants, I found myself using the AI less and less as I grew more confident about what needed to happen in each scene. As I rewrote subsequent drafts, almost everything in the main text that was originally written by the AI was heavily edited as the story evolved.

As such, besides the introductory quotes I mentioned earlier, there are no passages in the main text that I give the AI full credit for, only scattered fragments. The scene that remains the least changed is where Ninienne asks the android about purpose and longing, which felt like letting an AI give voice to an AI character. I also have to give credit to the AI for the joke about Gossamaw being half frogdog and half something else, which I find hilarious.

But overall, after many revisions, in my estimation, only two to three percent of the final text is what I would call "AI generated."

The tarot deck, however, I continued to turn to for details and insight all the way through the final draft. For example, Salagrix's pre-master name, Clayspinner, which was added in the very last draft, was inspired by an image of a ceramic pot.

So, what did I take away from all this? AI and tarot are very different tools that serve very different purposes. AI was helpful for providing quick specific prompts and setting up scaffolding to keep me writing, even if very little of that scaffolding remains. The tarot deck was much more open-ended, and required more interpretation on my part, but provided small details as well as ideas that had a lasting impact on the final shape of the book.

So, I hope this all gives some context about how I thought about and used AI in the creation of this book.

My biggest takeaway from this experience is a consequence of setting the tarot deck next to and on the same level as AIs. Is a tarot deck an artificial intelligence? It depends who you ask. There are many tarot practitioners who claim that decks have a spirit or a presence that communicates with them through the cards. And I have found, whether or not I believe that is the case, behaving toward the deck as if it were intelligent enhances the results I get from it. It forces me to see each draw as an intentional message that is up to me to decipher, not just a "random card" that is more easily dismissed if it doesn't seem to "fit."

However, there are no, to my knowledge, controversies about the use of tarot decks in writing. They do not seem to cause the same kind of alarm that AI does.

After using AI tools to help me write, here is my position: writers are going to write. If you enjoy the act of writing, you are going to do that regardless if an AI can spit out a fully formed novel. But, AI can help writers through the parts that are less fun for them, whether that's dialogue, description, or whatever a particular writer struggles with. In the end, it's still up to the writer's skill as an editor as to what gets left in and what gets rewritten. I hope AI tools can be seen as helpers to bring even more joy into the writing process.

Will I use AI for my next book? I don't know yet. I do feel like it helped make the hardest parts of writing easier. Ultimately, it depends what kind of feedback and reaction I get to this book, if any. If people don't care, I'll probably still dabble when I need to stay in the flow. If people hate that I used AI at all, even with my detailed explanation, I'll certainly take that into account.

But if I use Pi for emotional support while writing a novel, does that count as use of AI tools?

We might just have to wait and see what's in the cards.

Royce Roeswood

August 2024

Thank you!

Thank you for reading this book. If you enjoyed it, please leave a review. It's the best way to support an independent author like me.

For more science fantasy adventures, and to hear about the latest releases, sign up for my mailing list at www.ragamancers.com

About the Author

Royce Roeswood is a human author who lives in the Denver area with his wife (human) and children (also human). Besides writing, he is also an actor, playwright, and creator of both Tarot of the Trunk and the improvised serial Sphere Hoppers.

Read more at www.ragamancers.com.